Jasmine Grace

Book Three: Heartbeats in the Heat

Revved Up & Ready

Published by Jasmine Grace

Copyright © 2025 by Jasmine Grace

All rights reserved.

The story, all names, characters, and incidents portrayed in this production are fictitious. No identification with actual persons (living or deceased), places, buildings, and products is intended or should be inferred.

Cover Art by Gary Tussey

First edition 2025

ISBN (Paperback) 979-8-9892533-5-7

ISBN (Ebook) 979-8-9892533-4-0

www.JasmineGraceAuthor.com

For everyone who had a crush on the class clown.

Author's Note

It is my intention for this book to feel like an ooey gooey romantic escape from reality. I've included content warnings, so you can determine if this will be a safe space for you. One of the main characters has anxiety. I did my best to handle this with care and respect, and my hope is that you will enjoy this story as a lighthearted read.

Content Warnings

-Anxiety, anxiety attack on page
-Discussion and brief descriptions of motorcycle crashes and injuries from motorcycle crashes
-Explicit sexual content
-Marijuana use
-Profanity

Revved Up & Ready is a spicy, low-angst romantic comedy with no third act breakup. Intended for 18+

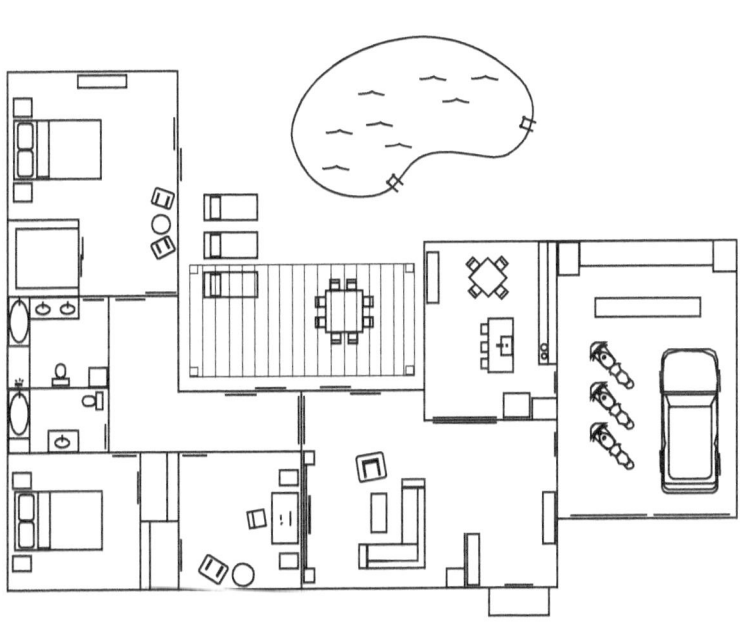

Chapter 1

Cam

Ten years ago, the Pacific Coast Highway –
Ventura, California

Nothing beats the full-body rush of winning a motorcycle race. It's like someone shook up a bottle of champagne and sprayed it straight into my soul. My mouth aches from smiling, every hair on my body stands on end, and my pulse is a drumbeat in my ears.

Although, the last two might be because I'm not wearing anything between my helmet and boots.

And, oh yeah, *I'm currently running from the cops.*

It's been one hell of a night.

Sadie

Ten years ago, a dorm room – *Corvallis, Oregon*

"Study break," I announce, plopping down onto Devon's bed with my laptop.

My roommate glances at me from her desk. "Not ready for a break."

"You said that two hours ago," I whine, tapping my fingers next to her mouse. "Hurry up and *get* ready. I'm *bored*."

She arches a brow but goes back to her project. *I'll have to be more persuasive.* Grabbing my favorite little orange pipe, I pack a fresh bowl and offer her some greens. She eyes the brightly colored glass and checkered lighter in my hand, considering for a moment before closing her computer. "*Fine*," she sighs—*like getting high on a Friday night is* such *an imposition.*

After a little smoking and a lot of coughing, she joins me on the bed to watch the video queued up on my screen—*Naked Guy Wins Street Race.*

It starts like a *Fast & Furious* movie—except with motorcycles, no budget, and garbage sound editing. The yellow hue of a streetlight casts over five people dressed head to toe in black, lined up next to their bikes. Small crowds gather on either side of the road, their voices blending into incoherent noise as they wait for the race to begin.

Devon tilts her head toward me. "Don't you hate motorcycles?"

"Yes, *definitely*. But this is different. I saw it over someone's shoulder in class this morning, so I already know what happens—no one crashes."

On the screen, a siren blares in the distance, adding to the clamor of voices. "Oh shit! Cops!" someone yells across the crowd. Soon, a chorus of "Cops! Cops!" rings out as people scatter, only a handful staying put while racers hurriedly mount their bikes.

Devon interrupts the video again. "What exactly is supposed to be so great about this?"

I shush her, pointing to the screen. "Pay attention, or you'll miss it."

A guy wearing a beanie and thick-rimmed glasses steps into the shot, his eyes as bloodshot as mine probably are right now. I start giggling in anticipation as he looks into the camera and—completely out of place against the chaos and sirens around him—deadpans, "Not the *fuzz*."

"Oh, my word." Full-body laughter bubbles up in my chest. "Not the *fuzz*."

Devon cracks a smile but fights her own laughter.

In the video, someone yells, "The flag. The *flag*!"

The camera zooms in on a girl typing on her phone, chewing gum as aggressively as possible. She pulls a green bandana out of her back pocket without glancing up from her screen, reaching it high in the air. Motorcycle engines roar, momentarily drowning out the approaching sirens as the pack of racers takes off, disappearing from view. For the briefest moment, my stomach twists with anxiety that someone could crash, but it passes as soon as I remind myself I know how this ends.

I squeeze Devon's arm. "Are you watching?"

She rolls her eyes. "Yes, I'm watching."

"This is where it gets good," I say.

The dispersing spectators slow down, their exclamations rising from the crowd.

"Holy shit!"

"That's one way to cut drag."

"Do you see that guy?"

The camera pans to reveal a sixth racer speeding across the starting line. He's wearing leather boots, a black helmet—and *that's it*. A handful of tattoos scatter his lanky frame, and a bright yellow smiley face has been edited into the video to cover the most interesting parts of his nudity.

"Do you think the smiley needs to be that big?" I whisper to Devon—*as if I'm afraid the guy on screen will hear me.*

"I'm *sure* it's an exaggeration," she answers.

The sound of sirens grows less insistent with each shot of the naked guy as he passes racers and puts distance between himself and *the fuzz*. I snort another laugh. *The fuzz.*

The video cuts to a view of the finish line from a rooftop. The six racers appear—two at the front, naked guy in close third, and the other three trailing behind.

Voices from around the camera take notice as naked guy gains on the lead duo.

"Oh shit. Is that guy?"

"Fuck's sake. That's Hacker."

"Show us the goods!"

Naked guy—Hacker—brings his front tire up behind the lead racers' rear tires and—using some kind of racing magic I don't understand—forces his way between them.

"How the—" Devon whispers as he pulls ahead at the last second.

He and his yellow smiley cross the finish line first, his front tire lifting into a wheelie.

On the rooftop, a girl with black space buns wearing a pink top and double-fisting red plastic cups runs to the edge and yells in a slurred voice, "No, not your *wheelie*. We want to see your *willy*!" When Hacker disappears off-screen, she steps in front of the camera, yelling, "Show me your willy!" With that, the video cuts off.

I turn to Devon with a cheesy smile, waiting for her response.

She releases what starts as an exasperated sigh, but her lips curl up halfway through, and she devolves into laughter. I follow her into giggles until we're leaning into each other, wiping tears from our eyes.

"Want to watch it one more time?" I ask.

"I cannot believe I'm saying this," she answers, regaining her composure, "but *yes*."

Cam

> Same night – ten years ago, the Pacific
> Coast Highway – *Ventura, California*

A motorcycle's been tailing me for a couple of miles, staying right on my ass—*my naked ass*—as I take the exit off the PCH. Fortunately, it's not a cop. It's my best friend, Luke. *If I'm lucky, he'll lend me his pants.*

The sirens pass, not noticing us ducking into an alley behind a Chinese restaurant that's closed for the night.

"What the hell was that?" Luke asks, his voice muffled by his helmet as he pulls it off.

"Could I get some pants?" I ask, covering myself with my hands, backing up between the stucco wall and a dumpster.

"Do I look like I have extra pants?" he says, dismounting his bike.

"You have more pants than I do," I shrug.

"Fuck's sake," he mutters, undoing his belt. "How did this happen?"

"They started the race early 'cause of—" I point toward the disappearing sirens with my chin. "I was still getting changed when they started the race."

Luke's pants get tangled in his boots, and he curses as he tugs at the laces. "I'll have to burn these socks now," he says, one socked foot landing in a puddle that dripped from the dumpster. "You could've skipped this race."

"And lost all our rent money?" I glance around the alley, making sure no one's watching.

A stern, dad-like tone creeps into his voice. "Excuse me?"

"I did *not* lose our rent money." I lift my hands to emphasize my point, realizing too late that now I'm just flashing Luke in a dark alley.

He makes a noise between a groan and a gag. "Dude, what the fuck?"

I cover up with my palms again. "Now we have rent handled through June because I *won*. Thanks for congratulating me, by the way."

He throws his jeans at me with more force than necessary, and they hit me in the chest with a thud. "I could kill you," he mutters.

The pants are a few inches too short and loose in the waist, but they beat riding the rest of the way home commando.

"We look like a couple of perverts," Luke says, now wearing a leather jacket, boxer-briefs, and motorcycle boots.

I fire up my bike. "At least *I* have pants on," I say, then take off before he can kick my ass.

Sadie

Nine and a half years ago, a frat party –
Corvallis, Oregon

"Did that guy just flash me?" I ask, swinging a hand to my chest in offense—completely forgetting I'm holding plastic cups in both hands and splashing *Malibu* and *Coke* all over my pink *Show Me Your Willie* t-shirt.

"He did," Devon says, recoiling. "Third one tonight."

"Did not think this Halloween costume through," I mutter, scanning the area for somewhere to put down my drinks.

"You really didn't," Devon agrees, eyeing me with a look that says, *I told you so.* Her *costume* could best be described as *hot girl in a black dress who thinks she's too good for this party, but showed up anyway.*

A cute guy, a few inches taller than me but still shorter than Devon, steps in front of us. He's wearing a pair of smiley-face boxers, fake tattoos, boots, and a helmet.

"Here," he says, taking one of my drinks so I have a free hand to deal with my spill.

"Got any napkins tucked in there?" I ask, nodding toward his boxers.

"None in here, sweetie," he laughs, "but I'm sure we can find something somewhere." He wraps an arm around my shoulder and looks to Devon. "Can I steal her away?"

Devon manages to sip her drink and glare down her nose at him simultaneously, then looks to me. "Do you *want* to be stolen away?"

"Sure, why not?" I giggle, leaning into his arm.

Devon nods, making a *should've-asked-her* face. "And what's your name?"

"I'm Jared—" he answers, pulling me in tighter. "Your friend's new boyfriend."

Devon scoffs, "You don't even know her name."

But I swoon a little inside.

Cam

Nine-and-a-half years ago, a dive bar –
Ventura, California

"You think any of these assholes realize they're dressed up as you?" Luke asks, finishing something behind the bar and nodding toward three guys wearing motorcycle helmets and some form of smiley-face underwear.

"Dressed *up* isn't the right term—at least, it shouldn't be," I laugh. "No one has committed to the look the way I did."

"They're probably not trying to catch the indecent exposure charge you barely avoided," Luke says, passing me a pint while wiping down the bar.

"Cowards," I scoff, accidentally blowing foam off the head of my beer onto the freshly wiped counter.

Luke glares at the dissolving bubbles, then walks off to help another knock-off *Race Naked* guy.

My phone buzzes, reminding me of the hundreds of posts I've been tagged in tonight. *It's fucking surreal.* That video went viral months ago, and it's still making the rounds. I scroll through the posts while I wait for Luke to get a lull in his line.

First up—someone with a highlighter and sharpie smiley face safety-pinned to a pair of tighty-whities.

Next—a girl in a bicycle helmet, jeans, and a smiley-face t-shirt.

Then—*Oh wow.* Someone who really did commit to the *naked* part of the costume. *Good for them.*

The next few are photos of people in *Race Naked* t-shirts they bought off the website I threw together in a rush when this whole thing started.

Finally, I land on one I haven't seen anyone else post—a blonde babe with her hair in space buns. She's wearing a pink t-shirt that says *Show Me Your Willie*, the fabric drenched like she spilled a drink on it. She's holding a red plastic cup, leaning toward the camera with a laugh.

I scroll through a few more posts but find myself going back to hers again and again—her smiling face, her tight, wet tank top. She even has dimples. *Fucking adorable.*

Sadie

Six years ago, an overrated steakhouse –
Portland, Oregon

"I thought you'd be excited," Jared says, stepping in front of me and placing his hands on my shoulders.

"I was—I am. I just—" I stumble over my words, not wanting to sound ungrateful. "We're celebrating my new job, and you said you'd plan something special for *me*."

"And I did, sweetie," he says, his voice hurt despite my attempts to soften the blow. He runs his fingers down my arm and squeezes my hand. "These weren't easy reservations to get."

A woman in a cocktail dress squeezes past us, making me realize we're blocking the entrance to the restaurant. I step aside, pulling Jared with me.

"I just—That Italian place is my favorite. You said you'd get reservations there," I half-whisper. "I don't really like steak."

"Is *that* what you're upset about?" He smiles, rolling his eyes like I'm an adorable little idiot. "I'm sure there's pasta or something here."

"It feels like you picked a place for you—like what I wanted was an afterthought." I search his face for some kind of recognition, but he just stares back. "Can you see how I'd feel that way?" I ask.

He throws up his hands, impatience flaring. "We have reservations here."

Stunned, I gape after him as he turns and walks into the restaurant without me. *Where did that come from?* It's unlike him to snap at me. Did something happen today that upset him? *Is he angry with me for wanting him to eat at my favorite restaurant? Maybe I am being ungrateful. I shouldn't have said anything—*

"Going in?" a deep voice asks.

Looking up, I find a tall man with bright red hair flashing a huge grin. He's standing between me and the restaurant door. His black button-up conceals the bottom half of the tattoos crawling up his neck—a roaring cheetah, traditional roses, and a checkered flag with the number *207*. *Holy shit. It's the* Race Naked *guy*.

I always thought he was good-looking, but in person? He's

unreasonably attractive. It's hard not to stare at how perfectly his features come together. His chiseled jaw and high cheekbones ground his almost-too-large mouth, and his nose, which has clearly been broken at least once, adds character. Tattooed fingers sweep through deep copper hair that falls onto his forehead, revealing intense blue-green eyes locked on mine.

My stomach gives a little flip. *Get it together. This man races motorcycles. More importantly—your boyfriend is inside. Even if Jared's being an ass for some reason I don't understand, I can't stand here and drool over Cameron Hacker.*

Cam

Six years ago, an overrated steakhouse –
Portland, Oregon

The gorgeous blonde blinks up at me through glassy, caramel-colored eyes, her cheeks flushing deeper with every passing second we stand here. *Does that little brown-haired fucker who just went inside have her on the verge of tears?* Normally, I'd break the silence, but I don't want to rush her, even if it makes me late to meet my agent.

"Um, hi," she says, and it's been long enough that I've forgotten what I asked her in the first place.

I introduce myself, and she stares at my extended hand for a moment before shaking it.

"Yeah, my boyfriend loves your videos," she says, offering a smile that doesn't quite reach her eyes.

It's tempting to focus on the fact that she recognizes me, but then I remember how it's tied to her boyfriend—who left her standing outside a restaurant on the verge of tears. *Not surprising.* My brand of internet shenanigans attracts assholes.

"Boyfriend loves them, but not you?" I ask.

"Oh, they're funny. I didn't mean to—*You're* funny." She stumbles over her words, her cheeks going even pinker as she tucks a strand of golden hair behind her ear. "I just hate motorcycles." She winces. "No offense."

"None taken," I laugh. "I might be some people's poster boy for motorcycles," *and if this meeting goes well, I literally will be.* "But there's more to me than that."

"Of course. I'm sure," she says, offering a genuine smile. Dimples appear in her rosy cheeks. *What a babe.* "If you wouldn't mind, I'm sure he'd love to meet you."

Right—the boyfriend. "Happy to. He around somewhere?" I ask.

"Just inside." She points over her shoulder toward the restaurant's entrance.

I bite my tongue, holding back from asking why the hell he's inside without her. Instead, I hold the door open and enjoy the view as she walks through. The light blue dress she wears is sweet with its floral print, but it clings to her curves in all the right ways. *Damn, that's a nice ass.*

"What brings you to Portland?" she asks.

I shrug. "Motorcycle race."

"Oh, of course. I'm so dumb," she apologizes, looking around the restaurant for her idiot boyfriend.

"I'm sure you're not du—"

She waves me off, asking, "Did you win?"

"Sure did."

"Figured you would have," she says, looking up at me with

another genuine, dimpled smile.

My chest swells with pride. *She figured I'd won.*

Sadie

Three years ago, Sadie & Jared's house –
Portland, Oregon

Jared's friends pause to sniff the lemon bars cooling on the counter as they pass through the kitchen to the living room.

"You'll have to wait a while for these," I say, shooing them away. "But there are chips and dip on the coffee table if you're hungry."

They disappear into the other room, followed shortly by the sound of a televised motorcycle race.

"You good, sweetie?" Jared asks, opening the fridge to grab a drink. "I know you don't like it when we have the races on."

"I wish you wouldn't watch that stuff," I say, shaking my head. "It's so *dangerous.*"

"Don't forget, if it wasn't for motorcycle racing, we never would have met," he reminds me, referring to the Halloween costumes that brought us together by accident.

"I remember," I admit, sighing.

Jared knows about the motorcycle accident I was in back in high school. Ever since, I can't wrap my mind around how anyone would risk their life just to go fast on two wheels. But he always tries to point to the time in college when I used to laugh at that *Race Naked* video as proof that I like motorcycle racing. *I don't.*

I've given up trying to explain that the video was an

exception, a silly moment among friends while stoned—one I could control, where I knew exactly what would happen. Cam Hacker wins the race, and no one gets hurt. It's something else entirely to watch a live race, knowing someone could crash and end up devastatingly injured, or worse.

Don't they know cars with seatbelts are an option?

"It's not like I'm going to get hurt from the couch," my boyfriend says, kissing my cheek. "Still better than me riding them, right?"

"Of course," I answer with a tight smile.

Baking—my oldest friend—keeps me distracted while they watch the race. *I can almost guarantee the dough will end up overworked with the amount of anxiety I'm channeling through the kneading.*

I've almost forgotten what they're watching when the living room erupts in gasps and shouts.

"He crashed, and it was bad," one of Jared's friends explains when I rush in to see what happened, his voice sounding more delighted than concerned.

A pit forms in my stomach, and the images of my own friends, sprawled on the asphalt between the motorcycles we'd just collided with, flash in my mind—*images I can't seem to shake, no matter how many years have passed.*

When I look up at the screen, a racer—number *207*—is laid out flat on the asphalt, his black-and-yellow leather jumpsuit scraped, one leg folded at an unnatural angle. My stomach churns. *I knew I shouldn't have looked.*

"Good thing he wasn't naked this time," Jared jokes.

How are they making jokes right now? My heart races when his words sink in. "Wait, that's—"

I only met the guy once, but his posts pop up on my feed

every now and then. I've been *aware* of him for so long. The realization that he's the one who crashed makes my stomach flip.

"He's reckless," one of the guys says. "Surprised this never happened before."

"Aren't you worried about him?" I don't dare peek back at the television. "He hasn't moved yet, has he?" I ask. "Is he okay?"

"Doesn't matter, he'll get even more pussy than usual after this," another of Jared's friends says.

How are they still joking about this?

I stand there, nervously wringing my hands, until they finally take Cam away on a stretcher. At least I know he's still alive.

Cam

> Three years ago, a hospital room – *Austin, Texas*

"Well, shit," Luke says as he steps into my hospital room.

"Yeah, shit," I agree, my voice flat.

"What's the damage?" he asks, pulling a chair up beside my bed.

"Broken femur," I answer, the same wave of defeat hitting me as when I first realized what happened.

"Fuck," Luke sighs, running a hand through his hair.

"Yeah, fuck," I mutter, dragging a hand through my own hair. "I *had* him, too."

"Pretty sure if you'd had him, you wouldn't have crashed,"

Luke ribs me, lightening the mood in that way he knows I
need.

"You could *try* a little sympathy," I say, tapping my fingers
on the IV line attached to my other arm.

He knocks my hand away. "Pretty sure you're not supposed
to mess with that."

I've been racing 600s in *USMoto* for years now, and up
until this morning, I had the best sponsorship lineup of my
career for this season. If I'd won the championship—*hell, if I'd
just been able to* finish *the season*—I would've been able to sign on
with a team and move up to the superbike class next year. I'm
not a *WorldMoto* guy, so racing superbikes in *USMoto* was my
pinnacle. *And it was within my reach.*

"Definitely out for the rest of the season, and most likely
next year too," I tell Luke with a sigh.

"It'll be fine. When you come back, you do one more year
in 600s. You're still racing motorcycles," he says, but it's not
enough to reassure me.

This was supposed to be the year I finally earned more
money racing than I do making dumb videos online. Now,
without racing, I'll have to double down on the influencer thing
to make ends meet.

Sadie

> One year ago, Sadie & Jared's house –
> *Portland, Oregon*

"But you *said* it was just going to be you and the guys," I
say, stepping forward so Jared can't leave the bedroom without

looking me in the eye.

"I can't control who brings their girlfriends," he sighs.

"Why didn't you invite me once you saw they were there?" My hands instinctively move to my hips, but I drop them, not wanting to *look* as angry as I feel.

"I don't know... didn't think about it." He gives me a look that makes me feel like an idiot for even bringing it up. "I'm allowed to do stuff without you." His tone is sharp in a way I barely recognize. *He never used to talk to me like this.*

"Of course you are," I reply, leaving out what I really want to ask. *But why didn't you want me there?*

"Good. We agree. Love you." He kisses my cheek and walks past me into the hall, ending the argument without resolution.

I'm left standing alone in our bedroom, the silence heavy with something he isn't telling me.

He never used to keep secrets. He never shut me down like this. There was a time when he invited me to everything because he liked my company more than anyone else's. He loves me, or at least, he used to. He was so sweet back then—staying up late with me while I baked, surprising me with flowers or even spontaneous vacations. But now? I can't even remember the last time he did something like that. The last time he made me feel special. *How long has it been since I last felt loved by him?*

I'm torn between needing to know what happened at that bar tonight and fearing what I might learn. *If it's what I think it is, I don't know how I'll get past it.*

I shut the door behind him and curl up in a ball on the bed, feeling small, lost in thoughts I don't want to face.

Hanna could have invited me, too, I guess. Jared has this

tight-knit group of friends he's known since college. Recently, they've all started dating younger girls in their early twenties—except for Jared, of course. *Maybe those girls just don't like me?*

My phone vibrates, and seeing Allie's name on the screen brings a moment of relief.

Allie: Remember I told you about my new landlord? The gorgeous jackass one? You will never guess who he's friends with.

Me: Please tell me! I could use some gossip right now.

Allie: The race naked guy! Do you remember him?

Me: Cam Hacker?

Allie: Yes! He just came over here and got coffee with stupid Luke. I think he's visiting.

I start typing a response about how Cam is Jared's favorite racer but delete it just as fast. If I bring Jared up, Allie's going to ask how things are going between us, and that's the last thing I want to talk about right now.

Me: Cam's a good guy, no? If they're friends, maybe your landlord isn't all bad?

Allie: Ugh. No. Luke sucks. Trust me.

Me: He sucks, but he's gorgeous?

Allie: A truly unfortunate combo.

Cam

Seven months ago, Allie's office, Turbine Café – Palm Springs, California

"You're supposed to be helping me," Luke grumbles, his words muffled by the nail he's holding between his teeth. We're adding storage to Allie's office in preparation for the bar they're opening together next month.

"I am helping," I reply from my perch on top of her desk, leaning against the wall.

He shakes his head. "Then would you assemble the stand in the box on Allie's desk?"

I open the box to find a book of coffee puns, mismatched highlighters and pens, a chipped *Turbine Café* mug—*now this is interesting*—a framed picture of Allie, her friend Devon, and a gorgeous blonde with a dimpled smile who looks vaguely familiar. She's wearing a yellow bikini that matches the gigantic tiki drink in her hand almost perfectly. *Do I know her from somewhere?*

I hop off the desk and show the picture to Luke. "Who's this?"

"That's the wrong box," he mutters, not looking up.

"But who *is she*?" I press.

"Her name's Sadie." He takes the frame from me, shoves it back in the box, and hands me the correct one. "Apparently, she has a shithead boyfriend in Oregon. Allie wants her to break up with him and move down here."

Setting the box down, so I can grab the photo again, I sigh, "Yeah, so do I."

Sadie

Six months ago, *Voyeur Café's* grand opening – *Palm Springs, California*

My reflection stares back at me from the glass front door of *Voyeur Café*. This is it.

First day of a new chapter.

Turning over a new leaf.

A fresh start.

Starting with a fresh page?

A blank *page.*

A blank slate.

Picking a mantra shouldn't be this hard.

Okay, no mantra.

I've got this—wait. Maybe that's the mantra.

I've got this. I've got this. I've got this.

Devon and Allie have been encouraging me to break up with Jared for what feels like forever. It started with a late-night, "Are you sure you're happy?" conversation when I was visiting, and turned into text messages every few days along the lines of, "Did you break up with that jackass yet?"

Being with Jared was comfortable, safe. So, I kept my head buried in the sand for an embarrassingly long time—not willing to admit what our relationship had become—*not willing to face who he'd become.* I'm ashamed that it took me so long to leave. I didn't want to live through the pain of redefining myself without him.

We had a life together, a routine, the same friends—*who I didn't realize were backstabbers*—and I couldn't imagine any *other* life for myself but one with him in Portland. I pushed everything else to the back of my mind for years—him slowly pulling away, doing more and more things with *our* friends that didn't involve me, refusing to *talk* about marriage because—*why aren't you happy with our life now? Don't I take good care of you already?*

It *should* have been enough to break it off, but I wasn't

ready to let go until I found out he'd been sticking his dick in someone else—*for months*. Suddenly, creating a life without him was my only option.

So, I told him to fuck off and moved out the next day.

Not really. I wish it was that easy.

What I *actually* did was yell and cry until my throat was raw for days after. The next morning, I went to the salon and had eight inches of my hair chopped off and the tips dyed pink.

Then, I made a thoughtful plan to move in with Devon in Palm Springs, which included two excruciating weeks sleeping in the guest room of the house Jared and I had shared for the last seven years. Now it's time for the final step of my plan—actually *starting* my new life.

I've got this.

Shouldering my way through the door with two gigantic roller bags, my eyes land on Cam Hacker. He's straddling a barstool, arms slung across its back, and *staring straight at me*. His eyes stay locked on mine as he leans forward and says something to Allie.

Her brows furrow, but then she spots me. "Holy shit!" she yells across the crowded bar, running all the way over to me and pulling me in for a tight hug. "Is that a fucking break-up haircut, Sadie Winslow?" she asks into my ear, still holding me tightly. "Did you finally leave that motherfucker?"

My lips curl into a triumphant smile. "Yeah. I left that motherfucker."

She takes my suitcases and starts leading me back to her office, but Cam steps out to stop us when we pass the counter. He takes over the luggage, urging us to sit down and have a drink. Allie starts bickering with him about something, but I don't hear it.

Does he remember me? No, why would he? That was six years ago.

Cam

> Six months ago, *Voyeur Café's* grand
> opening – *Palm Springs, California*

"*Shit.* I'm sorry." As I enter the back parking lot, I nearly step on Allie's pink-haired friend, Sadie, sitting on the sidewalk by the back door. She's the girl from the photo I found in Allie's office, but now that I'm seeing her in person, I'm certain we've met before.

She looks up at me for a moment, then says, "Um, hi."

"Seat taken?" I ask, pointing to the spot on the sidewalk next to hers.

She giggles, eyes dropping to her drink. "Nope."

When I sit down, the concrete's lingering heat from the Palm Springs sun seeps through my jeans.

I introduce myself, but she just shakes my hand without offering her name. "You're Sadie, right?"

"I'm sorry," she giggles again, her voice light and warm. "I should've said."

My brow furrows in confusion. "No need to apologize."

After a long sip from her drink, she sets it down between us and turns to face me directly, bringing her soft features into focus. "Let me try this again." She pulls her shoulders back, smiling brightly, and offers her hand again. "Hi, I'm Sadie Winslow."

I shake her hand for a second time, reintroducing myself.

Her last name doesn't ring any bells, but there's something about her dimpled cheeks that feels familiar.

She leans in closer, bringing her face near enough for the dim streetlight to reveal the caramel hue of her eyes and the freckles dusting the bridge of her nose. "Better that time?" she asks, her giggle making her eyes sparkle.

Leaning in too, I reply, "Absolutely. I really enjoyed it."

She lifts her drink, stopping just before it reaches her lips. "How do you feel about pineapple?"

"I'm for it," I say.

"Magnificent." She holds the smoothie-looking drink out to me. "You have to try this."

It tastes like pineapple and orange, with just enough alcohol to get someone her size drunk.

"That was a weak sip," she scoffs, rolling her eyes.

"Did you just call me weak?" I ask.

"I said you took a weak *sip*."

A joke about what my mouth is capable of crosses my mind, but I keep the humor to myself. "I'm not trying to take your whole drink."

She leans in further, giving me a glimpse of her cleavage. "I'm friends with the owner," she whispers. "Free drinks. You can finish this one."

When she shoves the drink back into my hand, I take another—much longer—sip, not stopping until she nods in approval.

"You know," I say, savoring the way her eyes widen with interest. "I'm friends with the *other* owner, and there's no way in hell he put this pineapple dream on the menu."

"If you're not getting off-menu drinks, maybe you should

have a word with *your* owner friend. Not fair if I'm the only one getting special treatment." She says this with a playful tone, and the warmth in her words radiates off her in an undeniably familiar way.

Has she been to races? Are we friends online? I'd remember that. Wouldn't I?

"Sounds like you have more pull than I do," I smirk. "Put in a good word for me?"

"I will. Promise," she says with a sincerity that feels a little too familiar. *Right?*

"We've met before, haven't we?" I ask, the question making me feel like an asshole. People recognize me in public a lot, and it's hard to keep track of everyone I've shaken hands with, hugged, or chatted with. But I remember *her*. I just don't know why.

Her eyes widen for a second before she looks away. "No," she drags the word out into two syllables, raising her voice at the end and tucking a strand of pink-tipped hair behind her ear.

I burst into laughter, knowing I'm right. "Well, aren't you an adorable little liar?" I tease, watching her cheeks flush.

"Did you just call me a liar?" she gasps, meeting my gaze with mock indignation.

"*And* adorable." I tap her lightly on the nose, and she giggles immediately. "Don't forget that part."

Her mouth drops open, and she blinks at me, unsure how to respond. Testing my luck, I tap her nose again, and she giggles again. *It's like I've found her giggle button.*

"You don't know I'm lying," she insists.

I finish off the last of her sweeter-than-pie drink before answering, "Yes, I do."

"Fine," she huffs, rolling her bottom lip between her teeth. "But if you don't remember how we met, I'm not telling you."

"It'll come back to me. I'm very—"

The back door of *Voyeur Café* opens, blasting the parking lot with the rowdy sounds of the party inside.

Luke steps halfway out the door, and for once, I'm not happy to see him. "Were you going to bring in extra booze from the truck, or—" He glances accusingly from me to Sadie and back to me.

"Oh, shit." I jump to my feet. "I'll be right in."

"It was my fault," Sadie says quickly, hiding her drink behind her like it's a crime scene.

"No, it wasn't," Luke mutters, shaking his head as he goes back inside.

"See? Adorable little liar," I call over my shoulder as I walk toward the truck. "I saw you out here and completely forgot what I was supposed to be doing. That's on me."

Sadie

Two months ago, Sadie & Devon's house—*Palm Springs, California*

Unknown 805 number: Heard Devon's moving in with her man soon. Think I could talk you into taking me as a new roommate in her place?

Me: I'm so sorry. Who is this?

Unknown 805 number: You apologize too much.

Me: You going to tell me who you are?

Unknown 805 number: It's Cam. Allie didn't tell you she gave me your number?

Me: Maybe she did, and I forgot. I'm sorry.

Cam: That absolutely did not happen. You've got to stop apologizing.

Me: Can't help it.

Cam: I'll help you overcome it when we're roommates.

Me: When we're roommates? Did you just decide you're moving in?

Cam: Pretty sure you agreed.

Me: Did not.

Cam: You sure?

Chapter 2
Sadie
Present Day

Go a whole day without apologizing - *from Sadie's list of things she's never done*

"Is it weird that I'm nervous?" I ask, pulling my feet up onto my new extra-cushy rose-colored couch and wrapping my arms loosely around my knees.

Devon's flawless face tightens in concern. "It's not too late to back out. I am sure with more time I could find someone far less absurd to take my place."

"I'm just not sure how to act when he gets here." I shake my head. "And Cam is *not* absurd. You can't say stuff like that about him."

"Sadie." She gives me a wry look. "How could the *Race Naked* guy not be absurd?"

"You're being unfair," I say, trying—and failing—not to picture the way he looked in that video. "It's just a catchphrase.

He probably hasn't done that in forever."

She arches a dark brow. "One naked race is too many naked races."

"Dev, it's not like—" The sound of a car door closing cuts me off. "He's here. *Shit*." My cheeks flush. As if I wasn't already nervous enough, now we're sitting here talking about an ancient viral video where he's naked in public.

"You think the wild motorcycle racer, internet-famous guy is going to make a good roommate?" she presses.

"*Devon*," I hiss. "He could hear you."

She rolls her eyes, whispering, "Okay."

The front door swings open, and Allie walks in, followed by Luke, and then *Mr. Race Naked* himself. He throws his arms wide and greets me with, "Hey, roomie!" at a volume that would be considered yelling for anyone else, but coming from Cam, it's just his regular voice. He extends a hand, pulling me off the couch and into a hug in one swift motion.

He's here. We live together now. This is the exact moment I've been nervous about all day—all week, actually. *Okay, ever since I agreed to let him move in.*

Since I have no idea how to act, I stare awkwardly up at him.

I'm sure I've been normal around him before. Why can't I remember how? What do I say? What if he doesn't like me? What if I annoy him—

"Luke and I were gonna get started in the garage," Cam says, beaming a smile that makes me feel welcome in my own home. "That good with you?"

Sure, that's great. Why not? It's your garage too. You're welcome to it—Of course he's welcome to the garage. He's welcome to the whole—Shit. I have to say something.

I clear my throat and force a smile. "Garage. Good."

As soon as the door to the garage slams shut behind him and Luke, Allie turns to me. "Are you okay? You're being weird."

I resist the urge to add an apology to my response. "I'm just a little nervous," I whisper, even though they can't hear me through the thick door.

"Really?" Allie—who's never been nervous a day in her life—twists her round features in confusion.

I swallow, wringing my hands. "What if he doesn't like living with me?"

Devon's lip curls in offense. "What if *you* don't like living with *him*? That should be your concern."

"That's not fair," I protest.

"No, she has a point," Allie says. "But you have nothing to worry about. Cam's a sweetheart and a huge Sadie fan already."

"Really?" I ask.

Allie laughs. "He couldn't stop talking about you in the truck on the way here. He's really excited about living with you."

"*Really?*" I repeat, still skeptical.

Devon's dark blue eyes narrow. "I am offended that you are so surprised by this information."

"In his mind, you two are besties already," Allie says, clapping her hands and making an excited squeal that has her brown ponytail bouncing. "You're gonna be the cutest roomies who ever roomied."

"That is a bit of a stretch," Devon says. "He *is* still the *Race Naked* guy."

"You've *got* to drop that," I roll my eyes. "It's not like he's going to strip down and ride laps around the pool on his motorcycle in our backyard."

Allie tilts her head to the side. "I mean…"

What have I gotten myself into?

She registers the tightening of my face and quickly changes direction, words tumbling out in a rush. "He's actually doing less of that stuff now. That's part of why he's moving out here. He told you, right?"

He did not. "Honestly, we've barely talked."

Devon gives me a side-eye but keeps her comment to herself.

"He wants to clean up his act. He's been struggling to get on a team since he broke his leg. His reputation—" she winces "—as a fuckboy doesn't help. But I *hate* to call him that. It's just his online persona. Having a solid homebase will help with that."

Devon's quiet, but I swear her eyes are asking: *Are you sure you want to live with a guy who's internet-famous for being a fuckboy?*

Allie's mood lightens when Cam and Luke's laughter floats through the wall from the garage. "Should we go see if they need help?"

"As fun as that sounds," Devon says dryly, "I have to get back to work." Turning to me, she leans down to my level and whispers, "You are allowed to be nervous, but I promise you don't need to be," before making her way out the front door.

Do you hear that, brain? I do not need to be nervous.

"He's perfect for you," Allie says, swinging open the door to the garage.

The house is a ranch-style, shaped like a capital *E* missing its middle prong. On one end is the garage, then the kitchen, connected to the entry by an archway, followed by the living room. Past that is an L-shaped hallway with my office first, then my bedroom at the corner, my bathroom, and finally, what used to be Devon's—but is now Cam's—bathroom and bedroom.

It only takes four of Cam's massive strides to cross the garage and reach us the moment we open the door. "Excellent timing, loves. Luke was starting to get on my nerves," he says.

He's already moved three motorcycles into the garage. *Who needs that many?*

Luke steps out of the black and yellow box trailer that's backed into our driveway—his muscular arms stacked full of cardboard boxes. "It's a lie."

"What is?" Allie asks.

"Whatever Cam just said." While the rest of us laugh, Luke only grunts and keeps going.

When I offer to help, Cam responds, "Nope. We just have some gear and a couple more motorcycles to fit in the garage." He dips his head a little closer to mine. "Very sweet of you to clear it out for me, by the way."

"I didn't—I mean, I guess I would have," I stumble over my words. The urge to apologize pops up, but I avoid it again. "I don't really have garage stuff."

"See? You're perfect for each other," Allie says, clapping her hands. "She doesn't have garage stuff, and that's *all* you have."

"Hey, I've got furniture too," he objects. "It'll be here in a few days."

My watch vibrates with a reminder. "*Shit.* I have to get on

a call. I'll see you guys later. I mean, I'll see *you*," I point at
Cam, "a lot later. Like, not a lot of time later. Just a lot of *times*
later. Multiple later times. I will be seeing you." *Dammit. For a
second there, I almost sounded normal.* "'Cause we live together now."
I finish with an awkward smile and bolt inside before he can
respond. *I've got to get myself together.*

When I log into the meeting, only two members of my team
are already on.

"—so fast to get engaged. I mean, obviously, they're
amazing together, but it's just so sad for—" my coworker
Hanna's voice cuts off. *Wonderful.* Never a good feeling when
the conversation halts as soon as you enter the room, even if
it's virtual.

"Sadie, how are you? Are *you* seeing anyone yet?" Hanna
asks. It's a thinly veiled attempt to garner gossip.

She introduced my ex to the girl he cheated on me with.
Kelee. Hanna and her boyfriend both knew Jared was cheating,
and they still came over to our house, eating meals I cooked,
without saying a word about it. *For months.* I've successfully
cut every other tie between my ex and me, but I can't exactly
get Hanna fired for being the opposite of a girl's girl. *I wish I'd
known she wasn't a real friend before I helped her get a job on my team in
the first place, though.*

Fortunately, our manager joins the call, and I'm saved
from trying to figure out a clever way to make it seem like
I'm seeing someone without lying. I alternate between trying
to hear what Cam's doing in the garage and puzzling over the
snippet of conversation I overheard.

It can't be that. Not so soon. But who else would *"so fast to get
engaged"* be about? Finally, I give in and pull up my ex's social

media.

My stomach drops.

A post from last night shows the woman he cheated on me with in a little white dress, and him in a suit, holding her left hand up to the camera. The caption reads, "One year down. The rest of our lives to go."

One year down? We broke up six months ago. One year down. Is he serious? Were they already—

Evidently, I'm committed to hurting my own feelings because I keep swiping through the photos. They had dinner at that fucking steak place he loves, then he planned a surprise party at our old house—*now their house*—with all of my old friends—*now their friends.*

He didn't even have the decency to buy her an ugly ring. It's stunning.

I don't care. I'm not upset. I shouldn't care. And I don't. This is me— not caring.

"Sadie?" my manager's voice comes through my computer speakers, and I barely hear it over the pounding of my pulse. *Wonderful.* "Do you have any insight on the timeline?" he asks.

Fucking rushed. Sketchy as hell. Wildly inappropriate.

Since my boss likely isn't asking about the timeline of my ex's engagement, I give a canned answer about teamwork and balancing time between projects. It satisfies him enough to move on.

The rest of the meeting passes in a blur, my entire body buzzing with something hot and awful. *Not jealousy. Maybe anger? Hurt? Ugh, hurt seems right. I hate that he's still able to hurt me.*

The moment the meeting ends, I click out before anyone can try and talk to me. Tears well in my eyes, but I refuse to let them fall. *I don't want to think about him. I am sick of thinking about him, and yet this—*

Cam leans on my open office door, a gigantic smile lighting up his entire face. "Allie and Luke just left, and I wanted to see if you—Are you crying?"

"No, I'm sorry." *Dammit, looks like I'll have to try for not apologizing on another day.* "I just—I really do not *want* to be crying."

"Got it," he answers cautiously, nodding his head. He glances around my office, and I realize it's because he's never been in here. *He lives here now, and I haven't even shown him around. I should—* "You want to go for a ride?" he asks.

"What do you mean?" I tilt my head. "Where to? Just to drive around?"

"No, a *ride*," he answers with an amused chuckle. When my response is to stare, he adds, "On a motorcycle—with me."

"Oh," I answer. The image of his body splayed across the asphalt race track after his crash burns behind my eyes. I've tried to forget this part of Cam—the motorcycle racer part. *Maybe the most significant part.* "I don't—motorcycles aren't—" *How do I explain this without offending him?* "It's probably not—"

He doesn't make me finish the thought I'm stumbling over. "How about a margarita?"

"Right now?" I ask, startled by his quick change of plans.

He tracks my movements as a tear rolls down my cheek and I push it away with a fist. "Yeah, right now," he says.

That meeting I zoned out of was the closest thing to work I've accomplished today. My screen has a flashing notification of a chat from my boss. My inbox is full of unread messages, and that doesn't even begin to touch the project I'm leading. Another notification flashes—a chat from Hanna. The last thing

I want to do is work today.

I could cross something off my list.

"I'm in." I exhale a heavy breath, feeling lighter already. "Give me five minutes."

"Can't wait," he says with enough excitement that I'm tempted to believe him, and then walks away down the hall.

Now, I just have to tell my manager I need the rest of the day off. *I just have to pretend to be sick. Should be easy.* I'll just say— what *do* I say? He just saw me on the video call, so he knows I'm not sick. *Although, not all illness is visible.* I could tell him I got food poisoning. *Seems too convenient.* Or, I could say I have a migraine. *But I've never had one before. Would he remember that about me and know I'm lying?*

I type out a message.

Hey, sorry if I seemed off during our meeting. My head is killing me, and I was wondering if I could...

No, too passive. I delete it and start over.

I'm not feeling well. I need to take the rest of the day off.

Hopefully, that'll be enough. I take a deep breath and press send. His response is immediate.

Get some rest! We'll catch up tomorrow.

That's it? Why haven't I been doing this all along? I never use all my sick time.

I grab my *Try It* journal off my desk and search for the

correct entry. The little checkered book holds a list I started this past summer. I wasn't expecting to rebuild my life this year and didn't know where to start. So, I've been compiling a list of things I've never done but want to try. Even though I think I'm well past a hundred entries at this point, crossing things off has yet to lose its shine.

~~*Fake being sick to get out of work.*~~

After changing into my comfiest leggings and a cropped sunflower yellow hoodie, I meet Cam in the kitchen, where he already has the blender going. I snag the tequila from the counter, pour myself a shot, and throw it back.

His laughter carries over the blender's whir until he presses the button to stop it.

"I'm not usually a mid-day drinker, but today is," I search for the right phrase and land on, "*Especially fucked.*"

"Oof, sorry." His smile drops into a grimace.

"Oh, my word." I rush to apologize, making sure his green-blue gaze meets mine. "It's not because of you. That probably sounded horrible. I'm sorry. The special fuckery has nothing to do with you. I'm really happy about this." I wave my hand between us, indicating *this*.

He smiles—over it immediately—and pours us each a margarita. Holding his glass up to mine, he says, "To those *later times* you mentioned."

I snort, tapping my glass to his. "Later times."

We've just barely settled onto the couch with our drinks when my phone buzzes with a notification.

Hanna: Hey, heard you're sick. I hope you're okay.

Before I figured everything out, I liked her. But she acted like my friend all that time, and *she knew*. It's a bit of insult to injury that she's reaching out right now, trying to act like she cares about me.

"So," Cam's voice breaks me out of my thoughts. He's leaning back on the couch with one leanly muscled, tattooed arm folded behind his head, watching me. "Are we gonna talk about what's happening on your phone that's making you look so murder-y?"

"Murder-y?" I ask.

"I'm surprised your eyes didn't burn a hole in that thing." He points to my phone. "Something's got you fucked up. You want to talk about it?"

I *should* talk to someone about this—should call one of my friends.

Allie would curse Jared, his new fiancée Kelee, Hanna, and everyone they've ever known. Devon would remind me that he was never good enough for me in the first place and not to waste my tears. And our friend Bea would probably make a point to validate each one of my feelings. *I have no idea what will make me feel better, but none of that sounds right.*

My eyes focus on my new roommate. *He's my friend, too.*

"It's kind of shallow, the thing I'm upset about," I say.

"I love shallow," he says, sipping his margarita.

Here goes nothing. "You know how I was in a relationship for a really long time?" I ask.

Cam nods, blue-green eyes focused heavily on me.

"And I finally left because he cheated on me?"

His brows shoot up. "Didn't realize that part. What an idiot."

"*Yeah*, what an idiot," I agree, realizing that might be the only insult I haven't mentally applied to my ex yet. "That *idiot* just got engaged to the girl he was cheating on me with." I hide my face by taking a big sip of my drink as soon as the words are out.

Cam's jaw drops, and he shifts forward from his laid-back position. "That motherfucker," he says, with a rare edge to his voice.

"It's fine," I sigh. "We're not together anymore, so he has every right—"

"It's not fine," Cam interjects, that same severity weighing down his tone.

"We were together for nine years, and you know what he'd tell me when I brought up marriage?" I ask.

Cam raises his eyebrows, inviting me to answer my own question.

"He said he never wanted to get married. He'd tell me that we lived together, and he took care of me." I roll my eyes. "And that should have been enough for me. 'Marriage is just a piece of paper, and it doesn't mean anything.'" The full-body *hot-angry-hurt* feeling from before returns, tears welling in my eyes. "I *hate* that I hate this. Does that make any sense?"

Cam graciously ignores my crying. "It makes complete sense."

"Being upset about this makes me look jealous, but I swear I'm not," I sniff, wiping my tears with a fist. "I realize I'm sitting here drinking and *totally not crying* because he got engaged, but I *am* over him—romantically, anyway. I'm still mourning the loss of the years I spent with him." My phone vibrates again, but I don't bother checking it this time. "I think I need another shot before I admit this next part."

Cam's quick to pour me one and one for himself, too. "Bottoms up, love," he says, holding his glass up.

"Bottoms up," I say as we swallow the tequila down.

"Alright, hit me with it," he says, striking a perfect balance between taking me seriously and lightening the mood.

"I don't want him back. *At all.* I'm honestly so happy I never have to see him again, but I'm not a big enough person to wish him well." I scan my new roommate's face for judgment, but find none. "*I've* been working through nine years of history, feelings, and betrayal, and the breakup seems like *nothing* to him. He started moving on before I even realized moving on was an *option.*" I release a heavy breath and admit, "I'm embarrassed." Checking him again for judgment, I only find rapt interest. "I hate that he's living in the house that used to be ours with his shiny new girlfriend—*ugh, fiancée*, and I haven't even been on a date since we broke up. It's been almost an entire decade since I kissed someone who wasn't him. He's winning the breakup, and I know I shouldn't—"

Cam holds a flat hand up between us, halting my rant. "Nope." He shakes his head for emphasis. "You lost me there. He can't be winning if he no longer has you."

I laugh, but Cam doesn't. *He meant that?* "You're very sweet," I say. "But I am the *most single* person in California, and he replaced me with a younger, better model."

"Woah, woah, woah," he stops me again. "She may be younger, but there's no way she's better."

My laugh is pained. "She's twenty-two."

"Younger, not better." He shrugs, resting his arm behind his head again.

My eyes narrow. "I am trying to feel sorry for myself. Could you quit encouraging me, please?"

He shakes his head. "I will drink with you about this all day and all night. I'll order takeout for lunch, dinner, and dessert. I'll listen to every word you say, but I'll also stand up for you. You're too important to feel sorry for yourself over someone dumb enough to fumble you."

I glare at him, but it holds no menace. "That sounded an awful lot like encouragement, Cameron."

"Alright, alright," he laughs. "I'll do my best to be less encouraging. Tell me what you would have to do to win the breakup."

"Trying to win the breakup is petty," I mutter.

He smirks. "I can get behind petty."

I draw my bottom lip between my teeth for a moment before I land on an answer. "I want him to be *jealous*. I want *him* to wonder about *me*. I want him to replay our relationship at night when he's trying to sleep and wonder what part of *me* was there the whole time that he just didn't see."

Cam's response is a nonchalant, "Okay."

"Okay, what?" I ask.

"Okay," he says again, shrugging. "Let's make him jealous."

Chapter 3
Cam

Moved to the desert so I can work on my tan. (Just kidding. You know I'm rockin' SPF 1000 every day.) - *caption from Cam's social media post - a picture of him standing on the seat of a dirt bike parked in front of a wind turbine, February 17th*

It finally came back to me. Sadie is the woman I met outside the restaurant after the first time I won the *Portland Moto Invitational.* I don't remember our whole conversation, but I do remember wanting to cheer her up then, too. *And that smile.* She had the warmest smile I'd ever seen. *Still does.*

Sadie blinks at me for a moment before bursting out laughing. "You're serious? Make my ex jealous?"

"Why wouldn't I be?" I ask.

"You say it like it's easy." She tucks her socked feet under her body and hides her hands in her hoodie pocket. "Did you miss the part of the story where he didn't want me?"

Anger on her behalf tightens my throat. "That is not what I heard."

"Stop it. Yes, you did," she says, shoulders slumping.

"You broke up with him," I remind her.

"As a technicality," she says, curling in on herself further. "He had a whole other girlfriend."

"Yeah, but he never broke it off with you." I nudge her toes with my knee. "He liked having you and took you for granted."

She nods, straightening the smallest amount. "He really did."

"He's an arrogant fucker," I decide, and she doesn't disagree. "Probably doesn't think you'll ever move on."

"That's essentially what he said—*how was I going to be okay without him? I need him. My life is nothing without him.*" Sadie pulls her shoulders back as her words get stronger. "He never admitted he was cheating—told me I was making a huge mistake leaving him. I still don't understand what he thought was going to happen." She shakes her head, pulling her hands from her pocket and tying her hair into a ponytail. "And now he's winning the breakup, and I'm day-drinking about it," she finishes with a frustrated sigh, followed by the final sip of her margarita.

As I refill her glass, I come back to my point—which is also arrogant, but hopefully in a more appealing way. "You think he'd be jealous if we could make him think you're dating me?"

"*You?*" Her mouth drops open. "That wouldn't—we're not—he would never—we would never—I don't think—"

I brush it off with a joke. "Trying not to be offended over

here, Sadie."

"Oh, no. I'm sorry." Her sincere eyes search mine as she reaches over and holds my hands. All my senses zero in on her touch. "It's not that he wouldn't be jealous of you. There's nothing wrong with *you*, but—no, that's not what I mean—well, no. There *is* nothing wrong with you. But you're *you*. We can't date." She releases my hands with the last sentence.

"I'm not asking you to *actually* date me," I say, *even though I wish I could.* "But we could pretend."

My reputation is no one's fault but my own. When that video of me went viral forever ago, I leaned into it, embracing the *Race Naked* persona. It's all over my branding, on my trailer—I even have a merch line dedicated to it.

That evolved into me publicly doing other reckless things—racing motorcycles where I shouldn't, getting naked in places I shouldn't, doing stunts I had no business doing. When I act like an unserious asshole, my engagement goes up, and I make more money to fund my racing.

It also made it easy to find women who were happy to hook up with me—to be able to say they slept with the *Race Naked* guy. Most of the time, I haven't had to find them at all. They come to me. *But I've never been successful at finding a woman who could see past all of it and commit.*

In my early twenties, it was amusing when people called me slutty. But as I've gotten older and stopped acting the part, the reputation stayed on anyway. *No wonder Sadie's hesitant.*

"You'd be helping me out if we could make it *look* like we're dating," I add.

Her brow furrows, and her plump lower lip drops into a little pout. "Helping you? How?"

In this idea's two-minute lifetime, I haven't considered how much I'll have to tell her for this to work. Suddenly, sitting face-to-face on the couch feels too vulnerable. "Want to go for a walk?" I ask.

She looks at the half-drunk pitcher of margaritas on the table and then back at me. "Sure?"

"I can make fresh ones when we get back. Don't worry," I say, helping her off the couch.

We pause by the door so she can put her sneakers on and I can grab a sweater. It's not cold here the way it is a couple of hours away by the ocean, but the February afternoon still carries a chill.

She leads the way, walking on the road instead of the sidewalk. "So, are you going to answer my question, or what?" she asks.

"Which one was that again?" I tease.

"How exactly is us not dating, but *looking* like we're dating supposed to benefit you?"

"Without boring you with my entire racing history—I need to improve my image, so I can get on a team and stop having to fund my racing myself."

She nods along but says, "I'm still confused. I think I'll be needing that boring race history. I'm sorry."

"So much apologizing." I shake my head.

She brings the back of her hands under her chin and bats her lashes innocently. "I can't help it."

Turning onto the next street, I explain, "I've been racing in *USMoto* in the 600 class since I was twenty-one—nine years ago. I was supposed to move up to superbikes—*which are 1000ccs instead of 600ccs*—a few years ago, but I crashed out and broke my femur. It—" I cut my story off when she winces.

"I remember that," she says, staring at the asphalt under her black and white sneakers.

Shocked, I ask, "You saw that crash?"

"Yeah," she answers, jaw working. "Jared and his friends were watching the race, and I—" She pauses, releasing a tight breath, "I heard them from the other room, and I knew something happened. I came in—" She shudders. "And I saw it. Saw *you*, laid out on the track. Your leg was—you didn't move for a really long time."

Sadie's response is visceral, and as much as it's tempting to be touched that she's upset about seeing *me* like that, it has to be connected to something deeper for her.

Wrapping my arm around her shoulder, I pull her close, pausing our walk. "I'm sorry," I say. It doesn't seem like the right words, but they're all I've got.

"Oh, my word. Do not apologize to *me* about that," she says, leaning into the hug for a long time before letting go. "I doubt you did it on purpose to hurt me—a girl in Portland you don't remember meeting that one time."

"I remember," I say. I may have just now placed the interaction, but I *knew* we'd met.

She eyes me skeptically. "No, you don't."

"You were standing in front of a steakhouse in Portland, wearing the tightest little blue dress." Her eyes widen as I recount the details, leaving out everything I remember about her ex. "Your hair was longer then, without the pink. And you said you hated motorcycles, but you thought I was funny."

Her cheeks flush as she draws her lip between her teeth. "Okay, you remember," she says, turning away and starting down the street again. "I still don't understand what any of this has to do with you racing superbikes and pretending to date me."

Pretending to date her. The idea just grew legs, but I'm holding onto it like a lifeline. "The crash took me out for the rest of that season and the next," I explain. "I lost my sponsorships, so when I came back to racing last year, I did 600s again and had to fund it myself. This is my first year in superbikes, and I'm paying for that too."

"Never thought about how much it costs to race," Sadie notes. "I guess I imagined they'd just pay you a salary or something."

"A lot of racers get signed by the motorcycle companies themselves, which would be the closest to what you're thinking. But I'm not a factory racer."

"*Ooh, I like the flowers on this cactus,*" she points, whispering, like she doesn't want me to miss the flowers, but also doesn't want to interrupt. *It's adorable.*

"*I like them too,*" I whisper back before returning to my story. "I pay for my bikes and gear using money I make doing dumb shit online, but I don't want to do that forever. I actually just got a call with a conditional offer from a private team owned by *Incite Energy Drinks* for next season. That's why I was going to go for a ride—clear my head so I could think it over."

"Oh, I should have—"

Cutting her off before she can apologize, I say, "I have a reputation problem, which is what I'm hoping you can help me with. The first condition from *Incite Energy* is that I have to clean up my image. The online persona—*that I know I'm responsible for*—has been a double-edged sword. I am lucky as hell that

I've found a way to fund my racing, but the stunt videos and other dumb shit make me look reckless—which isn't appealing for a legitimate team."

"Let's go this way," she says, pointing to the left.

Turning the corner reveals another row of white mid-century houses with perfectly tailored lawns. It's a beautiful neighborhood, but I'm looking at her more than anything else.

"What's the other condition?" she asks, light-brown eyes focusing on me.

"I have to finish top three for the season."

Her head tilts with curiosity. "You're good at racing, though, aren't you?"

"I'm amazing." *No one's ever accused me of humility.* "But it will be my first year in superbikes. It won't be easy."

"The image stuff—rebuilding your—trying to be—trying not to be a—" She gives up on completing the thought. "That's the hard part?"

"Hard*er* part anyway," I answer. "It's a bit like flipping a U-turn with a cruise ship. I've made myself into a punchline, and I can't be that anymore. I need racing to be the loudest thing about me."

"I like that plan for you," she says, matter-of-factly.

"Does that mean you want to help?" I ask, unable to drop the idea.

She gasps, hooking one arm with mine and pointing across the street with the other. "Look, it's my friend."

There's no one across the street, though—only more mid-century houses with neatly landscaped lawns. "Where, exactly?" I ask.

"He's the little black cat running across that driveway," she points again. "Sometimes he visits me in our backyard."

"Have you figured out where he lives?" I ask.

"No idea," she says. "He doesn't have a collar, but he's always around." When the cat disappears from view, she picks up her pace again, but leaves her arm looped in mine.

"Did you name him?" I ask, enjoying her closeness.

"He's not *mine*. I can't name him," she says, staring at the road beneath our feet.

"You absolutely did name him."

"No, I didn't," she says, fully turning her head away.

"I can tell you're lying," I laugh, tugging her closer with our joined arms. "What's his name? I need to address him properly if we ever run into each other in the yard."

"Fine," she sighs, but it's a playful sound. "I call him Boo, 'cause he spooks so easily."

"Cat named Boo. I can get behind it."

She nods but shifts the subject, tugging lightly on my arm. "I still don't understand how I could help you with your reputation."

Grateful I wasn't the one who brought it up this time, I answer, "People believe I'm a fuckboy. I've—"

She gasps, "Oh, I wouldn't say—"

"It's okay," I reassure her, guiding her closer to the sidewalk as a car approaches. "I said it, not you."

"Well, I don't like it." Her lips pull into a frown. "It's obvious that's not who you are."

"Was it obvious before we met?" I ask.

She bites her lip, looking away.

"It worked for me in the past, and I leaned into it—built a whole career around it. It's been a long time since I did anything deserving of the reputation—at least not the slutty part," I explain, wanting her to understand how different I am from my online persona. "But people still believe it. I've never had a girlfriend. If it looked like I was with you, it would show that I'm not reckless. I'm steady and committed. I moved out here to get away from the people I partied with and have a home base close to my best friend. What if it looked like I moved in with my girlfriend, too?"

She stares up at me for a while before a slow smile turns up the edges of her soft lips. "That would be very domestic of you," she says, eyes sparking with mischief. "Very steady, not *fuckboy-ish* at all." The word fuckboy comes out in a rushed whisper, like she hated it in her mouth. "And, not to brag— actually, *yes* to brag—I am a *magnificent* girlfriend. I am sure I could be a magnificent pretend girlfriend."

She's considering it. She's actually considering pretending to date me. "I've never been a boyfriend of any kind before. Maybe you could teach me how to act like a good one."

"That could be fun. I've never had a *good* boyfriend before," she says, followed by an excited gasp. "I should put that on my list. Hold on a sec." She stops walking, pulling her arm from mine so she can type on her phone screen for a few seconds before indicating we can start walking again.

"Gonna let me in on whatever that was?" I ask, tilting my chin toward her phone.

"Ooh!" she squeals. "Have I not told you about my list yet? Do you want to hear?"

Seeing her joy return is a relief. Her sadness felt unnatural. "More than anything," I say.

She giggles, as if I've made a joke. "I'm on a bit of a

reinventing Sadie kick right now," she begins. "My life got a little stale." She rocks her head side to side, scrunching her nose. "Okay, *a lot* stale. So, I made this list of things I've never done, and I'm trying to do as many of them as possible."

"I'm in," I say, looping her arm back through mine.

"What do you mean?" she asks, using her free hand to tuck pink-tipped hair behind an ear.

"*I'm in*," I repeat. "I'll help you. I'll do it with you. Whatever you need."

"You can't know that," she says through a bright, dimple-cheeked smile.

"I can."

"You haven't even seen the list," she says, rolling her head on my shoulder to give me a skeptical look.

"Don't need to." I smirk back at her.

"It *is* a pretty good list." She pauses to point out a cactus across the street that's shaped like a snowman before saying, "I'm adding things to it constantly."

"Can't wait to hear them."

"All kinds of stuff. I'm training for a half marathon with Devon and Bea because I've never run a race." Her speaking and walking paces both increase as she shares. "I'd never had a martini before, so Luke made me one at the bar last week. I want to see a ghost, but I can't exactly do anything to make that one happen."

Wondering how I can get her to show me the entire list, I say, "And now you've added *have a good boyfriend*."

She sighs, "I imagine that'll stay on the list even longer than *see a ghost*."

"Didn't I just offer?" I ask with a light laugh.

"You offered to *pretend* to be a good boyfriend," she says, pointing at flowers in another yard we pass. "Very different thing."

I pull her out of the way just in time to stop her from rolling an ankle on a section of uneven pavement. Big light-brown eyes blink up at me for a few seconds, and I forget what I'm supposed to be talking about.

"Sorry, I should watch where I'm going," she apologizes.

"You don't have to. I'm watching," I say, guiding us back to walking.

"You don't *actually* think we should pretend to date, do you?"

"I do," I answer, adrenaline pumping through me at the idea that this is within reach. "You deserve to fuck with your ex a little, and I mean it when I say you'd be helping me with my racing career. I need help fixing my reputation."

Her shoulders rise and fall on a heavy breath, but then her lips pull into a smirk. "You're his favorite racer. I think your videos are half the reason he started watching racing in the first place."

If I didn't already know my image needed work, being her ex's favorite racer would be proof enough. "Perfect, isn't it?" I ask.

That draws a dimpled smile out of her. "If he was scrolling his feed, and a picture of me with you came up, his head might explode." She sighs. "It's a fun idea, but it would never work."

Well, shit. "Wait. Why not?"

"Because we have friends who know we're *not* dating," she giggles.

"Until we tell them we are," I say.

She hesitates, and I'm dying for her next words. "My friends are nosy." She brings a hand tipped with light pink nails to cover her mouth. "That sounded mean. I'm nosy too. I don't mean it like a bad thing. It would be a really hard secret to keep."

"We could let them in on it," I suggest.

She rolls her lips together, shaking her head. "They wouldn't support it. They'd give me a hard time for putting so much effort into making Jared jealous." When she says they, I wonder if she really means Devon. "I'm already *embarrassed*," she lowers her voice on the last word. "I know I *shouldn't* care what he thinks—"

"Do you want to do it, though?" I interrupt her to stop her from talking herself out of this.

Instead of answering the question, she says, "I'm supposed to be more evolved than this."

"But you're not," I laugh, nudging her ribs with my arm. "It's okay. Neither am I."

She nudges me back. "It *does* sound like fun."

"And it's something you've never done," I remind her.

"You're not wrong," she says, pointing out the house with the pink door—her favorite—as we pass it.

"We won't tell our friends we're pretending," I say, liking that idea better anyway. "And then they won't judge you."

"They'll judge me for getting into a relationship so quickly—or not actually—well *maybe*." Her pace slows again as she stumbles through the thoughts. "It's possible I'm not giving them enough credit."

"Is your friends' judgment enough of a reason not to do something?" I ask.

"Yes," she laughs. "These friends are more like family than my actual family most of the time," she explains.

"Luke is like that for me," I say, turning us around so we can head back to the house.

"You think it's a good idea if we lie to all of them?" she asks.

Shrugging, I answer, "I think it's okay to have things that are only your business if you don't want to share it with your friends—even if those friends feel like family. It's alright to have secrets."

"Huh," she huffs a quiet laugh. "You want to know something else I've never done?"

"Absolutely," I answer.

"I've never had a secret," she whispers the information to me, like it's a secret in itself.

"Never?" I ask.

"You've pointed out before that I am a terrible liar," she reminds me.

She is. It's one of her cutest qualities. "It's a good thing to be bad at," I say.

"Maybe, but it makes it awfully hard to be mysterious." She lifts a flat hand up like a tray for the point she's about to make. "Or to keep a secret."

"You want to try it with me?" I ask.

She considers for long enough that I'm focusing on the rhythm of our steps as our feet hit the asphalt when she finally answers, "Sure. Let's do it."

Now I'm the one trying to hide my response. *She actually agreed.* I take a steadying breath and say, "I'll post something tonight."

"Tonight?"

"Didn't you just agree to do this?" I tease her.

"Yeah, I did. I—but *right now*? Our friends won't believe we got together in the last fifteen minutes."

"We'll ease them into it," I say, guiding her out of the street. Wrapping my arm across her chest just below her shoulders, I rest my chin on top of her head and lift my phone in front of us to grab a photo. It's a pose that could be read as friendly or affectionate, but either way, *we look damn good together.*

Chapter 4
Sadie

Have a secret – *from Sadie's list of things she's never done*

The black cat clock on the wall above my desk swings its tail with every second I get closer to being late for my morning meeting. I click the button to join the 9:00 a.m. video call with my team at 9:01. *Dammit.* Cam and I were up late last night talking through the specifics of our outrageous plan, so I barely woke up in time to brush my hair and throw on a presentable shirt before my meeting.

"Oh, good! You're here," my manager greets me the second I pop up on his screen. "I hope you're feeling better."

Feeling better? My brow furrows, and then I remember. I was *sick* yesterday. *Shit.* I unmute myself. "Yup. It's gone. All better." What the fuck do I mean by *"it's gone"*? What's *"it"*? I never even said what kind of sick I faked being. *He's going to know.* I quickly mute myself again, feeling like the sound of my anxious heart might be picked up by my computer's microphone. I wait for him to call me out for lying in front of the whole team, but he just says it's good to have me back and moves on.

Between the throbbing behind my eyes and a general sense of wooziness, this hangover is determined to make sure I remember each and every tequila shot. Maybe this is karma for lying about being sick yesterday. *Or, it's just the consequences of my own day-drinking.*

A text from Allie lights up my phone, but I'm determined to focus on the meeting today, so it'll have to wait. I don't miss it when my manager asks me a question, and I actually have an answer ready this time.

"It's been moving more quickly than expected—" My words cut off, distracted by the fact that Cam is suddenly standing next to me. *I didn't even hear him come in.* I try to ignore him until I can put myself on mute. "More quickly than expected. We're close to wrapping up—" I lose my train of thought completely when he leans in close, resting one hand on the back of my chair and setting a hot cup of coffee on the desk right in front of me. I look up and find him sporting a completely unapologetic smile.

"Sorry to interrupt," he whispers—not meaning a word of it—then leans in even closer and *kisses the top of my head.* The casual affection has my stomach flip-flopping, but he walks out of the room like bringing me coffee and kissing me in front of all my coworkers is the most natural thing in the world.

Oh shit. My coworkers.

Lifting my newly delivered coffee mug to the camera, I say, "Sorry about that. Forgot my coffee." Through some miracle of self-composure I don't usually possess, I manage to pick up exactly where I left off and give a solid answer to the question.

Fortunately, the camera on my computer isn't good enough to betray the pink that's flooded my cheeks. My likeness is surrounded by my coworkers' little video boxes—a few of them staring down at their phones, but almost everyone else is smiling. Except for Hanna, whose mouth is agape.

That's what this was. He did that for Hanna. At some point yesterday—after tequila shot three or four, but before our Thai food was delivered—I filled him in on as much of the story with Jared as I could handle repeating. He knows Hanna is going to run back to Kelee and tell her everything she just saw. Between that and the photo Cam posted last night, Jared will be able to put it together.

This just might work.

Once it's finally not my turn to talk anymore, I check Allie's text.

Allie: Cam just texted me to ask how you take your coffee. Told you you'd be the cutest roomies who ever roomied!

My first sip of the drink confirms her words—sweet enough that most people would probably hate it, and frothy foam on top. *He got it just right.* I type out a response.

Me: Thank you for telling him...

I delete it right away. *It's not enough.* Cam and I agreed to keep our social posting reasonably ambiguous at first, so we'd have time to reveal it to our friends in a way they might actually believe. This is the perfect opportunity to lay some groundwork. *Of course it is. He did this on purpose.*

> *Me: He just brought it to me during my meeting. It was really sweet.*
>
> *Allie: Yes! I love when my friends become friends with each other.*
> *Me: I really like him. A lot…*

I delete that one before sending, too.

> *Me: I know it's only been a day, but I think this is going to be a really good thing.*

It doesn't seem anyone on the video call is paying attention to me anymore, so I sneak a photo of the coffee, making sure to show off my fresh manicure, too—a variation of my usual lavender-colored left hand, rose-colored right hand combo with a thin gold horizontal stripe running across each finger.

As soon as my meeting ends, I get up to find Cam. When I open my office door, he's standing in the hallway, hand poised to knock, wearing nothing but a towel tied low on his hips. My eyes are level with the tattooed words across his chest that read '*No Risk No Story.*' More lettering peaks over the top of the towel, crossing the deep muscular *V* there, but I can't quite make them out. *I'm staring. Shit.*

It's rude to stare.

When I drag my eyes back up to meet his, water drips from his red hair onto his freshly shaven face as he smirks. Good*ness.*

I train my eyes on his.

"You want to finish your coffee out back with me?" he asks,

like it's normal to be hanging around the house in his towel. *Oh, my word. What if it is normal for him to hang around the house in a towel?*

"Yeah—sure—coffee," I stammer.

"Awesome. I'll put some clothes on and see you out there," he says, turning toward his bedroom. I've never seen his tattoos this close before, especially not the ones on his back. I get a good look at the pirate flag and crossed palm trees on his muscular shoulder blades before he disappears into his room. *At least this time he couldn't see me staring.*

When I turn back to grab my forgotten coffee cup, there's a chat from Hanna on my screen.

> *Hanna: Um, excuse me. Who was that gorgeous man that brought you coffee?!?*

A petty smile turns up my lips. *It's working.*

"Come sit here by me," Cam says when I meet him in the backyard. Right outside the living room's glass slider, there's a pergola with magenta papery bougainvillea flowers growing up the side. Underneath it is a sturdy oak patio set, and just beyond it is our bean-shaped pool. I join him on the loveseat-style rocker he's sitting on, and he drapes his arm across its back, barely grazing my shoulders.

"That was very sneaky with the coffee," I say, lifting my cup for another appreciative sip. "And really *good.*"

"Seemed like something a boyfriend would do." He shrugs, but the smile on his face betrays just how pleased he is with himself. *It's kind of endearing.*

I smile up at him. "It's something a *good* boyfriend would

do."

"No more bad boyfriends for you, Sadie," he says, a slightly too big smile spreading across his face.

"We can only hope," I say, opening my phone to show him the picture I took. "I was thinking I could post this." Nerves about what I'm about to ask tighten my throat, but I swallow them down. "Would it be okay if I tagged you?"

"Yes, it's okay," he laughs, pulling me closer to him. "Of *course* it's okay. This is exactly the kind of shit we need to do. I'll repost it."

Fresh nerves flutter through me. *The man has millions of followers.* So far, we're only hinting, but eventually, there should be no doubt in his followers' minds that I'm his girlfriend. *And they'll judge everything about me. What if no one believes we're actually dating because I don't look like the kind of girl a famous motorcycle racer would date?* It's an old thought—*that I'm not pretty enough*—one that I've worked really hard to overcome in the past year, so I don't let it take hold. If Cam thinks we're a believable couple, then everyone else should too.

"Look," I whisper, pointing past the pool to the white concrete breezeblock wall that surrounds our little backyard. Boo jumps off it, landing on the smooth, gray rocks below and takes a cautious step toward us.

"Does he get close enough for you to pet him?" Cam whispers.

"He's rubbed against my leg a few times, but any time I've reached for him, he's run away," I answer. "Maybe if we're quiet, he'll get closer."

My phone buzzes with another text—this one from Jared. *That was quick.* My gut twists with a mix of nerves.

Jared: Are you seeing someone?

"It's working already," I say, reading Cam the text.

Cam's smile is devious. "Good."

"I'm not sure what to say back, though. Should I confirm it? We haven't told our friends yet, but I doubt—"

"You don't need to say anything," Cam interrupts.

"That'll make him really mad," I giggle.

"Exactly. Let him believe you're so happy with me, you can't even be bothered to text him back," he says, then shares details with me about the reactions to the picture he posted of us last night. People are eating it up, speculating about whether or not we're dating. *It's not a surprise.* Even though I avoided reading the comments on that post in particular, I did a deep-dive scroll on his social media last night, and as far as I can tell, he's never posted a photo like that with a girl before.

"Let me get a picture of you now," he says, snapping a photo of me sipping my coffee.

"Are you going to post that one, too?" I ask.

"Maybe," he shrugs. "But I need a photo for your contact in my phone."

My response is a sigh of relief. Something about him posting a picture of me by myself makes me feel much more exposed than a picture of us together.

"Do you think he'll get spooked if I stand up?" Cam asks, pointing at the little black cat who's now a few feet closer to us.

"Yeah, but don't let that stop you," I answer. "Do you have to go somewhere?"

When Cam stands, the loveseat rocks in his wake. Boo

bolts across the yard and disappears from view. "I have to get to the track," he says.

"You have a race today?" I ask, following him into the house. My heart beats faster as I imagine him on a motorcycle. *Racing a motorcycle—crashing that motorcycle.* This is why I could never *actually* date him. We're barely even friends, and I get anxious just thinking about him on a motorcycle.

"My first race of the season isn't until the weekend after next," he says. "Just a training day. I'd invite you to join, but you have to work now, right?"

I huff a laugh. "I'm not going to watch you ride motorcycles."

His dark red brows furrow. "I guess we didn't talk about this, but if you're gonna act like my girl, you'll have to come to races."

"Come on," I laugh, trying to hide the nerves in my voice. "Not *everyone's* girlfriend comes to their races."

"I guess they don't *always* come," he says. "But races are the best. You'll miss out on everything if you never come."

"Nothing about a motorcycle race sounds appealing," I say, shuddering my shoulders in an effort to physically shake off the mental images of bloody asphalt. *It's been twelve years since my crash, but the memories have never left me.* "Actually, I'd say it sounds like the opposite of fun."

Cam tilts his head—like he's trying to wrap his mind around the concept of someone not wanting to watch a motorcycle race.

"It's just not my thing," I offer, doing my best to laugh it off. The last thing I want to do is unload my trauma on him right now.

Brow still furrowed, he grabs a leather jacket off of a hook by the door. "Most races are out of state—so if you can't travel for those—that's normal." He sighs, disappointment pulling his lips down. "But it'll be a pretty tough sell if you're *never* there."

He's not even a little bit wrong. *How inconvenient.*

He searches my face. "Maybe if you explained your aversion, I could—"

"No, you're right," I wave my hand in an unconvincing display of nonchalance. "I should be there as often as I can. I'll be—" I shake my head, rephrasing, "It'll be fine."

He laughs, but it's mirthless. "That's *obviously* bullshit. Why don't you just tell me why you don't want to go?"

"I don't like talking about it," I answer.

He slides his arms into the jacket. "You don't have to explain yourself, but all of this will be a hell of a lot easier if you talk to me."

I bite my lip while trying to force a smile. *I probably look unhinged.* "All good."

"Little liar," he laughs for real this time, but settles quickly. "This thing we're doing won't work if you don't trust me. I hope you tell me eventually."

Again, he makes an extremely valid point. So inconvenient. Still, I don't agree—at least not verbally.

He pulls me in for a hug, surrounding me with the warmth from his chest and the rich smell of leather. "It'll be fine, whatever it is."

"Don't know what you're talking about," I joke, clearly unable to mask my concern.

He gives me a *you're-not-fooling-anybody* look, and says, "First race of the season is next Sunday. It's only a two-hour drive from here. It'll be the easiest one for you to get to. Will you consider it?"

"Sure," I say, swallowing the lump in my throat.

He opens the door to the garage, giving me a broad smile before he leaves. "See you later, Sadie Winslow."

"Have fun today. Don't crash," I respond.

"Woah." His mouth drops open, and he steps back into the entryway, shutting the garage door behind him. "You cannot say shit like that to me."

"Why not?" I ask. "I don't want you to crash."

He flinches, pulling his mouth back in a grimace.

"Isn't it a good thing that I want you to be safe?" I point out.

"I'd be pretty fucking concerned if you were hoping I get hurt," he says, running both of his hands back through the sides of his hair. "Believe me when I tell you I am aware of the risks. I know how dangerous this is. I've *been* hurt. I've seen other racers hurt." He takes a step closer to me. "I *am* careful. I'm not fucking around out there. But when you say *don't crash*," he whispers the words, like he doesn't want the race gods to hear him, "all I hear is *crash*," again the word is whispered, "and it'll get stuck in my head. I can't be thinking about that while I'm out there."

"But I don't want you to *crash*," I whisper the word this time, too.

"Which I appreciate." He looks up to the side as tattooed fingers tousle his deep copper hair again. "How about this? Think of it kind of like how you don't tell a performer good luck before a show."

"So—*break a leg*?" I sputter a laugh. "That cannot possibly be better."

"It's absolutely not," he laughs. "*Have fun* was great. That's always a good one. If it's a race day, you can tell me to make sure I win, kick some ass."

"There's no racing version of break a leg?" I ask.

"Not officially, but a lot of people will say *rubber side down, stay on the bike, or head down, butt*

    up."

"Head down, butt up? What does that have to do with racing?" I ask.

"If you're doing it right, your ass almost never touches the seat during a race," he says, sliding his hands into his jacket pockets.

My brows lift in surprise. "Must take a lot of strength."

"It does," he says, voice dripping with amusement. "Part of the professional athlete thing."

Professional athlete. I've never thought of him that way, but I guess it's true. I know motorcycles are heavier than they look, and he has to lean his all over the track. Maybe all the tight, sinewy muscle I saw on his torso this morning wasn't just for show. *I wonder what the muscles on his legs look like.*

A mischievous smile turns his lips. "My personal favorite is *ride it like you stole it.*"

"Huh?" I ask, blushing like he's heard my thoughts.

"Things to say to me before a race," he reminds me. "My favorite is *ride it like you stole it.*"

I giggle. *There is no way I'm saying that to him.* "Okay, Cam." I lift my hand toward the garage. "Have fun. Stay on the bike."

"Thanks, love," he says, reopening and walking out the door.

Still, all I can think is—*Don't crash. Don't crash. Don't crash.*

Chapter 5
Cam

The cutest - *caption from Cam's social media post - a picture of Sadie sipping coffee in their backyard, March 1ˢᵗ*

"How'd you do?" Luke's voice comes through my phone.

Shutting the door to my hotel room, I answer, "Sixth."

"*Sixth*? That's—" He stops himself. "What happened?"

We both know that's the worst qualifying placement I've had in twice as many races.

Qualifying is crucial. Each rider gets a set number of laps alone on the track the day before the race. Then, our best lap time is ranked against the other riders to determine our starting position for the actual race.

Sixth isn't terrible, but it'll make it tough to get podium— top three—and it's not a great start for my first race on superbikes.

Rebuilding my reputation is important, but none of that

matters if I don't dominate this season.

I blow out a breath and explain to my best friend that I had a couple of decent laps but blew a tire on the last one.

"Shit," he says.

"Yeah, shit," I agree. Kicking off my shoes, I fall backward onto the bed.

"Ludlow?" he asks.

"First," I answer. Ryan Ludlow grew up on the track with Luke and me, but when Luke stopped to start spinning wrenches, Ryan and I stuck with it. He moved up to superbikes a year before I had planned to, and he won the championship the last two years.

Luke doesn't comment on Ludlow, just asks, "Hart?"

"She got tenth. Not bad," I say. Shane Hart's a wonder. She's barely older than I was when I started racing 600s, and now she's in her first year on superbikes. She's the only woman on the circuit racing 1000ccs, and Luke and I both like to look out for her.

"Do me a favor and don't mention my blowout to Sadie," I tell Luke.

"Why would your roommate care about that?" he asks.

"She's not just my roommate. We're—" I stop myself mid-thought. She hasn't been ready to tell our friends about us yet—doesn't like the idea of lying to everyone. "It's not that. I don't care if she knows my qualifying position—honestly, I'm not sure she'd even know what it means—but she's freaked the fuck out about my safety out there."

There's a pause before he says, "I get it. Is she coming tomorrow?"

"Not sure, but I want her there," I sigh. Having her in

my pit would mean more than she understands. It's only my team—mechanics and coaches, and sometimes a close friend like Allie—who I have down by the track with me.

Luke's quiet for a few seconds before asking, "What are you doing with her?"

"I like her," I answer, no hesitation.

"She's your roommate. You're not supposed to—"

I interrupt him. "Can we not do this tonight?"

"Fine," he sighs. But I know this won't be the last time he brings it up. "If she comes, it'll be her first race. Have you prepped her?"

"She's watched them on TV before, but we haven't talked about it much," I say. "The last few days have been a whirlwind, so we didn't get a chance." The last few days *have* been a whirlwind, but that's not the real reason we haven't talked about it. Every time I bring up racing or even motorcycles, Sadie either changes the subject, shuts down, or leaves the room.

"Well, if she's there, we'll take good care of her," Luke reassures me, likely sensing I'm not telling him the whole truth.

"Thanks, boss," I say.

"See you in the morning," he replies, ending the call. He used to be a race mechanic but gave it up to open his motorcycle shop and the bar he ended up sharing with Allie. He agreed to mechanic for me this season, saying he didn't trust anyone else to manage the bikes. *But I think he misses the track.*

I throw my phone aside and strip down to shower off the grime and sweat from qualifiers. A lot of athletes have routines they can't break—*won't break*—before race day. I never got into a consistent routine like that, but I do make sure I have a quiet night alone before a race. Most guys stay in their trailers at the track, but if I do that, I get into trouble.

There were years when all I did was race and party. I'd race on a few hours' sleep and somehow still pull out wins. Four years ago, one of the guys I partied with ended his career after a night like that. He made a stupid call and high-sided on a tight turn, scraping most of the skin off his clutch hand. His bike caused a pile-up, taking three other guys down with him. Fortunately, no one else was seriously hurt, but it was a heavy reminder that a tired racer is a dangerous one. *It's not only my life on the line out there.*

Now, I barely drink during the season—never the night before a race—and I don't have to sweat the random drug tests they throw my way. I make sure I have plenty of time the night before a race to wind down, watch a movie, and get a solid eight hours.

After my shower, I'm searching my phone for something to watch when it rings. A giant smile takes over my face. *She's never called me before.*

"Hi, love. What's good?" I ask, my voice warm.

"Do you have a jersey or something I should wear tomorrow?" she asks. "I mean, I know you don't wear a *jersey*, but it should look like I'm with you, right?"

Too surprised to properly answer her question, I ask, "You're coming?"

"Yes, silly," she giggles.

"You made it sound like you'd rather do anything else," I tease. She's avoided it every time I brought it up since.

"I guess, but I need to be there," she answers. "So, I'll be there."

Torn between excitement that she could actually show tomorrow and not wanting her to be uncomfortable, I remind her she doesn't *have* to come.

"I'm coming," she replies, determined. *But why didn't she want to come in the first place?* "Cameron," she says my full name to get my attention. "You got a jersey or what?"

"No jersey, but anything in black and yellow—those are my colors—would work. My number is *207*, and I've got boxes of *Race Naked* merch in the garage you're welcome to." The idea of Sadie wearing my colors, my number, anything with my name on it practically makes my dick hard. "Actually, if you go in my closet, all of that's in there. Just wear anything that's mine."

"I can't go in your room without you here," she says, and I can picture the scandalized blush on her cheeks. "That's so invasive."

"I just told you to," I say, digging through my bag for my headphones.

"Okay." Her giggles echo off the hall around her.

"I'm sorry I can't drive you tomorrow."

"No worries," she says, the sound of hangers sliding in the background. "Allie and I have it all worked out. Besides, you have to focus tomorrow. Can't have you worried about driving me."

"Driving you wouldn't be a worry."

"You get what I mean," she says, and I can picture her waving her pink-nailed hand dismissively. "Has *207* always been your number?"

"Since day one," I say, settling back onto the bed and

putting on my headphones.

"Was sixty-nine taken?" she jokes.

"It was," I answer, relieved it was. That number, with the *Race Naked* mantra, would've made it even harder to change my reputation. "February seventh was the date of my first race. When I had to pick a number at sign-in, it's all I could think of. Not the most creative thing."

"It's a higher number than most of the racers I've seen on TV. Isn't it?" she asks.

"Yeah," I answer, hopefully masking my surprise. I keep forgetting that even though she hates motorcycles for a mystery reason, she's watched a lot of racing—mine included. "As you move up, they offer lower numbers—double digits, or if you're really killing it—single digits. But *207*'s been good to me. I don't want to give it up."

"Well, I like it," Sadie says.

"Yeah?" I ask, running my hand along the tattoo on my neck of a checkered flag with my number over the top. "Why's that?"

"It's my birthday," she says, shyly.

Now I'm *definitely* never changing it. "My first race was in 2007, so that would've been your—what—ninth birthday?"

"Eleventh, actually. Guess I'm older than you thought," she says, closing my bedroom door.

Trying to guess what she picked from my closet, I answer, "Nah, I'm just bad at math. So, I was twelve, racing a barely-running dirt bike with Luke on February seventh, 2007. What did you do for your eleventh birthday? Do you remember?"

She hums quietly, bringing up the memory. "I think that was the year it snowed. It's not rare to get snow in Boise in

February, but that year it *dumped* on my birthday. School was canceled, so I spent the day baking with my mom. I forgot a whole sheet of cookies in the oven, and the house had that acrid, burnt smell all day," she laughs.

"Is your mom the one who taught you to bake?" I ask.

"Yeah, she's an amazing baker. I wanted to be just as good as her when I was a kid. Still do."

"Do you still bake together when you see her?" I ask, realizing I know so little about her family.

"I don't see her that much anymore," she says, rushing to change the subject. "Did you remember to pack sunscreen?"

"Sure did," I say, confused by the shift in conversation. "I'm the whitest person you know, and I'm covered in tattoos. I don't leave home without it."

"Good," she breathes, sounding genuinely relieved. "I've just been thinking about your safety tomorrow—from the *sun*."

"From the sun?" I ask, sitting upright.

"Yes," she drags the word into two slow syllables. "It's very dangerous—the *sun* is."

"Okay?" I answer, unsure where she's going with this.

"People *go out in the sun*, not thinking about the risks," she says in a rush. "Just because they haven't personally been hurt doing it—"

"Going outside?" I ask, trying to follow.

"Yeah, yeah, that," she agrees, though it doesn't feel like she should be. "Like maybe someone's spent their whole life—" She takes a deep breath. "*Going out in the sun*, and they've never—" There's a long pause I don't know how to fill. "*Personally* gotten—" another pause. "Skin cancer. *Yes, that's it.* Just because you've never gotten skin cancer doesn't mean you won't. Or maybe you got it once and survived. It doesn't mean you'll survive next time."

"I guess that's true," I answer, wishing I could see her expression. "Maybe a little depressing and unnecessary to bring up right now, though. Don't you think?"

"No, *not* unnecessary," she practically scolds me. "Cameron." She says my full name again. "You have to be very careful to protect yourself tomorrow—from *the sun*. You could get very, very hurt if you're not careful."

It finally clicks. She's doing what I asked—avoiding the *C* word—but in her own way, she's giving me a safety talk. *It's kind of adorable.* "You're right," I say. "I could. The sun is dangerous. But I'm really, really good at being safe," I stick with her metaphor, "in the *sun*. Some might even say I'm professional."

"You can never be too safe." She goes quiet again, and I feel lost without her body language. *I wonder how she'd respond if I tried to video call her.*

"The safest thing would be to just stay inside," she says.

"That would make it awfully hard for me to race tomorrow." I'm half touched, half hurt by how concerned she is. If she'd ever had a real conversation with me about this, maybe she'd understand why I need to race—how it feeds my soul—and I could explain the level of risk.

"I guess," she sighs.

Maybe sticking with her analogy is the way to get through to her. "But I have extra layers of *sun* protection."

"Yeah?" she asks, hopeful.

"Yeah. The helmet I wear is thick and padded. The sun doesn't stand a chance against it." Making sure she knows *I* know what we're talking about, I add, "You know, if *the sun* ever did manage to get through my helmet, I'd throw it away."

"*What?*" she gasps.

"I have backups for that exact reason. Every racer does." Searching for a way to keep her calm, I say, "If a helmet's compromised in any way—" I trail off, but she finishes the thought for me.

"If it was cracked *somehow*, and sunlight could get through?" she asks, being bolder than I expected.

"Straight in the trash. New helmet time. Same pretty much goes for my leathers and boots. Those are repairable, but I only wear them when they're in good shape." *Would telling her my suit has an airbag freak her out more?* I skip it. "When I'm out there—*in the sun*—I've got layers of thick, sturdy fabric and foam that protect every inch of my skin. From a sun flare."

I don't even know what a sun flare is, but she doesn't question me.

"Isn't that expensive?" she asks, some of the severity dropping from her voice.

"It is," I laugh. "That's one of the reasons you're helping me."

"So, by pretending to be your girlfriend, I'm helping you stay safe?" she asks. I hear a muffled sound in the background.

"Exactly," I say. "You feel a little better?"

"Actually, yes," she says, surprised. "*Oh shit*," she mutters under her breath. "*That still doesn't look right—ugh.*"

Before I can ask, she quickly ends the call.

It's the first time in years I wish I wasn't alone the night before a race.

When I wake up the next day, I find a text from her sent a little after three in the morning.

Sadie: Don't forget your SPF!

Chapter 6
Sadie

Go to a motorcycle race – *from Sadie's list of things she's never done*

"Stick with me," Allie says, reaching her hand back for me to hold as she weaves through the crowd. "We'll turn left up here," she adds, waving the hand I'm not holding to show me the correct direction.

The smell of freshly poured asphalt mingles with the concrete-y scent of the stadium as we pass through the fans gathered to watch the race. Engines roar louder the closer we get to the pits, where we'll be spending the entirety of Cam's race.

A girl wearing a white *Race Naked* shirt bumps into me, and I almost lose hold of Allie's hand. *I should've guessed I wouldn't be the only one here supporting him, but I didn't expect half the crowd to be in black and yellow.* A self-satisfied smile pulls at my lips. *I'm the only one wearing his clothes, though.* I catch sight of another woman wearing an oversized black and yellow hoodie with *207* printed across the back. *Maybe I'm not the only one. What if there are women here who—*

"Keep up, Winslow!" Allie yells, squeezing my hand and pulling me forward. We're not late, but she's thrilled to be here. She talked about what an incredible racer Cam is the whole drive, sharing anecdotes from races she's seen over the past year. I nodded along and did my best to act interested, like a girlfriend should—*even though I still haven't told Allie about that.* It was a good chance for me to practice calming breaths. *I can't let him know how scared I am for him. It'll only make him more likely to get hurt.*

90s alt-rock blasts through the sounds of engine revs, signaling we've made it to the correct pit. Allie runs to Luke, who's already been here for hours. Cam's nowhere to be found, so I set the cookies down on a folding table behind a stack of tires and try not to look as awkward as I feel.

The pits are areas designated for each racer and their teams, where they keep bikes, tires, and gear. They're lined up next to the track in a row of colorful tent shades, each coordinated with the racer it represents. A low concrete wall—like the ones you see along some freeways—is the only thing separating the pits from the track.

Some pits are three or four times the size of others, with Cam's being on the smaller side. His team seems smaller too, consisting of Luke, two guys I don't recognize, Allie, and me.

"There she is," I hear Cam's voice just as I feel him behind me, wrapping an arm around my waist and kissing the top of my head.

My heart flutters. We probably should've talked about how

to handle today. *Are we telling Allie and Luke? Was the photo of me he posted last night too obvious? Why else would he post a photo of just me? It's probably time to tell them anyway—*

Keeping my back flush to his chest, his arm loosely draped around me, he says, "She's the one I've been telling you about."

A tall, athletic, dark-haired woman I hadn't even noticed standing beside us reaches her hand out. "Shane Hart. Thrilled to finally meet you." *Finally?* We only just started *dating* two weeks ago. "If Hack sucks it up out there, you can always cheer for me instead."

Cam's chest shakes against my back with laughter. "We want me in first and her second," he says against my head. "Kid's a wonder. Spent about ten minutes in the 600s before she moved up to superbikes."

"Kid? I'm not that young," Shane says, smiling warmly at me. "Twenty-two."

Twenty-two. Feels like a lifetime ago. At her age, I was graduating college and moving in with Jared. *Ugh, Jared. Will there ever be a day when he isn't a part of every memory I recall?*

Shane heads back to her tent, which turns out to be the red and white one next to ours with the number forty-seven proudly displayed at the front.

Cam stays close to me, always having a hand on my waist, arm, or shoulder as he shows me around his pit—a proud smile on his face—and introduces me to his team. Rick—a friend who races 600s—is acting as a coach, and Beau—a quiet guy who looks about Shane's age—is here as a second mechanic.

Two identical bikes sit on stands in the middle of the space. Three helmets are lined up on the side next to a spare suit.

Everything has a backup. *How many times is he planning to crash?*

His brow furrows as he comes over to the massive stack of tires and picks up the container of cookies. "What's this?" he asks, opening the top.

"I'm sorry. I just thought it would be nice—"

He cuts me off. "Are you trying to *apologize* for baking me cookies?"

"I don't know the etiquette," I shrug.

He pulls out a rectangular sugar cookie with flood-decorated frosting on top. The design is black and white checkers—like a finishing flag—with the number *207* in yellow across the top. The cookie looks better than I thought it would, although the black is a lot grayer than I intended.

"The etiquette can fuck right off if it says you're not allowed to bring these to the track," he says, eating half the cookie in one bite. "Have you *had* these?"

I sputter a laugh. "Honestly, no."

Knowing a good night's sleep before watching Cam's race wasn't an option, I decided to try flood-decorating cookies to pass the time. I knew it wouldn't be *easy*, but I figured I'd pick it up quickly. *I did not.* There are three dozen poorly decorated rejects in the fridge at home.

He holds one out to me, the design *Race Naked* in black and yellow frosting. *There are only four of those. Lettering is hard.*

"Let's save this one," I say, switching it out for a checkered flag cookie.

"Shane!" he yells to the tent next door as he leads me over to his friend with an arm slung around my waist. "You've got to see this." He tilts the container toward her. "My girl made these cookies for me."

My girl. My heart flutters again, but I have to keep myself in check. *He doesn't mean it. It's not real. And I don't* want *it to be real.*

"Damn, look at these," Shane says, grabbing a cookie with a black track around the edge and *207* in the middle. "For next time, my number's forty-seven, and those are my colors." She points at the red and white tent above her as she takes a bite. "I didn't believe him when he said he just moved in with his gorgeous girlfriend," Shane says, shaking her head.

Girlfriend? Evidently, Cam's done playing it close to the chest.

"Why not?" I ask.

"Cause Hack doesn't really commit." She looks back and forth between my fake *boyfriend* and me. "Or, he didn't."

"Exactly," Cam says, squeezing my hand. "I didn't until I found her."

"I disagree," I say, feeling defensive of him. "He's more committed to racing than I've ever been to anything."

Cam's brows raise, but Allie bounces over before he can respond. *Did she hear the girlfriend part of that conversation?* "We need you, racer-man," she pops up on her toes and looks into the container of cookies. "Were you just *not* gonna share?" she asks with as much offense as anyone could muster over cookies and snags them from his hand.

"See you out there, boss," Cam says, giving Shane's shoulder an encouraging squeeze before we leave her tent.

Then everything happens in a blur. All of the bikes are lined up on their marks based on the qualifying laps the racers did yesterday. Warmers are placed around the front and back tires, and the racers zip into their suits and slide on their helmets before going out to mount their motorcycles. The voices of the announcers ring out, and a countdown timer starts. *Five minutes.*

Some of the racers have a coach, friend, or partner standing on the track with them. *Is that allowed? It must be if people are doing it.*

Luke steps up next to me. "I usually keep him company for this part."

"Oh," I say, not sure what to do with that.

He watches me with dark, skeptical eyes. *Has Cam told him we're dating? Can he tell we're faking? Does he think I'm bad for Cam?* "I think he'd like it to be you today."

"Me?" I squeak, looking across the track to Cam, where he stares straight ahead, fingers drumming impatiently against his gas tank. Between us is a minefield of places I don't belong. There are thirty racers lined up with people interspersed throughout, including interviewers and camera crews. *No, no, no. That can't possibly be what he meant.*

Luke watches me for a moment before nodding and stepping over the cement divider. "I'll walk you over." He holds out his arm for me to balance on as I step onto the track.

But my feet don't move. *How do I explain that I cannot go out there?* I want to be as far away from the racing as possible. Not *on the track.*

"You alright?" Luke asks, arm still poised.

No, not at all. But I can't say that, can I? I don't want to be here, but Cam was right. If we were truly dating, there's no way I'd miss his first race of the season, especially one that's so close to home. I had to come, *and now I have to do this.* Plastering a smile on my face, I grab onto Luke's offered arm, hoping he doesn't notice the way I shake as I step over the concrete barrier.

When my feet land on the track, the asphalt doesn't explode or suck me in—*so that's a good sign*. Luke doesn't say anything as he leads me through the small crowd and over to Cam. He grabs Cam's shoulder, nods, and walks away, leaving me staring at Cam through his helmet.

Cam motions for me to stand closer and lifts his visor. "Hey, gorgeous."

"Hey." I glance around, hoping no one's watching us, but find that many people—even some with cameras—are.

"It's alright," he reassures me, bringing a gloved hand to my waist.

Cam's an affectionate person—making sure to hug everyone in a room before he leaves, resting his arm on a couch behind anyone he's seated next to—so it shouldn't surprise me that *boyfriend* Cam is so hands-on. He'll probably have to start kissing me for real—not just on top of my head—at some point. *If I wasn't already twisted in knots over his impending race, I'd probably feel a dip in my stomach at the idea.*

Tilting my shoulders into him, I giggle for no reason and bat my lashes. "I have no idea what I'm supposed to do right now," I say without breaking my flirtatious smile.

Cam's head leans back with his full-body laugh. "You're doing amazing. I have to sit here on my bike—ready to go—until the race, and I'm terrible at sitting still. It's my least favorite part of the whole day. You keeping me company makes a big difference."

Conversation has always flowed seamlessly between us, but

now that it *matters*, my mind is blank.

Fortunately, Cam has no such problem. "You crossing anything off your list today?" he asks.

"Go to a motorcycle race," I say, running my hand up his leather-clad arm. The suit is so stiff it feels practically impenetrable. *If only that were the case.* "It's a little bit of a cheat, because I just added it this morning. Although, I am having lots of firsts. I've never stood on a race track before."

"You look really good on one," he says through a charming grin. "Especially in my shirt."

I chose a heathered gray long-sleeve with his number on the front and his last name on the back. The sleeves are rolled, and I had to tie it up in the back, hopefully making it obvious that it's his.

"It's very soft," I say, rubbing the fabric against my chest. "You might not get it back."

"I hope I don't," he answers.

When Luke and Beau appear to take off his tire warmers, adrenaline courses through me. *It's time. He's really doing this. I can't stop him, and he could get hurt. He could—*I cut off my line of thinking, not even allowing the word in my mind while I'm standing on the track.

Instead, I lean up on my tiptoes, grab onto either side of his helmet, and say the only race-related thing I can remember, "Rubber side down."

"Yes, ma'am," he says with a solemn tip of his head, at odds with his wide smile.

And then—because it seems like something a girlfriend should do—I smack a kiss on the lower part of his helmet just below the visor before rushing back to the pit.

"You guys are so fucking cute," Allie says, steadying me as I step back over the low wall. "*However*, last I heard you were just roommates."

"We are roommates," I say. "And also—" *Should I say I like him? Should I say we're dating? I should. He's telling people we're dating. It'll be weird if I don't.* Allie's green eyes search my face, and I can't bring myself to lie to my friend. "And also, he's great."

Allie's responding laugh is loud enough that everyone in our pit and the next one over turns to look at her. "Sure, that's all it is." She closes one eye in an exaggerated wink. "Just roommates, and he's great. You can't lie to me. I see what's going on."

I don't respond because I *can't* lie to her, but fortunately, she changes the subject and explains how to know Cam's rank during the race and what the screens in the pit show, including the livestream.

A wave of engines roar to life, and my gut drops. "Are they starting already?" I ask.

"Not really," Allie scoffs, rolling her eyes. "It's just a warm-up lap. They're precious about tire temperatures."

It's been so long since I sat through a motorcycle race, I'd forgotten all about that part. "I'm guessing they're not being *precious* so much as they're being as safe as possible," I say.

"Safe, precious, whatever. I just want to see some racing," she laughs, bouncing on her toes.

Before Allie met Luke, her opinions of motorcycles mostly mirrored mine. She thought they were dangerous and unnecessary, but as soon as she started riding on the back of one, it's like she forgot about the very real dangers these things represent.

She leads me back to the low wall. "This is the best part!"

The racers return from their warm-up lap and roll back onto their starting marks.

The green flag waves, and a moment later, the asphalt under our feet shakes as bikes rip past. They're so close together it looks like any number of them could run into each other. My heart pounds, and my breathing speeds. *I've got to pull it together. The last thing he needs is me losing my shit on the sidelines.*

Allie's jumping and saying something, but I don't hear her over my pounding pulse. *He's going to be fine. He is fine. He's safe— But, no, he's not. None of them are. Why do I even care this much? He's not my actual boyfriend. But he is my friend. And I don't want my friend to—This is fine—but it's not fine. It's not—*

My head spins, and I'm struggling to focus on the now-empty track in front of me. *What the fuck am I doing here? I should never have come.*

Abandoning my spot by the edge of the pit, it feels like the earth is wobbling as I manage to find my way over to the shade and slump back against a wall behind the stack of tires. Closing my eyes, I focus on my breathing. Well, I have the thought that I *should* focus on my breathing. *So that's something.*

There's nothing to be done now. He's out there, and he could—any number of horrible things could happen to him. But they won't. Right? Right? I reach for a logical way to reassure myself and find none. *This shit is dangerous. It's how people die.*

Pulling my legs in tight to my chest, I bury my face in my knees. *Motorcycles are so dumb. This is ridiculous. This is why I could never actually date him. This feeling. I shouldn't have to put up with being terrified.*

Breathing, Sadie, breathing.

I manage to breathe in for a count of four. Hold for the same. Breathe out for the same. Hold again. *He could just not do this. It's so dangerous. People die. He could*—I've lost track of my breathing. *Dammit.* I start again.

Breathe in for a count of four. Hold. And out. Hold. I get into a good rhythm, concentration on counting and breaths taking up all my focus. Eventually, my heart rate slows, and the pounding pulse in my ears subsides.

It occurs to me that I should go back out there, watch the race, be supportive, participate in the experience. But every time I consider it, my heart races again. So, I stare at my feet and go back to box breathing. *In for four. Hold. Out for four*—

"You're missing the race," Allie's too cheerful voice interrupts my fragile calm.

I give her the dirtiest *are-you-fucking-kidding-me* look I can muster.

"Oh shit," she says, eyes wide. "Never mind." She squeezes in next to me, wrapping an arm around my shoulder and forcing a water bottle into my hand.

I chug half the bottle before asking, "Is it over yet?"

She gives me a sympathetic chuckle. "About halfway."

"He's okay, right?" I ask, feeling silly for overreacting.

"He's crushing it, Sade." Allie's green eyes sparkle. "Right now, Cam is the happiest he's ever been. This is what he lives for. And he's *good.* He's already gained two positions. He's amazing, actually."

Allie would sit next to me like this for the rest of the race—for the rest of the day—if she thought it's what I needed.

But I don't want her missing any more of this on my account. "Should we have a cookie and watch this thing?" I ask with forced optimism.

"Fuck, yeah, we should!" she answers with genuine excitement.

Allie holds my hand as we each choose cookies and head over to the screens for an update. Luke points him out for us. "He's been dicing it up with Ludlow, the guy on the white bike right there, number two, for the last three laps."

"Still?" Allie sighs. "That guy's got to get out of the way already."

Luke chuckles. "Cam just has to be patient. He'll find his window."

I don't know anything about Cam as a racer, but in general, I doubt anyone would describe the guy as patient. *What happens if he's impatient?* My heart pounds again.

Luke explains that Cam is in third now—not fourth like he was when Allie left—because one of the front runners' bikes had a mechanical failure, so he's out. Before I can properly lose it about that, he says the guy rode his bike off the track. *No crash.*

I nibble nervously on the edge of my cookie as I scan the screens and land on a map showing the racers' numbers traveling around the track. *I like this one.* Can't actually see any motorcycles, but I can tell what's going on. I find *207* and watch it gain on *2* during the straightaways but lose ground in the turns. Sometimes the numbers get so close that one covers the other, but I try not to think about what that means Cam is actually doing.

"He's about to come through," Allie tells me, squeezing my

hand and pointing to the section of track next to the pit. "You want to watch?"

Deep breath in. "Sure." *Deep breath out.*

We line up against the low wall, making sure not to block the pit board that gives him information about his position, how close the person behind him is, and what lap number they're on. The crowd of bikes is much thinner than it was at the start, with the racers mostly in groups of three to five as they pass by the pits. *That's a little less stressful.*

Number two comes out of the turn first, but Cam is on him in an instant, passing him just like he did on the other straightaways. My fingers tighten on the low concrete wall as he flies by us. Adrenaline pumps through me, only now it's from excitement *and* fear. *He could totally take this guy.* By the time I've finished the thought, their bikes are disappearing around turn one, and I can't see well enough from where we're standing if he managed to keep the lead.

Pulling Allie with me, I rush back to the screens.

"There it is. Right *there*," Luke says.

Even though I'm watching the same screens as he is, I don't see what he's talking about. Cam's fallen behind bike number two, Ludlow, again. When Cam leans into the turn, it looks like his bike kind of skips, the tires jumping on the track instead of riding smoothly. *Is he crashing? No, no, no. He can't. This can't*—My chest tightens, and I squeeze Allie's hand.

"It's okay," she whispers. "Just a little chatter."

"What the fuck is chatter?" I ask.

I must have yelled my question because Rick answers me from across the tent in a reassuring dad voice. "It's what those little bounces are called. Cam knows his edge. It's nothing to worry about."

What would happen if he didn't know his edge? How is that nothing? Looking back to the screen, I see Cam level out and stay on his bike. And Luke was right because he pulls ahead of Ludlow as he comes out of turn three and maintains it into turns four and five, putting serious distance—in reality less than a second—between him and Ludlow when he pulls into the next straightaway.

Without Ludlow to contend with, Cam gains on the bike out front. I find myself deeply invested, wondering what he'll have to do to get to first. *If he's going to risk his life, he might as well win.* Now I wish I'd learned more about racing, or *anything* about racing before today.

Allie and I rush back to the wall to see Cam race past the pits again, and I have to stop myself from waving. *I don't want to distract him.*

"How does he get first?" I ask Luke when we return to the screens.

"Probably won't on this one," he answers.

My mouth drops open in shock. "I can't believe you just said that."

"Second place after starting sixth is great," he chuckles. "They're on the last lap. He's not close enough to get first in the next thirteen turns, but he'll keep pushing."

Last lap? Already? It feels like the race just started.

"He'll get twenty points. Solid start to the season," Allie says, then explains the points system while we wait, watching the finish line. The top fifteen finishers of each race get points, ranging from one point for fifteenth place to twenty-five points for first. All of their points for the season get added together, and that's how they determine the championship.

It happens exactly like Luke said it would. The first-place racer crosses, and even though it's only a second or so later, when Cam crosses, it's obvious it would have taken more than a lap for him to make up that distance.

When Shane crosses seventh, Allie says, "I like to root for her too. She's the only woman who races superbikes. There are a handful in 600s, but she's the only one at this level."

The only woman in superbikes. Cam's thirty, and this is his first year at this level. But she pulled it off at twenty-two? *She's impressive.*

Allie leans over, "This is the cutest part."

Cutest part of a motorcycle race?

The racers slow after they cross, lifting their visors. One after another, they swerve closer to the other racers, fist-bumping and even reaching across for hugs, congratulating each other on the race. *It is quite adorable, but I wish they'd stop letting go of their handlebars.*

When Cam pulls into the pit, the tightness I hadn't realized was still in my chest loosens. My hands and teeth unclench, and I take a proper deep breath, one that isn't a forced count. *He's safe. It's over.*

His smile is even more oversized than usual as he pulls back into the pit, mouth open wide, eyes crinkled, right on the edge of laughter. *I've never seen him happier, and this was only second place. What does he look like after winning?*

His team greets him with shoulder squeezes, hugs, and

congratulations. *I want to feel for myself that he's in one piece.* For the first time since the race's start, I remember I'm supposed to be his girlfriend. *Should I go up to him?*

"There she is!" Cam calls, pointing through his team to the corner of the tent where I'm standing. He leaves them behind, rushing toward me. *He's a much better liar than I am, doing a magnificent job of acting like he's into me—like he's my boyfriend.*

He's already taken off his helmet and unzipped his leathers, exposing his sweat-soaked undershirt and tattoo-covered neck. Red hair sticks to his forehead in a way that should look ridiculous, but doesn't. *He's safe. He's okay.* There's only a moment to take him in before he's gathering me up in his arms.

I've seen him pick Allie up before, hugging her and then swinging her around in circles, letting her legs fly out wildly until she erupts in giggles. That's not what he does with me. *At all.* His arms scoop under my ass, bringing me up flush against his hard, sweaty body so my legs wrap around his torso and rest just above his hips. I collapse against his chest, pulling him as tightly to me as possible.

He's safe. I don't let go, needing to keep feeling for myself that he's in one piece. *Can he tell I'm shaking with relief?*

When I finally loosen my hold enough to pull back, it brings my eyes level with his, our lips barely inches apart. He leans into me.

Is he going to kiss me? It's what a boyfriend would do. Should I kiss him? Do I want him to kiss me? I—

Cam gives my ass a solid squeeze then brings his teeth down in a light nip on my nose. I can't help the giggle that bubbles up in response. "It was amazing seeing you from out there," he says.

"You saw me?" I ask, not sure if I'm more shocked by that information, the ass squeeze, or the lack of a kiss. *Am I disappointed he didn't kiss me? No, I'm not.*

"Of course I saw you. You're much more important than any info on the pit board."

"That can't possibly be true," I laugh, squeezing him again. *He's safe.*

"It is," he says, dropping his forehead to mine. "Thank you for being here. I know it was hard for you."

"It wasn't hard," I say, the words getting stuck in my throat.

"Adorable little liar," he says, kissing the top of my head.

Chapter 7
Cam

Race season's off to a great start. – *caption from Cam's social media post – a picture of Sadie kissing his helmet just before the race, March 3rd*

"Morning, boss," I say, walking into Luke's motorcycle shop, *Voyeur Motors*.

He lifts his chin toward me in greeting, then continues with his work.

Leaning back on his worn leather couch, I check the text from my contact at *Incite Energy*.

Ian: What's going on with this Sadie person? Seems like a really good move.

Me: Dating her. Living with her. If it helps my rep, that's great, but she's my girl.

Ian: Love to see it. Keep up what you're doing.

It's working. Sadie and I pretending to date is having the exact impact on my image that we'd hoped for.

The changes are slow, but I can already see a shift. Normally, I'd have to strip down to my boxers and do a wheelie obstacle course to get the kind of reaction I'm getting off one photo with her. *It's refreshing how many people want to see me happy.*

There *is* a small, loud subset who would rather see me reckless or hurt. I made a career attracting douchebags, and dropping them is a fucking battle in itself. As long as their hate stays pointed at me, and not Sadie, I don't care.

Her ex is skirting that line pretty dangerously, though. He's been in my direct messages talking all kinds of shit. Normally, I wouldn't engage with things like that, but I'm close to breaking my own rules for that little fucker.

Some days, I wish I could scrap my social media altogether, but my online presence is key to staying in racing. It's funding this season and setting me up so that next year, I'll be on the *Incite Energy* team. I doubt I'll ever be free of it, but at least I'll be able to scale it back so it's not a second full-time job.

> *Ian: Looking forward to meeting her at a race soon.*
> *Me: Can't wait to introduce you.*

If she comes to any more. I still don't know what happened with Sadie at the race yesterday. She didn't show up by the pit board until halfway through, and she wouldn't talk to me about it last night or this morning when I asked how the race was for her. *Something isn't right.*

Slipping my phone into my pocket, I step over Luke's

sleeping pit bull, Betty, and find a spot at his workbench that gives me a perfect view of Sadie—who brought her work to *Turbine Café* today.

"I think I finally *get* it." I point through the wall of windows separating Luke's motorcycle shop from Allie's coffee shop.

He continues porting the intake he's been working on for the last fifteen minutes, but I know he's listening.

"You want to be close to her, keep her safe, talk to her whenever you want, and obviously, it's awesome to be able to see your girl all the time," I say, leaning across the worn wooden surface.

That grabs his attention away from the disassembled engine long enough to find his girlfriend through the glass, mouth turning into a half smile.

Sadie combs her fingers through the pink-tipped ends of her hair over and over as she reads something on her screen. *Must be something she does when she's concentrating.*

"But I never thought about how it would be to watch her work," I tell Luke. "I like learning her habits."

Luke nods, but the movement turns into a shake a few seconds later when my words register. He stops his work and stands up from his stool. "Are you talking about how nice it is to stare at Allie?" His voice is a mixture of confusion and irritation.

"Don't make it weird." I scoff, spinning the screw on a Crescent wrench, opening and closing it as I continue to watch Sadie. "I'm not staring at *her*. She's my best-friend-in-law."

He shakes his head. "That's the dumbest thing I've ever heard."

"She came up with it." I shrug, pointing the wrench toward

Allie.

He looks through the glass at her, then back to me. "Alright," he grumbles. "Not the *dumbest*." He starts toward his stool but stops again. "Who *are* you talking about?"

Betty—still mostly asleep—huffs a breath and rolls her heavy head onto my foot. *Maybe she thinks it's as ridiculous as I do that he had to ask.* Sadie kissed me at the race. *She kissed me.* Actually, my helmet, but that's almost more significant.

"Sadie," I answer.

He abandons his work altogether and moves over to block my view. "We talked about this."

Tilting my head, I ask, "Did we?" Even though we have. *Multiple times.* He knows I'm into her, and he warned me not to get into anything casual with her. *I haven't.*

The conversation with Ian was just another reminder that I need this to work, but Sadie needs it to work too. She needs the confidence boost of letting her ex and everyone else know she's moved on. She needs to prove to herself that she can do risky things and pull them off.

We need this to work, and if our friends don't know, it won't. She's nervous they'll figure out the truth and keeps telling me I won't be able to keep a secret from Luke because he knows me too well. *And if Luke knows, Allie will know. And if Allie knows, everyone will know.*

Her mind works like that—in dominoes. One small, fairly reasonable thing knocks down another small, fairly reasonable thing, and then another, and another, and eventually, it's a giant, unmanageable pile of things that are no longer fairly reasonable. Every time I see her start to spiral like that, I want to hold her and tell her she doesn't have to feel that way. I want to pick up all her dominoes, but I haven't figured out how yet.

"You know she's fresh out of a relationship." Luke's voice pulls me from my thoughts. "That asshole really did a number on her. She's not ready for—" he huffs a breath almost identical to the one Betty just let out, "—whatever it is you think you want from her."

"Not ready?" Frustration I rarely feel with my best friend heats my neck. "She tell you that? Do you often ask Sadie how she feels? Do you ask her what she wants?"

"Do you?" he counters.

"Yes," the word comes out loud enough that an elderly woman sitting at a table on the *Turbine Café* side of the glass looks up at me. I give her a sheepish smile and shrug.

"She's vulnerable," Luke says.

Making sure to lower my voice, I say, "Sadie is wounded, but she's working hard to heal. She *has* healed from so much of it already."

"And you think getting involved with you—*her roommate*—is helping with that?"

Now is my opportunity to sell this to Luke, so Sadie's dominoes can work in our favor. If Luke believes it, Allie will believe it, and then everyone else will follow. I spin the screw on the wrench up and down, up and down. Truth is, I don't know if it's helping her to be attached to me. *But I saw an opportunity to make her mine—in a way—and I had to take it.*

"Sadie deserves a man who knows how special she is. Have you heard Allie describe her as 'sunshine personified'?" Luke tilts his head in acknowledgment. "She's right. Sadie gives warmth and brightness to *everyone*. She spent years giving it to that *fucking guy* in Portland, and she got nothing back. But *I* can give it back to her."

Luke is stone-faced, giving me the harsh end of the protective big brother treatment I've seen him hit everyone else with over the years. Whether it's his actual little sister or anyone else who seems like they need someone to look out for them, Luke is a protector. *Not sure when he decided to adopt Sadie as his own, but it's not surprising.*

"I want to listen to her," I continue, "make her life better. I don't want to take anything from her. I want to be the man she deserves." Convincing Luke shouldn't be difficult because every word of my confession is true. *And he knows it.* "We're good together," I add when he continues staring at me without replying.

"And she likes you?" he finally asks.

The question stings for a second. The idea that someone like Sadie would be interested in slutty, wild Cam Hacker was hard for me to wrap my mind around at first. The thing is, *she's not. She's just pretending to be.* But I need Luke to believe it's real. Leaning over so I can look through the window at the woman in question, I answer. "Hard for me to believe, too."

Luke has never judged me for my past. He stood beside me while it was all happening, and he doesn't judge me now, either. "Allie was right." He shakes his head. "I'll never hear the end of this."

"Allie was right about what?" I ask, trying to find a way to shift my position without disturbing Betty. *My foot is falling asleep.*

"Yeah," he grunts. "She's been telling me for months that you two are meant for each other."

Months? "Maybe next time you should believe your girlfriend."

"Yeah, maybe," he says, returning to the disassembled motor on his workbench.

I lower down and lift Betty's head off my foot as carefully as possible. "Sorry, babe. I've got to be able to walk out of here." She huffs and returns to sleeping on the concrete floor.

When I stand back up, Luke claps me on the shoulder. "Good for you, man. I can tell you're happy."

Happy as long as this lasts, anyway. I'm setting myself up for a thorough heartbreak, but every time I look at her—every time I get to claim her as mine—I can't bring myself to be cautious.

Chapter 8
Sadie

Watch a scary movie all the way through –
from Sadie's list of things she's never done

Jared: What's going on with you and Cam Hacker? He's not actually dating you, is he?

It's not the first time Jared's texted me since Cam and I started this, but he's gotten more insistent since the race. He's jealous—which is exactly what I wanted—but it doesn't feel as satisfying as I thought it would. Since I showed Cam that one text and he suggested I stop responding, I've been better about it. I'm engaging with my ex less and less, but his constant texts are interfering with my ability to forget he ever existed.

"Still working?" Cam asks, setting a can of watermelon sparkling water—my favorite—on a coaster next to my mouse.

"Just finishing up," I answer.

He plops into the mustard-yellow vintage armchair in the corner of my office and cracks open his own can. "We should probably get on the same page before your friends get here."

After deleting three exclamation points from the email I just finished, I sign off for the day and spin my chair around to face him. "Are we not already?" I ask.

"It's the first night you're telling them—" He pauses, running tattooed fingers through his deep copper hair. "That we're *together*. Right?"

My heart races, and I try—*and fail*—to swallow the anxiety that immediately tightens my throat. *It's time.* I've skirted around the dating thing with my friends so far, able to handle Devon, Allie, and Bea individually, *but all three together?*

Allie will probably ask me directly if we're dating. And I'll hesitate because it's hard to lie to my friends. Devon will see me hesitate and call me on it. Then I'll choke further. Bea will try to defend me, but I'll feel bad that she's defending me for—

Cam leans into my eyeline, a playful smile on his wide mouth. He taps me lightly on the temple. "Could I participate in this conversation?"

My responding laugh comes out on a heavy sigh, releasing some of the tension in my body. "I'm afraid I can't do this," I admit. "What if I *can't* lie to them?"

His oversized smile returns. "Just don't lie. That's what I did with Luke."

I take the first sharp, bubbly sip of my drink. "So, we're not going to—you don't want to—" I can't bring myself to ask. "I don't think I understand."

His giant hand engulfs mine, giving a gentle squeeze. "Say as many true things as possible. You don't have to lie *much* to make this believable." He gives my hand one more light squeeze before releasing it. "If someone asks what's happening between us, what would you say?"

Allie *has* asked me that three times already, and I've dodged it every time. My mind is completely blank, my heart races, and my teeth dig into my lip hard enough to hurt.

"It's okay," he comforts me, though I'm not sure I deserve it. "Let's try something else. Forget what you'd say to them for a second. Why don't you try telling me what *is* happening between us?"

"I can do that," I answer, more of the tension easing. "We are pretending to date to make my ex jealous, help me feel less like a failure after my breakup, and to help you change your reputation so you can get on that team and keep racing without making a bunch of dumb videos on the internet."

"And how did that start?" he prompts, flipping the tab back and forth on his can in a motion I'm unsure he's aware of.

"We had an incredible conversation the day you moved in." The memory draws enough of a smile out of me that I have to stop clenching my teeth. "It seemed like we'd be a good match to help each other out, and pretending to date you sounded like a lot of fun." My cheeks flush with the admission.

He nods along with each of my words. "You can keep most of that. Tell them we're dating—leave out the *fake* part and the reasons why." He breaks off the tab and switches to tapping it against his can. "And, you can tell them exactly what happened if they ask *how* this started between us. Does that make you feel any better?" he asks.

I nod, trying to convince myself as much as him. "A bit. Sorry I'm so bad at this."

"You're not bad at this. You're *great* at this." He's emphatic, holding my stare. "This is working. People are starting to see me differently. I'm getting amazing responses online, and *Incite Energy* is happy. *You're* making it work." With each compliment, my spirits lift little by little. *Maybe I'm not bad at this. Maybe this isn't just him doing me a giant favor—*

"Is it working for you?" he asks. "Your ex losing his mind?"

"He's mad," I answer, realizing I don't know what a solid moment of triumph would look like for me. Even though the idea of him continuing to race turns my stomach, there will at least be an obvious moment when this has been a success for him. I'm not sure what that would look like for me.

"Knew he wasn't over you." Cam shakes his head. "Still can't believe he had you for that long and wasted it."

The plastic strawberry-shaped timer I brought into my office from the kitchen rings out in the most obnoxious way possible, shattering the calm.

"Cookies!" I jump up, running out of the room.

Fortunately, the house isn't large, so I make it from my office, through the living room, and to the kitchen before there's any chance of burning. My socks slide across the oversized white tiles on the kitchen floor as I reach the oven. The wash of hot, sweet-smelling air that hits me when I pull its door open is a familiar comfort. Using a spatula, I test underneath a couple of cookies. *Not quite.* When I shut the door and stand up, Cam's there, leaning on the counter.

"Smells incredible, love."

Love. I can't decide if I like or hate that he calls me that. It's sweet—kind of endearing, even—but it's not specific to *me.* I think I've heard him call just about every one of our friends love at one point or another. *Why do I want him to have a special name for me, anyway?*

"What'd you make?" he asks.

"In two more minutes," I say, setting a timer, "these will be strawberry shortcake cookies with lemon cream cheese filling, hopefully baked to perfection. They're tart and sweet, and the way they feel in your mouth is just—" turns out I don't have a word for that, so I make a satisfied *hmm* sound instead.

He settles himself lower against the gray and white marble counter, bringing his slightly crooked nose to my eye level. "Are they your favorite?" he asks.

"They're Bea's favorite. But not mine. Well, not my *favorite*, favorite." I squat down to look into the oven, making sure the little confections don't get offended and decide to burn. "I make these every time I wish it was hotter outside because they taste *exactly* like summertime."

"Summertime in March." He nods. "Can't wait to try."

"Oh, these aren't for you." The second the words are out, my hands fly up to cover my mouth.

His brows lift with a slightly shocked chuckle. "That works too."

"Oh, my word." Still staring through the oven door, balancing on my toes and resting my fingers on the oven's handle, I look up at him. "That sounded so mean. I'm so sorry."

"You don't have to share everything you bake with me. You spoil me too much already," he says, taking a bite from a rosemary focaccia muffin I made at lunchtime.

"I promised Bea she could have as many as she wants. But it's not like she'll know how many I made. Of course, you can have one." The strawberry timer goes off, and I open the oven to test the cookies again. This time, the bottoms are browned to perfection. I grab a yellow plaid oven mitt and pull out the baking sheet, holding it out to Cam. "Look at these fluffy little beauties."

"They are gorgeous," he says, his voice trailing off wistfully. "Too bad I won't be able to try them."

"Stop it, yes you will," I laugh.

Before he can respond, my friends knock at the door and let themselves in.

"What are you doing here?" Allie's voice carries into the kitchen when Cam goes over to greet her.

"He *lives* here!" I call out.

"Yes, but it's girls' movie night. Cam doesn't qualify," Allie says, rounding the corner from the entryway into our little kitchen. Devon, Bea, and what feels like every dog in Palm Springs follow her in.

"Don't worry. I'll be out of here in a few minutes," Cam says, leaning against the wall by the dining table and scratching Betty behind her ear.

"I maintain that you shouldn't have to leave," I say, although admittedly, it's mostly that I want him here as a buffer.

"It's all good. I get to lift weights with Luke," he says, crossing the short distance between us to pull me in for a hug. "Although it's hardly as much fun as *eating your cookies* and watching a movie." His hands linger on my hips, just an inch shy of inappropriate, as he gives me a soft kiss right on top of my head.

He's just putting on a show for my friends. Good*ness,* when he flirts with me like that, it's hard to think straight.

"That was an awfully chaste kiss to follow up your cookie-eating comment," Bea observes, her voice rich with amusement.

"Bea!" I exclaim, because what else can I say? *What else am I supposed to do?*

Cam looks down at me. *No, down at my lips. Oh, my word. Is he going to kiss me? In front of—*

He snakes his arm around my waist again, lifting me against him with a strength I often forget he has. He leans in but passes my lips, leaving a burning kiss on my cheek instead. I practically melt on the spot when his lips touch my skin for the first time. "It's hard enough to leave her tonight," he says. "If I gave her a proper kiss, you'd never get rid of me."

My cheeks flame redder than his hair as I watch him walk away.

The second he shuts the front door, Allie says, "We've waited long enough. You have to share every single detail about that right now."

My eyes go wide. *We're dating. He's my boyfriend. That's the story. So why can't I get the words out?*

"How about we go out back first?" Bea suggests, pulling a joint from her denim jacket pocket, saving me from having to respond.

"You can talk and smoke," Allie says, sliding open the back door. Spaghetti—Allie's giant, curly-furred puppy—runs outside, chasing Dandy—Bea's fluffy little white dog. Boo, my black cat friend who was sleeping on top of the breezeblock wall that surrounds our backyard, dashes away immediately.

Once we settle at the table, Betty—Luke's stocky gray pit

bull—shuffles underneath and rests her head on Devon's feet.

"I love that you're her favorite," I say.

"I am not," Devon says, but she cracks a smile. "I probably just have the biggest feet."

"*Details*," Allie insists, her green-eyed stare laser-focused on me.

My phone buzzes with a text, and I read it instead of giving in to Allie.

Jared: A year ago, you were begging me to marry you, and now you're too good to return my texts?

Fucker. I never begged. I just wanted to know where my life was going. Is that how he actually remembers me—as someone who begged him to marry me? I keep trying to remember him as the kind, loving man he used to be, but the way he talks to me now—was any of it ever true?

"You alright?" Bea asks.

I tilt my phone toward her.

Her eyes scan the screen briefly, then she declares, "He's clearly obsessed with you."

"Wait, is Cam texting you?" Allie asks, leaning forward and propping her chin on her hands.

"Not Cam," Bea says, handing my phone to Allie before lighting the joint.

"Eww, I fucking hate him," Allie mutters after reading it.

When Devon gets the phone, she stares at the screen for a while, then starts scrolling up. The joint makes its way to me, and I take a hit just as she asks, "Why are you writing him back?"

He's probably texted me at least three or four times a week

since I moved out. I used to write back every time. Now, I've cut it down to about once a week. *I'm proud of that.* "Actually," she continues before I can respond, "why haven't you blocked him?"

Could I do that?

She answers my unasked question. "You do not owe him anything. He doesn't deserve to insert himself in your life like this."

If I block him, how will he know Cam and I are dating*? How will I know if it's working?* Of course, I can't tell my friends any of that, so I say, "I've never blocked someone before."

"Never?" Allie asks.

"Nope." I shake my head. "Who have you blocked?"

"I block people all the time," Devon says, her perfectly styled blonde hair settling around her shoulders as she tilts her chin up. "Anyone who does not deserve to contact me."

"Guys I used to date," Allie adds, and Bea nods in agreement.

"That explains it then," I shrug. "Jared's the only person I've dated in the last decade."

"*Is* he though?" Allie asks, turning the conversation back to Cam.

Something true. Say something true. Technically, I dated a few other people in college before I met Jared. "He's not," I say, "but I'm going to have the munchies in about twenty minutes, so I need to order dinner right now."

Allie begrudgingly agrees to wait for the story until after dinner is handled. But the second I'm done ordering the Thai food and we all hit the couch, she's back at it.

"So, what the actual hell is going on between you and

Cam?" she asks, pulling a blanket from the basket by the couch. "And why haven't I heard every single detail yet?"

I'm being ridiculous now. I have to tell her Cam and I are dating. I have to tell all of them. I have to do it.

"She's allowed some secrets," Devon comments dryly.

"Oh, please," Bea laughs, amused. "You're just as indignant that Sadie hasn't let you in on her current cohabitation situation as Allie is."

Cam's advice echoes in my mind: *Tell the truth.*

"He's gorgeous," I rush out. *Oh, my word, Sadie. It doesn't have to be the* first *true thing that comes to mind.*

Bea is far less invested in whatever's happening between Cam and me than the others, so when she asks, "Is it just a physical thing?" it's with genuine curiosity.

"No, definitely not a physical thing." *That's true. But is it too true?* "I mean, it's not *just* physical." My cheeks flush at the thought of Cam's sensual non-kiss.

"Yeah?" Allie snickers. "You getting your cookies eaten all the time?"

Actually, no one's ever *eaten my cookies*, but I can't admit that. The shame I feel because Jared never wanted to has always been enough to keep it to myself. *But if I said it now, they'd assume Cam won't. And I just can't imagine Cam being the kind of man who wouldn't—*

"If it isn't just physical," Devon asks, ignoring Allie's invasive question, "Does that mean you *are* dating him?"

Yes. The answer is yes. This whole scheme with Cam only works if I say yes. Right now. Yes.

"Mmhmm," I nod. *Chicken.*

"Yay!" Allie squeals, waking Spaghetti and Dandy, who

had just settled down. Both dogs wag their tails excitedly, coming over to the couch. Betty, on the other hand, continues to snore against Devon's foot, which she found again the second we moved inside. "I love it when my friends become friends, but this is next-level dream come true. I secretly hoped this would happen."

"You were not secret about it," Devon says in her usual deadpan tone.

"No one told me," I say.

"Wanted you to get there on your own," Allie says, grinning and throwing herself across Bea's lap to give me a tight hug.

Something else I didn't consider—Allie loving this idea. Now I feel guilty for getting her hopes up. At some point, I'll have to tell her—tell her what? That this was fake all along? Or do Cam and I just keep pretending forever and say we broke up at some point? My gut twists.

"And you went from being nervous about living with him to what—moving down the hall within a few days? A week?" Devon asks, nonplussed with the pile Allie's made of the rest of us.

Truth. There's something true that will satisfy her skepticism. There has to be.

"I want to hear this too," Allie says, crawling back to her seat, propping both hands under her chin.

I'm grateful for the distraction the dogs provide as Spaghetti immediately ducks her head into the space Allie's arms create and demands attention again. Taking a steadying breath, I try to remember what Cam and I practiced. "It was almost immediate," I say. "It started that first night he moved in. I'd never really sat and had a conversation with him before then—"

"Exactly," Devon interjects.

"*Exactly*," Allie repeats, with the emphasis of someone who's made a point that Allie definitely has not.

I continue with another truth. "He's so easy to talk to—"

"So am I," Devon cuts in.

"Not right now, you're not," Bea says lightly, amused. "Let her finish, for fuck's sake."

"Fine," Devon huffs.

"He makes me feel safe." *A truth I didn't realize until it came out of my mouth.* "And we just make sense together." *A half-truth. We make sense as a pretend couple, but in reality, I could never love someone I was constantly in fear of losing to a motorcycle accident. He deserves someone better for him than me.*

"All they needed was some time alone to get to know each other properly," Allie picks up where I left off, filling in blanks I couldn't have pulled off. "They're both these delightful sweethearts. Cam has so much to give, and did you know he's never had a girlfriend before?" Allie looks to Bea and Devon, who both shake their heads. "Women throw themselves at him constantly—"

I flinch, hoping no one notices, but Devon eyes me in a way that shows she did.

Allie continues, "I've seen him turn down at least a dozen, and I've only known him a year. He wanted someone he could have a life with, and he *found* her. Right here." She reaches across Bea again to squeeze my leg. "Obviously, they make an incredible couple."

Devon considers for a long time before asking, "And this is a good thing for you?"

"Yes," I say, knowing it's the right answer. But when I

think about it, I realize it's another surprising truth. I'm having a great time with Cam. "I'm really happy."

Devon narrows her eyes, holding my stare for a long moment before nodding. "Okay, let's watch this movie."

Did I do it? Did I pull it off?

Bea queues up the movie, and Allie heads to the kitchen for the cookies. *No one's asking me questions anymore. I think I pulled it off.* I check my phone.

> *Cam: Hope that wasn't too much.*
>
> *Me: You were great. They're thrilled.*
>
> *Cam: All of them?*
>
> *Me: Okay, Allie is thrilled. Bea is intrigued, and I doubt Devon's on board yet.*
>
> *Cam: Sounds like a perfect start. Told you you'd be amazing.*
>
> *Me: Did you? I feel like I would've remembered being told I'm about to be amazing.*
>
> *Cam: If I didn't, I should have.*

"Is that Cam?" Allie giggles, overjoyed about us in a way I should've seen coming. "See if he'll send you a gym selfie with Luke."

Devon curls her lip. "Eww."

"Don't be such a downer," Bea giggles, pressing play on *The Shining.*

"Wouldn't Luke do that for you?" I ask Allie.

"I mean, yeah," Allie answers, "But he'd be cranky about it. Your thing with Cam is fresh—plus he actually likes taking selfies."

If we were really dating, would I still be this embarrassed about asking him for this? Probably. But she has a point, and I don't want to do anything that would make it seem like we're *not* dating.

> *Me: You can tell me to fuck off if you want, but any chance we could get a selfie of you and Luke?*
> *Me: Please know, I'm cringing as hard as possible.*
> *Me: Allie's request.*
> *Me: I'm so sorry. Please ignore this.*

"He's not writing me back," I say.

"Probably because he knows you're supposed to be watching a movie," Devon says, smoothing Dandy's fur.

"Give him half a second," Allie says.

And that's all it takes before my phone buzzes with his reply.

The picture is a classic *flash-photo-in-a-gym-mirror*, featuring an overly flexed Cam with a not-paying-attention Luke in the background. It's completely ridiculous.

My stifled laugh draws my friends closer, and Allie and Bea burst into laughter when I turn the phone their way. Devon doesn't look, but she gives us an indulgent smile as she holds Dandy close to her stomach and reaches for the remote. Cam's next photo shows up while Allie and Bea are still looking over my shoulder.

This one's a proper selfie, with one of his lean, tattooed arms extending toward the camera. His smile is more subdued than the usual too-wide grin—more of a sensual smirk. His blue-green eyes seem to be looking directly at me, and the harsh gym lighting reflects the droplets of sweat on his collarbones in an unreasonably appealing way. Good*ness*.

"Aww, Luke's not even in that one," Allie pouts.

My phone buzzes again, and I clutch it back, eager to see what it is without anyone else interfering.

Cam: Don't pretend these aren't for you.

"Is that a dick pic?" Allie asks. "Is that why you're hiding it and blushing?"

"No!" I squeal, mortified. "He's not taking dick pics at the gym. He's not a creep."

"But he *is* taking them?" she teases, waggling her brows.

"What are you getting at?" Bea asks, arching a brow. "It sounds like you want to see her boyfriend's dick."

My boyfriend. I blame the flutter in my stomach on excitement over our ruse working.

"No, of course not," Allie answers. "I just want to make sure Sadie's getting the full benefit of dating Cam. Besides, I've already seen it. We all have."

"What do you mean, *we've all seen it?*" I ask, slightly horrified.

"In his old video," Allie says.

"You couldn't actually *see* it," I say. "There was a smiley face covering everything."

Allie's mouth drops open. "Do not even sit there and tell me you've never seen the other version of that video."

"What other version?" I ask, though I have a sinking feeling I know exactly what she means.

"You clearly never looked hard enough. It's out there," she says, smirking at me. "But if you want to see it now, just ask Cam. I'm sure he has the original footage."

I gasp. "I am *not* asking him that."

"You're right," Allie says, and for a brief moment, I think she's being reasonable. But then she adds, "You deserve fresh dick pics. Special just for you."

"You must be the only woman on the planet who thinks receiving a dick pic is a good thing," I respond.

"Obviously, I'm not talking about *unsolicited* dick pics," Allie laughs.

"Wait a minute," Devon joins in. "Are you *soliciting* dick pics?"

"Yeah," Allie says, like it's the most obvious thing in the world. "Are you *not?*"

Devon blinks at her, before saying, "No."

"You're missing out." Allie shrugs. "It's like long-distance foreplay."

"You two work on either side of a glass wall and live together," Devon says. "You're never more than fifteen feet apart. You don't need long-distance foreplay."

Allie smirks. "We find opportunities."

Bea shrugs as her lips curl into an amused smirk.

"Oh, my word. We are not talking about this." I bury my face in my hands.

"No, we are not. We're watching a movie," Devon says, pressing play again.

I try to focus on the opening scene, but all I can think about now is Cam's dick. *It's a problem. A big problem. Well, maybe not that big. Probably. Whatever. My preoccupation is a big problem. He's not really my boyfriend. He's just my friend. I shouldn't be thinking about him like this.*

Once it seems like no one else is paying attention to me or

my phone, I text him back.

Me: Thanks for sending those. Allie is the most embarrassing person I know.

He responds immediately.

Cam: Cute how you keep saying they're for Allie.
Me: They are!
Cam: Uh huh.
Me: At least she's finally shut up about dick pics.
Me: Which I am not asking for!
Cam: You sure?
Me: Cameron! I am not asking you to send me pictures of your junk!
Cam: Your loss.

Chapter 9
Cam

Training hard or hardly training? - *caption from Cam's social media post — a video of him and Luke messing around at the gym, March 6th*

I try to be quiet as I shut the front door, not wanting to wake Sadie. *But she screams.* Calling out to her, I rush through the living room and down the short hallway to her bedroom.

When I throw open her door and flip on the light, she recoils from the brightness, then snorts a laugh. *I did hear her scream, didn't I?*

"Did something happen?" I ask, scanning her room for anything that could have scared her. It's just her usual setup— soft blankets, pastel paintings, a sunflower-printed rug. The most dangerous thing in here is the sharp corners on her dresser.

"This is so embarrassing," she groans.

I sit on her bed so we're facing each other, gently pulling

her pink-and-purple-tipped hands away from her wide eyes. "Are you okay?" I ask.

"I'm fine. I'm being ridiculous." She shakes her head, dropping her hands to her lap, revealing a thin yellow shirt that does nothing to conceal the shape of her pointed nipples. *Fuck. I can't be thinking about her like that right now.* "I shouldn't have screamed when I heard the front door," she admits.

"That's why you screamed?" I ask, confused. "What am I missing?"

She sighs, the tension leaving her shoulders. "It might not have been the *best* idea to get high and watch the scariest movie I've ever seen."

I fight back the urge to laugh at the most adorable thing she could have said. "The movie freaked you out?"

"Yes, don't judge me," she says, pouting.

"I'm not. I would never." My brow furrows. "Which movie was it?"

"*The Shining.* I wanted to check *watch a scary movie* off my list."

"And did you?" I ask.

"Not yet, but I should," she says, leaning over to her nightstand. Her tank top hangs loosely around her cleavage, which I try very hard not to stare at. She slides open the top drawer, eyeing it like something might leap out at her. When nothing does, she pulls out a pink-and-white checkered notebook. "I don't like being scared. *At all*," she explains. "Even a little bit. But a lot of the best things I've done, I did while I was scared." Sitting back down, she adjusts her tank top, exposing even more cleavage. *Was that intentional?* "So, I'm trying to do more of it. Being scared. A scary movie seemed like a less aggressive way to… I don't know… build that skill?"

"That's admirable," I say, forcing my gaze to stay locked on her eyes. "A lot of people aren't willing to do anything that scares them."

"Don't admire me too much," she laughs. "Mostly, I've always wanted to watch *The Shining* because it plays at the drive-in during that one scene in *Twister*."

"That's adorable."

"No one's around to hear you say sweet things to me, you know," she sighs. "Anyway, I was trying to sleep, and I kept hearing sounds. Or maybe just *thinking* I heard them. For all I know, it was just Boo running around the backyard." Her eyes dart over my shoulder to the dark L-shaped hallway beyond her open bedroom door. I look, too, but there's nothing there. "I can't stop thinking about the creepy ghosts, and feeling like they're going to *get me*," she whispers, the last two words barely audible.

"I won't let anyone get you," I say, pulling her fluffy blanket tighter around her hips.

"You can't protect me from ghosts," she murmurs. "*No one can.*"

"First of all, watch me," I say, resting my hand on the bed beside her legs. "Secondly, I don't think the ghosts in that movie actually hurt anyone, do they?"

She shakes her head.

"Maybe they were there to warn her of the real danger."

"Pretty sure that wasn't it," she laughs, her voice light again. "If they *were*, they were really creepy about it." She flips open her notebook and starts browsing the pages. "This isn't in any order. I just write them as I think of them. So, it always takes me a while to find the right one to cross off." She pauses on a page. "I should probably just remove *'see a ghost'* altogether at this point." Her voice drops, sounding more to herself than to me. "I forgot that was even *on* here. I should probably start bowling if I ever want to bowl a perfect game. It's not a full moon, is it?"

"It was last night, so almost," I answer.

"Hmmm, I don't think that would count," she taps her pen on the page.

"Plus, I'm too scared to go outside right now."

Struggling to follow her logic, I ask, "What does that have to do with bowling?"

"Oh, that's not about bowling." She cuts herself off. "It's something else."

"Now I'm dying to know," I lean forward. "But you're not gonna tell me, are you?"

"No, of course not," she laughs, pulling the comforter over her face.

Wanting to be closer to her, I move fully onto her bed and lean back against the headboard. When I place my arm on the pillows behind her, she drops the comforter and stares at me silently for a long moment, eyes narrowed, jaw firm.

I almost break the silence, but there's something happening behind her eyes that I can't quite place. Her face is clear of makeup, and what I thought were a few light freckles turns out to be a lot more. Her lashes are soft, her brows almost unnoticeable. The waves in her hair have fallen by this time of night, and her pink-tipped blonde hair now reaches her shoulders. *She looks soft and beautiful like this.*

Her teeth drag over her plush pink lower lip, and I want to

drag mine across it. *Would she like that?* She liked it earlier when I kissed her cheek, but that wasn't the same. I probably should have kissed her on the lips then. It would've made the most sense for the story we're telling. But I don't want our first kiss to be in front of anyone else.

Her voice is quiet when she asks, "Do you want to read my list?" Her arms are wrapped tightly around her knees, as if she's building up the nerve to share it with me.

I try to mask my eagerness, answering with nonchalance, "Thought you'd never ask."

She giggles, tucking her hair behind her ears and handing me the notebook. The silver lettering on the front says *Try It*, and the matching sprayed edges of the paper are starting to wear off. The first page is blank, but the second is filled with a list of things—about half of them crossed off.

> ~~Move to California~~
> ~~Leave Jared~~
> Bake a perfect cookie
> Call Mom
> Get two tattoos
> ~~Take a pole class~~
> Go a whole day without apologizing
> ~~Start smoking weed again~~
> ~~Learn how to roll a joint~~
> Fall in love one more time
> ~~Change my nail shape~~

Each one is a small insight into her inner world that leaves me more curious than before. *How long has it been since she called her mom? Who taught her how to roll a joint? Are there photos or videos from this pole class she took? Can I see them? Can I convince her to bump up the* "no apology" *day to the top of the list? I even want to know what her old nail shape was.*

I don't ask any of that, though, skipping over the most intriguing one—*fall in love one more time*—and opting for a safer question. "Why two tattoos?"

"Getting one didn't seem adventurous enough." She shakes her head as soon as she says it. "That's not really it. I just feel like if I'm going to do it, I should *do* it. Does that make sense?"

"It really does," I say, relieved that she's willing to entertain the conversation. "Do you know what you want to get?"

"I have a few ideas, but nothing solid," she answers.

"What are these ideas?" I ask. "You got pictures?"

"No pictures, just thoughts. I think I should get something baking-related, and Allie always says I'm like a ray of sunshine. It's my favorite way to think of myself, and that…" She trails off, suddenly shy.

"I've heard her say that," I nudge her shoulder with mine. "I think it's a perfect description for you."

"Really?" She looks at me, her face lighting up.

"Yes, *really*." I lean down, making sure she has to look me in the eye. "You're warm, bright, beautiful, and impossible to ignore. Pure sunshine."

"Well, that's—I'm not really—You don't have to—" she stammers, clearly uncomfortable with the compliment.

"Is '*learn how to take a compliment*' on that list somewhere?" I ask, lifting it between us.

"No," she says, pressing her lips together, trying to hide a smile.

I pass the book back to her. "Add it."

She opens her mouth in mock offense but shuts it again when I hold her gaze. "Fine," she rolls her eyes, her cheeks turning pink. "I guess you have a point."

"I do," I say, watching her jot it down. "Now give it back. I wasn't done with that."

She hands it to me without protest, and it's flipped to a later page. Just above *learn to accept compliments* is written: *Block Jared*

She wrote that recently, but why hasn't she done it? Last time I read one of his DMs, he said she's *not worth anyone's time. If that's what he's saying to me, what kind of awful shit is he saying directly to her?* She'll hate that I'm asking, but I have to know. "Why haven't you blocked him yet?"

"What?" she asks, her eyes darting around like she's been caught doing something she shouldn't.

"Jared," I say. "Why haven't you blocked him yet?"

Her brows furrow. "It never occurred to me until tonight. Devon suggested it, but I have to think about it."

"Why?" I press.

"Why what?" she responds, crossing her arms as she shifts away from me.

"He's not good to you," I say, running my hand through my hair. "He shouldn't be *allowed* to contact you."

"You don't know that. You can't—"

I cut her off. "Sadie, the guy—"

"You *interrupted* me," her mouth falls open.

"And *you* were defending him. Someone has to stand up for you."

I expect her to snap back with something like *"You're not my boyfriend"* or *"This isn't your business,"* but instead, she watches me quietly for a long time, her shoulders rising with deep breaths. Finally, she scoots closer and says, "He's the worst, but *I* decide when I block him."

It's not the answer I wanted. I hate that he still has access to her—that he can hurt her again. But she's giving me a clear *"back off"* message. This won't be the last time we talk about this, but for now, I change the subject. "By the way, whenever you're ready, I'll take you."

Her brow furrows, confused.

"To get two tattoos," I explain.

"Oh, right." She nods, relieved. Still tucked under her comforter, she drops her legs to the side, resting them on mine. "I'd like that a lot. I can't think of anyone better to go with."

Pride swells in my chest, but I move on, flipping the book open to the next pressing issue. "I'm amazed you haven't crossed off bake a perfect cookie yet."

"I'm not interested in lying to myself," she laughs.

"I've never eaten one of your cookies that wasn't perfect," I say, resting my hand on her knee.

Her eyes fall to my hand, and she rolls her lips to suppress a smile. "Well, you must not be much of a cookie connoisseur."

"Sadie, I know perfection when I taste it." My eyes drop to her pink lips. "I'm sure I'll taste it again soon."

Her caramel eyes widen, and her chest—*I'm no longer able to resist*—rises with a soft, shaky breath. *Good. I'm getting to her.* Her next words come out breathy, "Let me know when you find the scary movie one."

"Of course." I grin, turning back to the notebook. *This might be my favorite thing I've ever read.* It's a wild collection of experiences, from simple things—*win a game of Monopoly, stay awake for twenty-four hours*—to things she wants to learn—*drive a stick shift,* to things she wants to accomplish—*hold my breath for three minutes, run a half marathon,* and even things she can't control—*see a ghost, find five dollars on the ground, see two shooting stars at once.*

Pride swells again when I find *let someone read my list.* I point out that she can cross it off too. *I'm the first person she's shown this to.*

The item that made her blush and hide behind the blanket is *dance naked under the full moon.* She's already been brave enough tonight, so I don't bring it up. *Have a good boyfriend* isn't crossed off yet. Even though I don't deserve to feel it, a sting zaps through my ribs. It's a sharp reminder that this thing between us isn't real. *I'm not getting to her.*

It's almost one in the morning, but I'm not ready to give her up yet. "You save me any of those strawberry shortcake cookies?" I ask.

"Of course," she laughs. "I saved you two."

"You want one?" I ask, already getting off the bed and heading down the hallway.

"Sure," she says, but there's a waver in her voice.

When I turn around, she's curled back into her protective ball.

"You want to come with?" I ask.

"No, I'm fine." She shakes her head, obviously scared.

"Alright, I won't make you," I say, walking toward the kitchen.

"Wait!" she yells out, and I'm back in her room in an instant. She rushes to explain, "They're on your nightstand. I forgot I put them there. I hope that's okay—that I went in there.

I'm sorry. I probably shouldn't—"

"All good, sunshine," I say, leaving the room again. I raise my voice as I walk farther down the hall. "You're welcome in my room anytime." I flip on my light switch. "Especially if you're bringing treats." Sitting on my nightstand are two cookies on a plate I recognize as one of her favorites—blue with daisies and a cursive *S* in the center. "Are you sure these cookies aren't perfect?" I call out, picking up the plate. Underneath, there's a note in the same neat handwriting she uses for her list.

Promise I'll always share my cookies. — S

I lift the plate to my nose as I make my way back to her. "They smell perfect. They look perfect. They were made by you—" I stop myself from saying you're perfect as I enter her room again.

She's shifted into the space I left open, making it easier for me to join her on the bed. "They're not perfect," she sighs.

"Let's taste them to be sure," I say, sliding next to her.

Sadie leans her head into my shoulder, laughing. "Yes, please." She takes the smaller of the two cookies and devours half of it in one bite.

Matching her enthusiasm, I take the other one. *Holy shit.* "Cross it off," I say, mouth full of strawberry cream cheese perfection.

"No, it doesn't count," she protests.

"Why the hell not?" I ask.

"Because this is someone else's recipe," she says, her hand covering her mouth as she takes another bite. "I tweaked it, but

I didn't come up with it from scratch."

"The list didn't say you had to invent the recipe," I remind her.

"It's *implied*," she laughs, leaning into my shoulder again, finally allowing herself to relax there.

I'm caught up in the soft curves of her face, the pout of her lips, the sparkle in her eyes as they flutter closed. *If I don't move, will she fall asleep on me like this?* I want to reach out—run my fingers through her hair, cup her cheek, pull her closer. But I can't stop thinking about *have a good boyfriend*—and how it hasn't been crossed off. It's a sharp reminder that I'm *not* getting to her.

Carefully, I nudge her off my shoulder and onto her pillow, then stand.

She blinks at me, still dazed. "I guess we should sleep, huh?"

"Yeah, I've got to be sharp for practice tomorrow," I say, though I don't have to be there until noon.

Pulling her knees up to her chest, she mutters, "Sure, yeah, me too. I mean—not for practice. I'm not racing motorcycles tomorrow. You know that—I have work."

There's an uncomfortable twist in my gut as she stumbles over her words. She's probably still scared and doesn't want to be alone. It doesn't feel right to leave her, but I can't invite myself into her bed.

Resting my forearms on the doorframe, I ask, "Was thinking I'd sleep with my door open tonight. Would that be okay with you?"

"Uh, sure." Her brows furrow.

"And I could leave your door open too," I add, drumming

my fingers on the wood. "For airflow," I explain.

It's March in Palm Springs, so the days are warm but the nights are cool. All the windows are closed, and airflow isn't really a concern, but making sure she doesn't feel alone is.

After a few seconds, she catches my meaning and smiles. "Yeah, airflow. That's a good idea."

Her bedroom is at the corner of the L-shaped hallway, and my room is at the end of the other side. Our doors open toward each other. We can talk with our doors open, even if our bathrooms are between us.

Once I'm in bed, I call out to her. "Hey, sunshine?"

"Yes?" her sleepy voice responds.

"You doin' okay?" I ask.

"All good. I'll let you know if—" She pauses, and I stay still, not wanting to miss her words. "I need help with airflow," she finishes.

She's half-asleep, so I assume the silence that follows means she's already drifting off. But I stay awake a little longer, just in case she needs me.

Chapter 10
Sadie

Run a half marathon - *from Sadie's list of things she's never done*

Cam: Don't forget, rubber side down!

"One lap is a quarter mile," Devon says, looking cheerier than I've ever seen her. "Today's run is only two and a half miles, so you only have to do ten laps." *When did she forget the meaning of* "only"? *Ten laps sound like an eternity.*

"How long has it been since you went for a run?" Bea asks, pulling her dark, shaggy hair into a loose braid.

"I've never *willingly* gone for a run," I admit, a little embarrassed. "I guess the last time I ran at all was in high school."

Bea's lips curl into an encouraging smile. "Then let's just do whatever feels good in your body today," she says. "I'll stick with you, and Devon can join us after she finishes her miles."

"We are here for you today, Sade," Devon adds, "I'm happy to stay by your side."

Even though I know the offer is genuine, I gesture toward the track. "Go ahead," I tell her. "Enjoy yourself. This might be easier if I'm not comparing myself to my athletic, *runs-for-fun* friend the whole time."

Her smile returns. "I will come meet you in about twenty minutes," she says, and then she's off, moving at a speed I didn't know humans were capable of.

"She's a powerhouse, isn't she?" Bea comments, securing her braid. "Ready?"

"As I'll ever be," I answer.

She takes off at a pace that's easy for me to match—more like a slow jog than a real run. *Maybe this won't be so bad after all.* "What made you want to run a half marathon if you're not in the habit already?" she asks.

"It seemed like a big accomplishment," I answer, enjoying the slightly soft feel of the track beneath my brand-new running shoes. "I wanted to do something significant."

It's true, but not all of it. I once told Jared I wanted to train for one, and he said, "*Aw, sweetie. That's not you.*" That's the real reason it made the list, but it's not about trying to prove anything to him anymore. Now, I just want to prove to myself that I can do something this hard.

"I like that," Bea says, nodding in approval. "Let's get you a medal, babe."

We turn the first corner, and I find myself really enjoying it. I'm not big on intense cardio—usually, I go for long walks in the evening or take the barre classes Bea teaches for exercise—but this is fun. I get why Devon loves it.

"You're doing great," Bea encourages as we round the second corner.

So, what's that? Half of a quarter mile? An eighth of a mile. I just have to go that far nineteen more times. No big deal.

Devon passes us around the third turn, offering encouragement as she flies by. "You're doing it, Sade!"

"On your left!" someone yells out. I can't tell which side they're coming from. *Shit.* I always mix up left and right. For some reason, my brain just won't learn the difference. I lift my hands into "L" shapes to see which one looks correct. *The one that makes a proper* L *is left, so I need to move*—but then they shout again. "On your *left*!" As they brush past, I finally realize which side is left. *Dammit.*

Bea mutters that the guy was an asshole, and I make a note that he passed me on the side she wasn't on, just in case he does it again.

By the time we round the final turn and start lap two, I'm starting to feel the workout in my legs. This isn't necessarily *hard*, but I've dropped any delusions of being a natural-born runner. Bea's pace is more challenging than I thought.

When Devon passes us again, she barely seems winded and offers more encouragement in a voice that isn't the least bit breathless.

I, on the other hand, wheeze, "Thanks," wiping sweat from my forehead with a sweaty arm. *It's ineffective.*

On our fourth lap, I have to slow to a walk for a while to catch my breath. Bea graciously joins me, and Devon calls out that I'm amazing as she flies past.

By lap six, my legs hurt all over, and I'm questioning how much I really want this.

By lap seven, I'm wondering how *anyone* could possibly want this.

At the start of lap eight, Devon finishes her run and joins us in the walk-jog we've settled into. She and Bea launch into a conversation about work—Bea works for Devon at her interior design business, and they're in the middle of interviewing designers to add to their team.

I can't do this.

I have to do this.

I want to quit.

What if I quit?

I hate everything.

They apologize for not including me in the conversation, but all I can do is breathe heavily at them, marveling that they're able to talk at all. My throat burns. My legs ache. My feet hurt. There's a constant stream of sunscreen and sweat dripping into my eyes. *Who's fucking idea was this?*

Lap nine comes.

Amazingly, so does lap ten.

We reach the end, and I collapse onto the grass. "How—do you—do this?" I ask, panting between words.

Devon tosses me a water bottle, and I sit up just enough to gulp some down. "I've been doing this my whole life," she says. "I run every single day. You did *amazing* for your first time."

"You deal with this throat-burning sensation every day?" I ask, bewildered.

"Oh, I totally forgot about that part," she says, almost

wistfully. *Psycho.* "If you stick with it, the throat-burning eventually stops."

"No way," I huff out.

"No, she's right," Bea says, offering me a hand.

"I don't want to get up. Ever," I say.

"Alright," she says, lying down beside me on the grass. "We can stretch right here."

I follow her lead, leaning into a hamstring stretch. "Okay, *this part* feels good," I admit.

Devon joins us on the ground too, following the same stretching routine. "You should probably take a couple of rest days before we meet up again, but go for walks if you can. What's your schedule like on Wednesday?" she asks.

Now that my breathing is back to normal, I *almost* feel like I had a good time running. I look between my friends, their hopeful faces encouraging me, and muster the words to commit to another run. "I could be here by four-thirty."

"Perfect," Devon chirps.

I've always admired her drive. She's passionate about her business, her friends, her boyfriend, running—everything. *She knows what she wants and how to get it.* I've never felt that kind of fire about anything, which is why I started my list. I want to spend more of my life on things that light me up, but first, I have to find them.

After stretching, Devon and I get into her car for the short ride home. "I am really proud of you," she says as she pulls out of the parking lot.

"I'm hardly the first person who's ever run two and a half miles," I wave her off. "I didn't even run the whole thing."

"That's not the point," she says, shaking her head. "I'm

proud of you for how many new things you're trying. It seems like every day you are experiencing something new. *You* wanted your life to change, and *you* are making it happen. You are very impressive that way."

I want to argue, to point out that I'm not that impressive, but I look over at her. The subtle smile on her face shows she means it. Even if I'm not proud of myself, or don't think she should be, *she is*. I can't shoot her down. It'd be rude.

Devon is more comfortable with silence than anyone else I know, so she doesn't interrupt my thoughts or push me for a response.

Eventually, I find one. "Thank you for being proud of me, Dev."

"It is easy to be proud of you," she responds.

The rest of the short ride home is filled with talk about running. She asks how I felt, what I liked, what I hated, if I like the app she recommended to track my data.

When we turn onto my street, Cam's out front, working on one of his motorcycles in the driveway. My stomach drops. I've done my best to block out anything motorcycle-related since I went to his race—going so far as parking in the driveway to avoid them. I know he rides. I know he *races*.

It's his whole life—*his identity*. But it terrifies me. He's not even my real boyfriend, and I worry about him constantly. He left town this past weekend for more races, and I was anxious the whole time, until I heard he won one and placed second in another—*meaning he survived both*.

Devon either reads my mind or has the same thought. "Remember in college, you said you would never date someone who rides a motorcycle? Does it not bother you anymore?" she asks.

"It does bother me. I hate it," I say without thinking.

Devon shifts the car into park and looks at me. "So, you hate a core part of your boyfriend's identity—his career?"

"I mean, I don't hate *him*," I laugh, trying to lighten the mood. *How the hell do I change the subject? I don't have a good answer for this. Cam and I have never—*

"I didn't think you hated him," she answers, steady and unyielding, not letting me off the hook. "Have you talked to him about it?"

"No," I answer, relieved to say something factual.

"But he knows about the crash you were in during high school, *right?*" she presses.

Not wanting to answer, I look out the window, watching Boo run across the neighbor's fence. *I'd rather be hanging out with him right now. He's great at minding his own business.*

"That is not healthy," Devon says, her voice taking on her *'you-know-I-know-what's-best'* tone. "He should know how upsetting motorcycles are for you, and *why.* You were already in an unhealthy situation for too long, and you haven't even blocked your ex yet. You shouldn't put yourself into something else that's harmful—"

"*Hey,*" I jump to Cam's defense, deciding that's more pertinent than her harassing me about blocking my ex. "He's not Jared. He's not *harmful.* He doesn't fucking cheat on me. He doesn't lie to me."

"I never said he did," Devon answers.

"Don't compare them," I snap, crossing my arms.

"It's natural to compare your current relationship to your past ones. It would be a healthy thing to do, actually," she says. "You have to learn from the past to make your current relationship better. It's not about Cam being Jared. I know he's not," she softens her voice just slightly. "But you are making the same mistake of not communicating your needs. You're not telling him—"

"Stop." I cut her off. I love Devon, but right now, I wish she'd mind her own business instead of pushing me to dig into things I'm not ready to face. *Cam and I aren't really dating, but there is something real between us.* We *do* communicate, and I happen to think we do it well. Even faking it, he's a better boyfriend than Jared *ever* was.

"I know you mean well, but I can't do this right now," I say, glancing at Cam standing in the driveway, his jaw clenched as he watches us. He makes a *you alright?* face, and I sigh, offering him a half smile.

"You'll have to face this eventually," Devon says, stubborn as ever. "You have trauma around this, and you—"

"Okay." I unbuckle my seatbelt. "Love you. Thanks for the ride and the run. See you Wednesday."

Her reply is, "Love you too," but her face says *you're-being-irrational.*

As soon as I'm out the door, Cam walks over to me. I should tell him he doesn't have to put on a show of affection for Devon's sake. Even if she thinks we're dating for real, it doesn't matter. She's not on board because she thinks being with him will hurt me. *And she's right.* But when he wraps me in a big hug, I'm swept up into him, his body grounding me, and some of the tension melts away. It feels good. *Too good.*

"No, no. I'm all sweaty," I laugh.

He buries his face in my neck. "Don't care. I'm expecting

hugs next time you show up at a race. I'll be a thousand times sweatier then." Setting me down on the driveway, he asks, "How was your run?"

But I barely hear the question. I'm stuck on the thought of hugging him after his race again. *Because I'll have to go to more races.* Last time, it was less of a hug and more of me clinging to him in relief that he survived. I felt like *I* barely survived the race, and all I did was watch half of it from the sidelines.

My head spins, and I steady myself with a hand on his chest.

"Hey, hey, Sadie," his voice is soothing as he wraps his hands around my biceps, dipping his head to look into my eyes, concern lining his face. "You alright? What's going on?"

"I'm fine," I say, looking down. *I can't look at his face right now.*

"That's obviously not true," he says, releasing my arms. "Was it something Devon said? Are you two okay?"

"Devon made some really frustrating and accurate points about some things I don't want to talk about," I say. Her words repeat in my head: *He should know how upsetting motorcycles are for you, and why.* "And I *still* don't want to talk," I finish, trying to focus on steadying my breathing as I walk toward the house.

"You don't have to," he says, following me.

This is why we could never actually date. More of her words come into focus: *So, you hate a core part of your boyfriend's identity—his career?* Already, it's everything I can do not to imagine him bloody and broken on a racetrack. *If we were actually dating, actually in love*—I cut off the thought. *We never would be. I can't allow it, and he wouldn't want it either.*

"You don't have to, but I think you need it," Cam continues.

I turn on him. "I am *fine*. Sometimes the idea that you race motorcycles—" I take a steadying breath. "It makes me—" I search for kind words, but come up empty. "It's reckless. It's unnecessary. You're endangering your life for no reason, and it stresses me the fuck out."

He moves to speak, but I hold up a hand to stop him.

"No, thank you. All you need to know is that I've committed to doing this with you. I'll show up again at some point, I'll support you, and I will deal with my own anxiety. And when your season's over and my ex is married to someone else, we can stop this." I gesture between us. "And then I never have to think about motorcycles again."

He flinches, like I've physically hit him. *Shit. That was mean. I should apologize. I should—*

His jaw tightens, and he exhales a heavy breath. "You can't keep avoiding every tough conversation. You hate motorcycles, but you won't tell me why. You won't block your ex, and you won't tell me why. These things weigh on you, and you'll have to carry them alone if you don't—"

"Why is everyone up my ass about blocking Jared?" I snap, gesturing out the window toward the place Devon's SUV was parked. "Did you two *coordinate*?" I couldn't explain this to my friends—they don't know about Cam and me—but at least he'll understand. "If I block Jared, it ruins everything. That was the whole *point*."

"The point was to make him *jealous*, not to let him keep disrespecting you," Cam says.

Okay, so he doesn't *get it.*

"It's not that he's disrespecting me," I explain. "He's confused. It wasn't that long ago when we were together. I don't want to hurt him."

"I'll show you why I'm up your ass about blocking your ex," he says, holding out his phone. "*This* is the asshole whose feelings you're trying to protect?"

My stomach drops when I see the screen. There's a conversation between Jared and Cam. I hadn't thought Jared would stoop this low, but I'm not surprised.

> *Jared: You're a joke.*
>
> *Jared: Are you fucking kidding about Sadie? Do you know anything about her?*
>
> *Jared: You're an idiot if you're dating her. She was begging me to take her back last night.*

My blood boils. "I never begged him to take me back. I wouldn't—I don't want him back." I say more to myself than to Cam.

> *Jared: You're wasting your time with her. She's not worth it.*
>
> *Jared: She's a waste of time.*
>
> *Cam: Stay away from her.*
>
> *Jared: Just trying to help you out before you waste your time with that boring bitch for years like I did.*
>
> *Cam: You are useless. Get fucked.*

My heart thuds heavily in my chest, shame rushing to my face. *That man used to love me, right? He had to. I wasn't delusional for those nine years, was I? He must have loved me at some point. But what the hell has he turned into?*

I hand Cam his phone back. "Why didn't *you* block him?"

"Because I don't trust him, and I want to know what he's up to," Cam says, dipping his chin to meet my eyes. "You deserve so much more, so much better. He doesn't deserve any part of you." Cam taps the phone screen. "You want to win your breakup? Moving on with your life without him is the best way."

"You don't know what you're talking about," I breathe.

He doesn't argue. He just says, "Alright." Then he walks back out the front door to his motorcycle.

Jared was terrible to Cam, and Cam didn't defend himself. He defended *me*. I was awful to him just now, and he didn't defend himself then either. *He defended me again.*

Today was supposed to be about running, trying new things, finding my passion. Instead, I've alienated two of the people I care about most. *That really got away from me, didn't it?*

Before my shower, I text Devon:

> *Me: Hey, I'm sorry. I shouldn't have been that way with you.*
> *Devon: I understand.*
> *Me: I'm not ready to have that conversation yet, okay?*
> *Devon: I understand that too. Here when you need me.*

A separate notification buzzes on my phone. I hope it's Cam, but I know it's not. If he had something else to say, he'd probably knock on the bathroom door. No, it's the worst person possible.

> *Jared: You know Cam Hacker's using you. He doesn't really want you.*
> *Me: Get fucked.*

I switch back to my text with Devon:

Me: Okay, how do I block someone?

Chapter 11
Cam

Only twelve days until I get to race again, but who's counting? — *caption from Cam's social media post — a video of him doing a wheelie on a street bike, March 18th*

Sadie's mouth drops open in surprise when I set her coffee on the desk during her meeting. Even though this has become our routine since we started pretending to date, she didn't expect me to follow through today.

After she gave me a piece of her mind last night, I left for a ride and didn't come back until late. We haven't said a word to each other since. But I brought her coffee anyway. Didn't want to raise suspicions with any of the coworkers she's told me are deeply invested in our *relationship*.

I kiss the top of her head like I always do before heading to the garage to swap rain tires onto my race bike.

Last night was a reality check. I care for Sadie. I'm

attracted to her. I always have been—even back when we first met in Portland all those years ago. But I needed to remember something important: She's my *friend*, not my girlfriend.

She's doing me a huge favor—pretending to be with me—even though she thinks racing motorcycles is *reckless* and *unnecessary*. I'm not convinced her desire to *win* her breakup was enough to start a fake relationship with me, especially since she's still hung up on that guy. *It's because she's so damn sweet.*

I don't know how to move forward with her. She tenses up when she sees my bikes or when the conversation turns to racing. But racing motorcycles is all I've ever had, and before I met Sadie, it was all I ever wanted. *Without it, I don't know who I'd be, and frankly, I don't care to find out.*

The door to the garage opens, and Sadie steps into the cold concrete room. She cups her coffee between her sweater-covered palms as she crosses to me. She stops a few feet from the bike. *She never gets too close to them.*

"What's good, Winslow?" I ask, glancing down at the bolt I'm tightening on the front wheel.

"Um," she says, dragging the toe of her white sneaker in an arc across the floor. "Thank you for the coffee."

"Of course," I say, suppressing the urge to flirt—just to see how quickly I can make her blush or giggle.

After a long pause, she says, "You make it better than Allie does."

"Not true," I say, giving the tire a spin with my palm before standing up.

Her eyes track my movements, her chin tipping up when I reach my full height. She's biting into her bottom lip, hard enough it must hurt. *The movement always makes me want to kiss the pain away.*

"I have to load my trailer," I say, pressing the button on the wall to raise the garage door.

The rain was more of a mist earlier this morning, but it's picking up now—thick droplets. A rarity in the desert.

"Are you riding in the rain?" she asks, her voice high with concern.

"Some of my worst performances have been in the rain. I'm not as experienced with it as racers from other parts of the country," I explain. "I need the practice."

"That's so dangerous. You can't—" She cuts herself off, taking a deep breath. "I'm sorry."

"I get it," I reply with a shrug, even though I don't fully understand.

"I shouldn't have said what I said last night." She steps closer, tentative. "I'm not being fair to you. You love this." She gestures at the bike between us, and I swear she doesn't even realize the slight curl in her lip as she does.

"I do," I nod.

"And just because I don't understand—*and I really, really don't*—doesn't mean it's reckless," she adds.

"What don't you understand?" I ask, surprised she's even talking about this.

Her eyes scan the bike from handlebars to tailpipe. "How do you ignore the danger?"

"I don't," I answer.

"What do you mean you *don't?* You still race. You have to ignore the danger to do that," she says, her concern sharpening.

"You put your life in danger every time you get in a car, don't you?" I ask, slipping my hands into my front pockets.

"That is *not* the same," she retorts.

"No, it's not," I agree. "But the point is, I don't let the danger stop me from doing what I need to do. People die in car crashes every day. Do you think about that risk every time you start your engine?"

She looks like she wants to argue but instead shakes her head, admitting reluctantly, "No."

"Then why is the risk the only thing you think of when I'm on a motorcycle?" I ask.

Her shoulders tense, fingers tightening around her coffee mug. She steps back, just slightly.

I round the bike to stand closer. "What happened to you?"

Her mouth opens, but no words come out.

"There was something that happened, right?" I step close enough that the scent of her coffee fills my nose.

She nods.

"Will you tell me?" I ask gently.

She stares at me for a long moment, but I know she's focused on whatever thoughts are racing in her mind. After a long sip of her coffee and a heavy exhale, she says, "When I was in high school, I was dating this guy. His name was Travis. He was *so hot*." She giggles, a flash of her old self. "He had this shiny black motorcycle, and he used to take me for rides after school."

I hide my surprise that she's been on the back of a motorcycle as she takes another sip of coffee and gathers her thoughts.

"He used to race his friend on this side road behind the school, and I'd sit on the sidewalk with the other girlfriend, cheering him on." She swallows hard. "One day, they suggested we should ride with them for a race."

Racing two-up is fucking dangerous. My chest tightens.

"The other bike was ahead of us, but only by a little bit." She grips her cup tighter, her breaths shallow. "I told him I wanted to win, and that he should pass them on the turn. We were so close, and—and I don't know—I've thought about it a thousand times since, but I still don't know what happened. One moment his front tire hit their back tire, and the next we were all sprawled out on the asphalt."

This story is over a decade old, but the urge to check her body for injuries rushes through me. I pull her into my side, using my hand at her waist to draw her closer. She leans into me, still clutching her cup like it's her lifeline.

"We all had helmets on—so no brain injuries. But everyone was mangled and bloody. The guy on the other bike broke his wrist and messed up his leg pretty bad. His girlfriend and I both got road rash all over our legs. She broke a few ribs, and I broke my arm." She swallows again, eyes dropping to the floor. "And Travis—*he lived*," she adds quickly, "but he didn't get up off the street until the EMTs came and picked him up. It took a year of physical therapy before he could walk again. He had a walker at graduation."

"I'm so sorry that happened to you," I whisper, gently taking the coffee from her hands and setting it aside so I can wrap my arms fully around her.

Of course she's scared of motorcycles. Of course she's scared of racing. Fuck, of course she's scared of her boyfriend—even a pretend one—racing motorcycles.

I want to tell her that what happened to her is different from what I'm doing. *I'm racing in protective gear. I'd never race two-up. I'm a professional.* But none of that matters to her right now.

My hand rubs slow circles on her back as she stays pressed against me, and I feel a sense of relief that she trusted me enough to share this. When I no longer feel the thudding of her heart in her chest, I ask, "I take it that was the last time you were on a motorcycle?"

She pulls back, looking up at me. "That was the last time I *touched* one."

No wonder she always looks at my bikes like they might explode and hurt her.

Hoping to lighten the mood, I suggest, "You want to try touching one now?"

"Promise it won't bite me?" she asks, a faint smile playing on her lips.

"Promise."

"Okay," she giggles, reaching a finger toward the closest bike, tapping the seat. "I did it." She whispers, her dimples appearing as she smiles wide.

"You sure did," I say, a proud smile tugging at my lips.

"It's interesting," she muses, still relaxed. "But the crash didn't bother me as much for the first couple of years. I went to therapy and that helped a lot. And then in college, I actually—" She glances away, a groan escaping her lips. "This is so embarrassing, but I thought your *Race Naked* video was hilarious."

That's the last thing I thought she'd say, *but I love it.* "You've seen that?"

"So many times. *Not the Fuzz*," she quotes, laughing and hiding her face against my chest. "I can't believe I just told you that. *So* embarrassing."

Grateful she's laughing again, I tease, "You're not the one who had their dick out in a viral video."

"Are you embarrassed about that?" she asks.

"Not at all," I admit with a chuckle.

"You shouldn't be. It's iconic." *She was watching my video ten years ago, and now she thinks it's iconic.* "I think I liked it because there were no corners—no turns like the one I crashed on—*and* no one crashed. So I could watch it and enjoy the racing, knowing the outcome. Other than that one exception, my throat tightens every time I see a motorcycle. And then you—" She cuts herself off. "Well, being around all this again has brought a lot of it back up."

"It makes a lot of sense," I say, still holding her close and thanking her again for sharing with me.

"It only seemed fair after everything I said last night." Before I can tell her how little I care about that, she adds, "I crossed it off my list last night—*block Jared.* Thought you should know. I'm sorry about that too. I hate that he's saying those things to you. You don't deserve—"

"Do not ever apologize for him." I rub my thumb across her palm, giving her hand a gentle squeeze.

She swallows thickly. "Okay, but I'm sorry for what I said. You defended me, and I—I just want to say thank you. It meant a lot to me."

"I'll always defend you," I promise, releasing her hand.

Her lashes flutter, and she looks down, voice soft. "Well, have fun today. Rubber side down and wear your SPF." She giggles at herself. "You don't really need sunscreen, do you?"

"I'm covered head to toe no matter what," I smile.

"Okay, then," she says, starting to turn away.

"I won't be out there alone today," I tell her, hoping to reassure her. "Shane, Ludlow, and I are practicing together. If the conditions get too dangerous, we'll call it. I promise."

Her mouth curves into a soft smile. "That's good."

"We have to go slower in the rain," I add, leaving out the part where I'm still riding well over one hundred miles an hour.

"I like that," she says.

"Practice makes me a better racer—a safer racer."

"Dammit, I guess I like that too," she says, pointing toward the house. "But are you *sure* you don't want to stay home and hang out with me all day instead?"

"I wish," I sigh. It's doubtful she realizes that's the most tempting offer I could have gotten. If it weren't for the rainstorm, I'd have said yes in a heartbeat. Leaving her is hard, but I can't let this chance slip away.

Just as I'd hoped, the rain has turned into a heavy downpour by the time I make it to the track. A rare and needed opportunity.

"What's up, dickhead?" Ludlow greets, coming over to help unload my trailer.

"Just looking forward to racing circles around you, asshole," I laugh, pulling him into a loose hug and patting him on the back.

"You two are so weird," Hart mutters from under the canopy.

"You know you're going to get wet, right?" Ludlow smirks.

She runs a hand over her still-dry hair. "Not yet, I don't."

Under the canopy, I check my phone before slipping into my leathers. There's a message from my *Incite Energy* rep.

Ian: Can't make it today after all. But keep it up! You're right on track.

I don't dwell on his absence because I get a text from Sadie that shifts my focus.

Sadie: Rubber side down, Hacker! Stay on your bike.

"Your pretty pink-haired girlfriend got you smiling like that?" Hart asks.

"You know it." I'm grinning hard at my phone.

Me: I'll come home in one piece. And a better racer. Promise.

Luke always says working on motors is his meditation, and racing has always been mine. It doesn't matter what's going on in my life—the second my tires hit the track, my mind settles. *I've never felt more at peace or more alive than I do on a bike.*

This year, I'm racing the BMW 1000RR—an absolute beast of a machine. It's our first time in the rain together, and I start off even easier than I usually would on a wet day. This may be my only chance to find my edge on this bike in these conditions, so I'm dialing in.

I find my groove, leaning into each turn, pushing my speed a little more with every lap.

Slow is smooth. Smooth is fast.

I've hit the bike's limit for these conditions on about half of the turns, but I want to see—

Ludlow low-sides off the track, but he's fine—already standing by the time I've pulled over to help.

I didn't tell Sadie it's more common than usual to crash in the rain. She was already so fragile, and I didn't want to scare her further. It didn't seem like she could've handled the explanation that a low-side—when the bike slides out from under you—is usually a very recoverable crash. She's imagining a rarer high-side—when you get flung over the handlebars, like the time I broke my femur—or, worse, an even rarer collision, like what she experienced.

Ludlow's back on the track in no time, and I follow him out to finish my laps. Once my trailer's loaded and I'm changed into dry clothes, I text Sadie.

> Me: *Safe! See you soon, sunshine.*
> Sadie: *Yay!*

A picture comes through next—Sadie's purple-tipped fingers petting Boo between his jade-colored eyes.

> Sadie: *He let me pet him!*
> Me: *He loves you.*
> Sadie: *He might.*
> Sadie: *Drive safely!*

The whole way home, I'm working out ways to help her understand the reality of the situation. Yes, racing is dangerous, but not in the way she thinks. Ludlow crashed today, but he recovered immediately. He's not hurt. The kind of tragedies she fears are extremely rare. The slight risk is worth getting to feel alive on the track.

Chapter 12
Sadie

Bowl a perfect game – *from Sadie's list of things she's never done*

"I hate running," I mutter, closing the door behind me after my four-mile run.

"Then why keep doing it?" Cam asks, startling me as he steps out of the kitchen. His hair is wet, and he wears nothing but low-slung sweatpants that almost reveal the tattoo near his abdomen. *What does it say?*

"Because I don't *actually* hate it. I just complain because it's hard, but I want to prove to myself that I can," I answer, walking past him.

He sips a can of watermelon sparkling water, leaning casually against the doorframe. "What is it you want to prove you can do?"

"Something that feels *big*."

"Have you ever won something?" he asks, brushing a

droplet of water from his expressive brow.

"I'm not trying to win the half marathon," I laugh.

"I figured the big thing would be *finishing*, not winning. But for me," he presses a hand to his chest over the '*No Risk No Story*' tattoo, "winning is the biggest thing there is." His head tilts. "Actually, that's not true. Going fast is the biggest thing. It feeds my soul. Winning is second."

"Cam," I say, filling a cup with ice, "it sounds like you're suggesting I race motorcycles."

"Never say never." He shrugs. "But no, I was thinking go-karts."

"Go-karts? Like at mini golf?" I ask.

"A lot like that, but they make bigger, faster ones that are a hell of a lot more fun," he says, tracing his thumb around the rim of his can. "People race them competitively."

I shoot him a look, swallowing an entire glass of water before refilling it under the filter.

"It's one of the safest ways to race," he explains. "The center of gravity is extremely low, and the ones I'd have you racing top out at around sixty-five miles an hour. I don't know anyone who's been injured racing one."

"Safe is good," I nod. "But what about it makes you think I'd like it?"

A broad smile fills his mouth as he pushes off the wall, like he's been waiting all day to talk about this. "You get to go fast—that sixty-five is *a lot* when you don't have a car body blocking the wind. And I think you could win some races."

"You think *I* could win races?" I ask.

"If you decide to do something, you follow through." His eyes—more blue than green today—focus intently on me.

"You'll put in the work."

"I'll consider it," I answer as I walk away to shower.

His confidence in me is a surprise, *but maybe it shouldn't be. I used to like going fast. Maybe if I felt safe enough, I'd like it again. Would he race with me? Teach me? Would it be part of our arrangement?*

I'm still rolling the idea over when I get back to my bedroom after the shower. Collapsing onto the bed in my towel, I check my phone and find a text from Hanna. I'm still not a fan of hers, but I don't harbor the anger and hurt I used to. She helped my ex cheat—*which is abhorrent*—but holding it against her isn't worth the energy anymore.

> *Hanna: I get to see you soon!*
> *Me: You see me on the call every morning?*
> *Hanna: No, in real life! I'm coming to Palm Springs in July.*
> *Me: What for?*
> *Hanna: I wasn't supposed to say anything, but it's not like you'll care now that you have a sexy motorcycle racer boyfriend. Kelee and Jared are getting married there! Don't tell anyone I told you though!*

Instead of the gut drop I used to feel about Jared and Kelee's relationship, I'm overcome with petty amusement. He refused to visit my friends here because he *doesn't like the heat.* And now he's getting married in Palm Springs—*in July.*

Laughter bubbles up, uncontrollably. I wipe tears from my eyes, trying to catch my breath. *This is hilarious.* Either he's so in love with his fiancée that he'll endure anything to make her happy—which, fine, *good for them*—or Bea's right, and he's obsessed with me.

It's not lost on me that I've spent a significant amount of

energy making him jealous, too. But no matter how it started, pretending to date Cam is helping me move on. He treats me better than Jared did, and even just pretending to be with him is raising my standards for the next guy.

My *not*-boyfriend enters the room then, plopping down next to me on the bed. If he feels awkward about me lying here in my towel, he doesn't show it.

"You've got to share this joy with me, sunshine," he says. "What's got you laughing so hard?"

"We are definitely winning the breakup," I say, laughter returning. I fill him in quickly. Jared's taken up enough of my life already. Even though he's the reason we started this arrangement, talking about him now seems like a waste of valuable time with Cam.

"Think I could talk you into going to *Voyeur Café* for a drink with me?" Cam asks.

It's not a date, but my heart flutters anyway.

"You're lucky you came in when you did," I answer. "If I'd had the energy to change out of this towel into pajamas, the answer would have been no." I lie, and for once he doesn't catch me. "Give me fifteen minutes."

We're going to the bar our best friends own, which doubles as a coffee shop during the day. It's not a dressing-up situation. So, I end up in a floral-print midi-length dress with a thin cream-colored sweater over top, deciding it could lean casual or dressy.

When I meet him in the living room, he looks nicer than usual too. He's wearing an olive-green linen button-up with charcoal-colored pants, and his hair is combed into place instead of left in a wild tousle. *Oh, my word.* Is *this a date?*

That question is answered the moment we step inside *Voyeur Café*. A short girl with perfectly coiled dark brown curls rushes straight into Cam's arms.

She giggles as he picks her up in a tight hug.

Whelp. I hate this.

Jealousy I don't deserve burns the back of my throat.

He's never had a girlfriend before, but he has to know—

He sets her down unceremoniously, and she stumbles to regain her balance. Fixing her hair, she scoffs at him and then addresses me. "He's so dumb," she says conspiratorially.

Cam steps behind me, draping an arm across my stomach. "Sadie, this is Skye. She's a pain in my ass and Luke's little sister. Skye, this is my girl, Sadie."

His girl. Maybe my jealousy was premature.

"I've been wanting to meet you for so long," Skye says, surprising me.

Before I can respond, Allie appears. "Okay, perfect. I can't believe I didn't think of this sooner. Skye can stay with you guys."

"Yes, *please*," Skye says, pointing at her big brother. "I'm only in town one night, but their couch sucks."

"I guess our couch is comfier than—" I start.

Allie cuts me off, "Not your *couch*. Don't you guys have an extra bed now that you're together?"

It's a logical assumption, but it's not true. At all. Shit.

"Actually, how does that work since you were roommates first? Which bed *are* you guys sleeping in?" Allie asks.

Cam and I both answer, "Mine," at the same time.

We're caught. This is it. What will Allie think when she finds out I've been lying to her? What will Skye think? She just met me, and—

"This is pretty much the *only* thing we disagree about," Cam laughs. "My bed is better—it's bigger, softer, and my bedding's much nicer—"

"It is *not*—" I protest, not actually sure what his bedding feels like, but knowing Devon custom-ordered mine from one of her specialty interior design places.

"See?" Cam says, "She won't admit that my bed is better, so we end up switching back and forth constantly."

Without thinking, I offer, "You should stay in my bed. You can help me convince Cam it's better."

The conversation moves on to plans for the rest of the evening—*bowling, randomly*—but I barely hear a word of it as I realize what I just committed to. Sure, Skye can sleep in my bed. But that means I'll be sleeping in Cam's—*with him.*

It's still all I can think about in the truck on the way to the bowling alley, when we rent those ugly shoes, and he plugs my name in as Sunshine to show next to my score.

But if *he's* nervous, he doesn't show it. He plays the part of my boyfriend without a hitch.

It's natural and easy, and for a few brief moments, I indulge the idea that this could be real. *It would be just like this, wouldn't it?* But just as quickly, I shake it off. I might feel better after we talked about the reasons racing scares me, but that doesn't mean I'm no longer scared.

He pulls me into his lap after I bowl an eight. "Not bad, Sunshine."

"Got a long way to go if I'm ever going to hit three hundred," I laugh, leaning into him.

He runs his hand up between my sweater and dress, holding onto my low ribs. "I think I need to get you one of those bowling shirts—a yellow one with *'Sunshine'* embroidered in cursive on the front," he says.

"Oh, you *do*?" I ask.

"I do," he says, nodding solemnly. "If you're going to bowl a perfect game, you need the gear to pull it off. Actually, I should get you a ball and shoes, too. And lessons."

"That's a lot of things for *you* to do so *I* can—"

"*Cameron*," Allie's voice cuts in. "Quit flirting with your girlfriend. You're up next."

He lifts me from his lap and sets me on the seat next to his. "It'll be a strike, just for you."

"I'm so happy he found you," Skye says, leaning in from my other side as soon as Cam walks away.

"Found me?" I ask.

"He's been looking," she says, spinning to face me. "I think he always wanted a girlfriend." She glances up to make sure he's not coming. "We always joke that I was his prom date, but I was only ten. I remember he ended up babysitting me while Luke went. He asked a girl he liked, and she said no. He made me spaghetti for dinner, and we danced in the kitchen to Britney Spears. My mom still has a picture of us on the fridge from that night."

"That's so sweet," I say, imagining a seventeen-year-old Cam spending prom night with his friend's little sister. "But also, kind of sad."

"Yeah, it's both. He's such a good guy," Skye agrees. "That's why I'm glad he has you now. He deserves the happiness."

The sound of a ball hitting pins draws both our attentions, and we see Cam with his arms in the air. He rushes back over, moving me back into his lap. "I told you I'd get a strike for you." Narrowing his eyes at Skye, he asks, "She talkin' shit?"

"Of course," she says, shoving him in the arm. "You're the *worst.*"

Bowling is such an unexpected good time, I completely forget about sharing a bed with Cam until Skye gets in his truck with us at the end of the night.

After I get her settled with fresh bedding, I walk the short distance down the hall to his room. "I'm sorry I committed you to this without even asking," I whisper, closing his bedroom door behind me.

"You know I don't care," he says, sitting at the end of his bed, wearing nothing but those low-slung sweatpants again. "Are *you* gonna be okay?"

"I'm good. No reason we can't share the bed," I say, standing awkwardly in front of him.

He gestures toward his en suite bathroom. "You can change in there if you want."

"Oh shit." I glance over my shoulder toward my bedroom. "I left all my pajamas in there. I didn't even think about it."

"You're welcome to anything in my closet, remember?" he says.

I'd almost forgotten about that. "I thought that was just for your race."

"It's for always."

Always. Sometimes I think he forgets there's no one else around to hear him.

He tilts his head toward the closet. "You want me to find something for you?"

"Oh, no. Sorry, I—just give me a second." Feeling his eyes

on me, I grab the first t-shirt I see—a bright yellow *Race Naked* shirt. When I change, I realize it barely hangs past the black undies I hadn't remembered being *quite* this cheeky.

"My bedding *is* nicer than yours, for the record," he says, peeling back the covers for me.

"It is not," I argue again, twisting to avoid pointing my ass at any mirrors as I slide under the sheet.

"No, it's not," he admits, "But it made for a good story, didn't it?"

"It did." I smile. I enjoy pretending with him more and more lately. *But sitting next to him in his bed doesn't feel much like pretend.*

He runs his hand over his forehead, pushing his hair back, pausing for a moment as deep copper strands slip past the tattooed letters on his knuckles.

"What does your hand say?" I ask.

He pulls it down in front of his face, like he has to look to remember, then holds both hands out to me in loose fists with his thumbs touching. "Braaap."

"Braaap?" I repeat, wondering if I heard him correctly.

"Yeah, it's the sound a motorcycle makes when you rev it."

Altogether, his fingers spell *B-R-A-A-A-A-P-!*

"Wait, seriously?" I ask, finding it particularly ridiculous to have an onomatopoeia for an engine rev tattooed on his knuckles.

"Seriously," he answers, wiggling his fingers so the letters move in a little wave.

Taking one of his hands in mine, I trace my fingertip over the dips and rises of his knuckles. "*Braaap*. It's kind of cute, actually."

"I'll take cute," he answers, his smile almost boyish.

I wonder if he'll answer questions about more tattoos. Every other time I've been tempted, it felt too invasive to ask, but now, sitting together in his bed, the situation is inherently vulnerable. "How about the one under the B-R-A-A? Why get a horseshoe on your hand?"

Cam doesn't hesitate. "The horseshoe is because I'm a lucky motherfucker. It's my *job* to race motorcycles," he chuckles, as if the idea is surreal. "There are hundreds, maybe thousands, of racers out there who would crush it on the track if they had the same opportunities I've had."

For me, motorcycle racing would be a literal nightmare of a job. It's easy to forget that for him, the opposite is true.

"Braaap is there partially because it's funny, but mainly because it represents the most important thing to me," he continues. "The horseshoe is to remind me how lucky I am that it *gets* to be important."

I set his hand down and look up, finding he's shifted closer. His head tilts toward me, his eyes locking on mine with a heat I've never seen before. A flutter runs through me. *He doesn't usually look at me like that. Hell, I can't remember the last time anyone looked at me like that.* My eyes drop to the wide line of his lips. *It's been a decade since I had a first kiss, but that's what this look is, right? He's looking at me like he wants to kiss me.*

Swallowing thickly, I tap the bird on the back of his wrist. "And what about this?"

His mouth opens into an oversized smile, followed by an amused chuckle. "You looking for a tattoo tour?" he asks.

"A *tattour*?" I respond, snorting at my own terrible pun.

He gives me an *oh-my-god-you-adorable-little-nerd* look and says,

"I'm down, but you have to share with me too."

"*Cameron.*" I tilt my head toward him. "You know I don't have any tattoos."

"Sure," he answers, his eyes tracing from my face down to my t-shirt-clad body and further. "But *every* body tells a story."

I look down at myself—the exposed parts of my arms, my hands, the shape of my hips and legs under the blanket—and shrug. "Not sure what story there is to tell."

"I'll help you find it," he says, shifting his leg under the covers to tap my socked foot with his shin. "Do you always sleep in socks?"

"Lately, I do," I chuckle.

"Why now?" he asks.

"I don't know. I just—" *Maybe I shouldn't brush this off. Deep breath.* "Actually, you like the house really cold."

"You *don't?*" His shocked voice echoes around the sparsely decorated bedroom and probably down the hall. *What must Skye think we're talking about?*

"I *thought* I did until you moved in," I say, rubbing my feet together self-consciously.

"What were you keeping it at?" he asks.

Hiding my face behind my hands, I answer, "Seventy-two."

Cam is off his bed and moving toward the door in an instant.

"You don't have to change it for me," I protest, pulling off the covers. "I shouldn't have said anything. I don't want you to be uncomfortable."

"You're ridiculous." He grabs the door handle, pointing at me as I try to scoot off the bed. "And *stay in bed.* Evidently, it's cold out here."

"*Seriously*, don't change the thermostat for me. I'm having fun buying cute socks," I say, wiggling my toes to show off the fuzzy, mint-green ones I got last week.

Cam's mouth drops open in mock offense. "You've had to buy new socks because I keep the house so cold?"

I try explaining again how little I mind it, but he walks out to the hall—presumably adjusts the thermostat—then reappears and shuts the door behind him. "Are you cold right now?" he asks.

Glancing down at my bare legs, I answer, "Surprisingly, no."

His brows lower skeptically as he comes to the end of the bed. "I'd better check," he says, running both of his warm, wide palms up the sides of one leg and down the other. He passes over the scars left there from my crash, and I'm grateful it's a story he already knows. I never liked them—what they represent, or how they look. *Jared certainly never made me feel any better about the latter.*

Finding my legs satisfactorily warm, he gives a nod and returns to his spot on the bed next to me, holding his wrist out for my inspection. He jumps back into his *tattour* like nothing happened. "This bird is a swallow. You know when people ask what superpower you'd choose?"

I nod, holding his hand just above my lap, taking in the details—thick lines, heavy black shading, red belly and yellow wings, eyes represented by little *c*-shaped curves, like the bird is soaring through the air with its eyes closed.

"My answer has always been flying. It's the only thing that seems like it would be more freeing than ripping around turns on a motorcycle." His lips curl into a grin as he explains,

"There's something about the spirit of a bird—they can go as fast and as far as they want, whenever they want. I appreciate that."

Cam picks up one of my hands in both of his, cradling it above his lap. *What could he possibly want to know?*

Smoothing his thumb over a thin pink horizontal line on my forearm, he asks, "This is from an oven rack, right? Baking battle scar?"

I nod. "They don't last *too* long, but I always have at least one."

"Do you remember the first time you got one?" he asks, turning my wrist in the light.

"I haven't thought about that in forever," my words come out on a delighted breath. "My mom and I used to make cookies together before Christmas—classic ones like gingerbread, snickerdoodles, and peanut butter. *She* can make a perfect cookie." My lips roll together as my shoulders shake with silent laughter. "My mom is a little scattered. Her kitchen is always a wild mess, so she often can't find an oven mitt and uses kitchen towels instead to pull things out. I was probably six or seven, and I'd seen her do it so many times, but I hadn't noticed how she would fold the towel over and over again so it was thick enough to protect her hands." Cam winces, anticipating what I'll say next. "I tried to pull out a tray of cookies with only one layer of thin kitchen towel to protect my hands. That didn't burn me, but it hurt enough that I dropped the towel, and when my arm swung down, the inside of my wrist hit the oven rack."

"Have you called her lately?" he asks, running his thumb along the scar.

The question confuses me until I remember *Call Mom* is on the first page of my to-do list. I could tell him I don't want to talk about it, *but I'm being nosy tonight, too.* "Not yet," I answer. "But I should."

He nods along, clearly curious but not pushing.

Deep breath. "I'm not that close with my family. I talk to my older and younger sisters maybe three or four times a year. We pretty much only see each other at the holidays, and that works for everyone." I shift, adjusting the pillows so I can lean on my side and face him. "A few years ago, Jared didn't want to come home with me like he usually did. He had a ski trip with friends over New Year's and couldn't do both. Honestly, I didn't care that much. *I guess that should have been a sign.*" I roll my eyes.

"Maybe," Cam shrugs.

"But it made my parents angry. They held it against me that I *let him get away with it,* and after that they did not hold back with their feelings about him. It became really hard to talk to them because they wanted me to move on before I was ready, and they had no patience for me to figure it out on my own." I flinch. *That memory still stings.* "It sucked because when I finally *was* ready, our relationship was so soured, I couldn't even tell them. I'm sure my sisters did, but I haven't talked to my parents since I moved down here. I didn't even go home last year."

Cam blows out a breath, brows narrowing as he considers. I brace for a speech about how I need to be the bigger person, but instead, he just says, "That must be really hard," and changes the subject, knowing I need to move on. *How does he already know me so well?*

"Tell me about this haircut," he says, running his fingertips through the pink ends and shaking me from my distraction. "In every picture of you from before, your hair's long and blonde. Why the pink?"

As Allie put it—this is a breakup haircut. *But do I want to tell him that?* Pulling my knees against my chest, I look up into his blue-green eyes and find that sincere *tell-me-all-your-secrets-so-I-can-keep-them-safe-for-you* look.

Chapter 13
Cam

Luckiest guy around - *caption from Cam's social media post – a video of Sadie jumping into his arms after he bowls a strike, April 4ᵗʰ*

"I had a hair appointment the morning after my breakup," she answers, tucking the pink strands behind her ears. "I'd had the same hairstyle since high school, and it can be such a pain to deal with when it's long."

I give her a skeptical look.

Something passes behind Sadie's soft brown eyes as she blinks up at me, her lips tipping into a soft smile. "I needed a good change. I lost the security of a relationship, my friends, my home, and my city, all at once."

A smile full of pride for her turns my lips. "I can understand that."

"Short hair seemed a lot freer, too, and I was right," she says, her face brightening as she shakes her head side to side—

the cropped pink tips swinging up to brush her chin. "The pink was a spur of the moment decision, but it's my favorite part now. It's so happy."

"It suits you," I agree, brushing my thumb across the brightly colored tips again.

"I actually considered getting a tattoo." She drags her teeth across her plump lower lip as she tracks my movements and then drops her eyes to my lips.

Lowering my voice, I ask, "You're just about ready, aren't you?"

Maybe I'm an asshole, but I enjoy the hell out of the way her throat works on a swallow before she asks, "For what?"

"For your first tattoo," I say, fighting a smirk. "What would you have gotten?"

Her eyes narrow for just a second before she answers, "A whisk," running her finger along the outside of her right forearm. "Right here."

I let the back of my fingers follow the path up her arm. "That would be perfect for you."

"Even if it isn't that, I definitely want a baking tattoo."

"Or two?" I ask.

"Or two," she giggles, leaning into the pillows and my arm behind her. "But I don't think I want the first two to both be about baking."

"*First* two?" My brows lift in surprise. "You're gonna send it, aren't you?" I ask.

Her shoulders rise with her proud giggle. "Maybe it's just because I spend so much time looking at you these days, but I have a feeling I'm really going to like having tattoos."

I'm too hung up on *"spend so much time looking at you"* to think of a response. Her eyes drop to my lips in the same way I've seen a few times already tonight. At first, I thought it was coincidence. But as she licks them, I'm starting to believe she wants me to kiss her as badly as *I* want to kiss her. I manage to resist, saying, "Your turn," and softly squeezing her shoulder.

Either the touch or my words shake her focus, and her eyes drop from my lips to my bare torso. "Is that Betty?" she asks, fingertips dancing along my lower ribs where a representation of my best friend's blue pit bull is tattooed.

"Hell yeah," I answer, suppressing a groan as she continues running teasing traces around my ribs, up and down the edge of my obliques. "Up until you, she was the most important woman in my life."

Her breath catches, pausing her movements for just a second, before she asks, "Is that really why you got it?"

"Partly." I nod. "I do love Betty."

"She's the best."

"She really is," I agree. "The tattoo is for Luke more than anything, though. He doesn't want any, but I still wanted something that honored him. He's more than my best friend. He's my brother—*my family*."

"Aww." A smile warms her face. "You two are really cute together."

"Cute?"

"Yes, *cute*," she insists, her hand now resting at my hip. Looking up, she asks, "Would you ever get a tattoo with me?"

"Say the word, and I'll make the appointment."

"You don't even know what we'd get," she says—as if my immediate answer means I'm not taking her seriously.

"Doesn't matter. We'll figure it out." I hold her gaze. "I'll be proud to have matching tattoos with you."

Her lips roll together as her cheeks warm with a blush. "Okay," she answers.

"Can't wait," I say. My eyes snag on some long-healed scars on the side of her leg. Having a good idea what they're from, I decide not to ask. Instead, mimicking the way her fingertips have been mapping my tattoos, I run my fingertips across the bridge of her nose and across her cheeks. "Tell me about your freckles."

"My freckles?" Pink hair brushes her shoulders as her head tilts. "They exist—not sure what else to say about them."

"What's your favorite memory with them?" I ask.

She rolls her bottom lip between her teeth. "My dad loved my freckles when I was little. He'd always say the best kids have freckles."

I tap her nose. "I like them, too."

"I like yours," she giggles, tapping my nose in the same place.

"There was a short time as a kid when I didn't like the way I looked," I say, running my hand over my face. "Got picked on for being pale, freckled, and redheaded."

Sadie's brows and lips tip down. "I hate that."

"It's okay," I say, hoping she understands I truly mean it. "I figured out quickly I couldn't change any of that, so I decided to own it. I used to get the gnarliest sunburns, though. Never remembered to wear sunscreen as a kid. Luke's mom has these giant aloe vera plants in her front yard, and she'd cut off a piece and rub raw gooey aloe all over me—straight from the plant."

"You two were always inseparable, weren't you?" Sadie

asks.

"Yup, I was at their house way more than my own growing up. I'm an only child, and my parents are older. They gave me a lot of freedom." A smile forms with the memories. "Darlene Pine is a hell of a woman—loves the shit out of her kids. She has her issues—wasn't always able to take care of them the way she wanted. If you ask Skye, Luke did a lot more raising her than Darlene did. But she gives everything she *can* to her kids, and from the first day I showed up on her porch looking for Luke—she's included me in that."

"So that's why you say Skye's like a little sister to you?" Sadie asks.

"Yeah, I've known her since she was two or three. Luke and I would bring Skye along to everything, take turns keeping an eye on her. I'd even babysit when Luke had dates in high school and Darlene wasn't up to taking care of her." Something undecipherable passes Sadie's face at that last comment, and she drops her hand to my wrist. I lower my voice, "Don't tell her I said this, but I think she's turned out to be pretty awesome."

"You and Skye are even cuter than you and Luke." Sadie snorts a laugh. "Do you have a tattoo with her, too?"

"Yup," I answer on a low chuckle, "I took her on her eighteenth birthday. I don't think Luke has ever been more pissed at me than he was then, and I even—" cutting myself off from telling her I crashed and ruined his first motorcycle, I say, "I've been a pain in his ass for a long time."

"Which one is it?" she asks, searching my torso and arms.

"Down here," I say, pulling my pant leg up to reveal my right calf.

"She wanted exact matching tattoos in the same place." Rolling my foot to the side, I show her my Skye tattoo—on the inside of my ankle, there's a bundle of orange poppy flowers in a finer line weight than most of my other tattoos. It's underneath the front tire of a giraffe doing a wheelie on my shin whose neck goes all the way up to my knee.

"Why those flowers?" she asks, shifting forward to get a closer look.

"They're poppies, the California state flower, and when Skye was little, I used to fuck with her and tell her it was illegal to pick them." Sadie tilts her head, tsking. "One time she was sneaking around the yard—didn't realize Luke and I were watching—and she picked one. I played siren sounds from my phone, and Luke ran out of the bushes and scooped her up to *hide her from the cops.*"

"*Not the fuzz,*" Sadie giggles under her breath, then shifts immediately to scolding me, "What a couple of assholes. She wanted a tattoo about that?"

"Eventually, it became a thing we tease each other about. They're still her favorite flower, so the tattoo is a way for her to have them without *the cops* coming to arrest her."

Sadie's dimples appear as her whole face lights up in a smile. "That's really sweet."

"It's just family."

Her eyes narrow. "You're not very good at taking compliments either, Cam."

"No idea what you're talking about." I shrug. "Got another tattoo you want to ask about, or are you gonna explain why you always have purple nails on one hand and pink on the other?"

She tries to hide her flinch behind a shake of her head.

"You go. Tell me about the tortoise and the hare," she says, smoothing pink-painted fingertips over the brightly-colored, old-school style tortoise and hare that race each other across the outside of my left forearm.

"I always liked the story," I say, bringing my arm down between us, so she can inspect it further. *So, she'll start touching me again.*

She does—tracing lines around the outline of the oak-colored hare and olive-green tortoise.

"The hare seems like the clear winner," I say, watching her face as she watches her fingers trace around my arm. "And he *would* have been if he had any respect for his opponent. But he doesn't think the tortoise is a real threat, so the hare lets off the gas. He rests. The tortoise keeps his head down and works slow and steady the whole way. He wins because he never gave up. But *also* because the hare fucked up. In the tattoo, neither of them is winning. There's no finish line because things don't always turn out the same as the original fable."

She flips my arm over, confirming my statement. "I hadn't even noticed."

"The story is full of racing lessons, but it applies to regular life too. *It's not over 'til it's over. Never get too cocky. Never give up—even if it seems like you can't win. Focus on your own progress.* You ever heard the phrase '*slow is smooth, smooth is fast*'?"

She nods.

"It's true—good racing advice and good life advice. When I get you out on the go-kart track, I want you to remember it."

"*When*?" she giggles, dropping her mouth open, pretending to look offended. "You're assuming I'm willing to race go-karts."

"I know you well enough."

Her eyes narrow, and she tries and fails to draw her lips into a frown. "*Dammit, Cameron.* You're right. I *do* want to try it."

"Good, because I already reserved a track."

"You did?" she tries to look offended again before burying her face in my chest as she snorts a laugh. "I can't even be mad at you. I love not planning things. That's magnificent."

"Everyone's coming," I say. "Luke, Allie, Bea, Rhett, and Devon."

"*Everyone?* Not just us two?"

I nudge her shoulder. "You have to have people to race."

"Now I'm nervous."

My heart races when she buries her face in my chest again. Running a hand down her back, I say, "You don't need to be. You're going to be a great racer. Plus, you and I are getting there an hour before everyone else, so you have time to practice."

"Isn't that cheating?"

"Nope," I say, releasing her as I pick up her left hand—the one with purple nails. "Why did you get uncomfortable when I asked about your nail polish?"

"I did not—" She starts to deny, but stops herself, taking a deep breath. "Okay, I did. Because it's dumb."

"Doubt that."

She draws her knees up, but instead of holding them tight to her chest, she drops them across my thighs—leaning her head on my shoulder. "It makes me *feel* dumb is a more accurate way to say it."

I'm not always a great listener, but it's easier with Sadie. I want to know her so badly. Pulling her closer, I rub my hand up and down her biceps and wait for her to continue.

"I have a really hard time with left and right," she says, staring at her lap. "For some reason, it doesn't stay in my brain. I can't seem to learn or memorize it. I have an innate understanding for up and down, but left and right changes depending on which way I'm facing." She finally looks back at me. "If someone says *take a left up here*, I have to think really hard to figure out which way that is, and half the time I end up getting it wrong anyway."

I had no idea. Why does she feel like she has to hide that?

She holds her hands up in front of us with every finger tucked in but her index and thumb on each hand—making a field goal shape. "This is the easiest way for me to tell." She wiggles the extended fingers on her left hand. "See? The left hand makes an actual capital *L*, but the right hand doesn't. So, if I hold my hands up like this, I know which is which, but that's embarrassing. Most people know their left from right. *It's so basic.*"

She's not dumb. "Was there someone who made you feel bad because of that?" I ask, avoiding her ex's name.

Her chest lifts on a sad laugh. "Yup, so I started painting my nails like this." She holds her hands up closer so I can see.

"Pink and purple?" I ask.

"Lavender, for *L*, or Left," she wiggles her left fingers. "And rose, for *R*, or Right," she says, wiggling her right. "Sometimes I do rose gold on the right if I'm feeling fancy."

"That's *clever*," I say, rubbing my thumb over the smooth polish of her *rose* hand. "You don't have to do it anymore if you don't want. I doubt anyone in your life now would give you a hard time for making *L*s with your fingers." The fact that her ex *did* has my blood boiling.

"It works pretty well, actually," she says, "and I like having a signature thing like that. Maybe someday I'll get *L* and *R* tattoos instead."

"Or you could just use my tattoos," I say, tucking her into my side and bringing my hands out in front of us. "There's already the R from *braaap* on my right hand."

"Ooh," she giggles, tapping the lightning bolts tattooed on the back of my left hand. "*L* for lightning. Too bad it only works when we're facing the same way."

"You can always come sit in my lap when you need to check them," I offer.

"I'll keep that in mind." She blushes, looking down.

She stares at the text on her shirt for a second before leaning forward and scanning my body again. "Do you have a *Race Naked* tattoo anywhere?"

"None you can find with my pants on."

Her eyes go wide as her hands go to her mouth. "Is it on your ass?" she whispers through her fingers.

"Not quite," I say, enjoying the hell out of her bashful reaction. "You want to see it?"

A naughty smile curves her lips. "I do."

All she asked to see is the tattoo, so I fold the blanket to cover my lap, but not the side of my leg before sliding my pants down to expose the tattoo. On the outside of my right leg, all the way at the top of my thigh, almost to my hip, there's a pin-up girl wearing a *Race Naked* t-shirt.

"She's so pretty," Sadie gasps, reaching out to trace the lines with her fingertips, but pulling her hand back at the last second. "I'm sorry. That feels more personal. Is it okay if—"

"It's okay," I tell her. "You can touch me." I leave out the *"anywhere and anyway you want"* half of that sentence, but the thought ricochets around my mind as she traces the lines of the tattoo—pointed toes, shapely legs, cheeky shorts, half-moon shapes of the imaginary woman's breasts that peak out under the pink t-shirt, *Race Naked* lettering, dimpled cheeks, and finally over the blonde space buns.

"But the girl in the video had black hair," Sadie says, breaking the meditative way I'd focused on her touch.

"It's not supposed to be the girl from the video," I say, surprised she remembers.

"But that's pretty much what she was wearing. Only her shirt didn't say *Race Naked* of course because that hadn't happened yet."

I can't remember the last time I explained this tattoo to anyone, and I know I've never admitted the next part. "The reference photo I used was actually of a girl who dressed up *as* the girl from the video for Halloween that year. She'd made a shirt that said *Show Me Your Willie*, but I liked *Race Naked* better for the tattoo."

Sadie's face goes blank, swallowing thickly as she stares at the pin-up on my thigh. "Was she a friend of yours?" she asks.

"Never met her," I say, wondering if the photo is still taped on the wall in the back of my trailer. "She tagged me online. A lot of people had costumes based on the video that year."

"She was blonde, and she had a pink *Show Me Your Willie* shirt?" she asks.

My eyes narrow. I know I just told her those exact details. "Yeah, if I remember correctly, it was wet, too. She was holding two red plastic cups like the girl in the video. Maybe she spilled one."

She tilts her head, brow furrowed, glancing back and forth between the tattoo and me.

After she opens and closes her mouth a few times without saying anything, I ask, "You alright?" as I pull my pants back up.

"Yeah," she says, drawing the single syllable out until it sounds like a question more than an answer. She returns to her place next to me at the head of the bed and presses herself back in under my arm.

Trying to figure out what's just come over her, I search her face and find her eyes dropping to my lips. *She wants me to kiss her.* I am *dying* to kiss her. She's in my bed, snuggled in under my arm, watching me—and I am struggling to find a reason not to.

"You should probably kiss me," her voice comes out so quietly, I'm half convinced I imagined it. *Did I imagine it?* "I mean, it's a good idea," she continues. "Well, maybe not— but, yes—no—" as she stumbles over her words to explain it away, I realize she *did* say it. *She told me to kiss her.* "It's just that everyone knows we're—*thinks* we're dating—eventually it'll happen, and I think it's better—"

With a light grip under her chin, I tilt her face up to meet mine, halting her rambling. I'll never understand how we went from her asking about my pinup tattoo to asking me to kiss her, but I'll just take it as further proof I'm a lucky motherfucker.

"I think it's a great idea," I speak into the quiet between us, drawing her in until my lips find hers. Sadie is sunshine, and her kiss is just as bright and warm as the rest of her—lighting a fire inside me.

She was trying to make the excuse that we should kiss once before we have to do it in front of anyone else. *But this is not some trial run.* This is me finally taking the chance to rain affection on the girl of my dreams. Drawing her closer with a hand at her low back, my tongue meets the first taste of hers.

I keep thinking she'll pull back, say it's enough, but she doesn't. Instead, a quiet moan passes her lips as she rolls her body against mine and digs her fingernails into my shoulders. Her lips and tongue move in tandem with mine, as hungry for me as I've been for her.

I've passed up a dozen opportunities to kiss her—times I could have gotten away with it in front of other people with the excuse that we're supposed to look like we're dating. But that wouldn't have been right. She deserves better.

Needing to feel more of her, I grip her lush hips and slide her gorgeous body over mine until she's straddling me. The motion breaks our kiss, but we're both leaning in for more without a second thought. Her lips are even softer than they looked, and she tastes even sweeter than I expected. *I could drink her up all night.*

Letting my hands slide from her thighs to revel in the curves of her ass, I use the hold to line her up over my rigid cock. By now, the blanket has slid down so that only the thin fabric of her panties and my pajamas separate me from her heat. Rocking against her, I sink my teeth into her lower lip.

She cries out softly into my mouth, and I am done for. "Cam," she gasps, pulling back and panting for breath through swollen lips.

My chest rises and falls as I search her face. She can't possibly think this is only a test to make sure we aren't awkward when we have to kiss in front of our friends. *She can't. Everything else with us could be questioned, but this moment is real.*

After a few seconds, her lips tip into a sly smile I've never seen on her before. She braces herself with hands on my chest, and my cock throbs when she nibbles her bottom lip and rocks herself against me in a long hard stroke. *I knew she'd be amazing like this.* She rocks against me again—once, twice, then picks up a slow, sensual, teasing rhythm.

Breathing out a curse, I dig my fingertips into the plump skin of her ass and pull her down more firmly against me as she continues. I watch her—in awe that this woman is doing this with *me.* "You should probably kiss me," I repeat her words from before.

Her movements still.

Fuck.

"This is um—I should probably—we probably shouldn't," she's back to rambling excuses. I hate that she's pulled away, but more than that I hate that she's feeling anxious.

Releasing my hold on her, I bring my arms back to cross behind my head.

Another gasp escapes her as she's removing herself from my lap, this one much less delicious than the last.

Looking down, I see that her movements have drawn my pants down, exposing the tip of my cock and the tattoo above it on my upper pelvis. *Ride It Like You Stole It.* I drop my hand to fix the waistband, discovering she's also wet enough to leave a damp spot behind. Not sure—and honestly not caring—which of those three things had her gasping, I say, "You're welcome to anytime."

Chapter 14
Sadie

Learn how to take a compliment – *from Sadie's list of things she's never done*

"Why are you the cutest person who's ever lived?" Allie asks when I step into Devon's backyard, wearing my peach-colored '90s cut bikini and a wide-brimmed Panama hat.

"Stop it, I am not." I wave away the comment, sitting down next to her, Bea, and Devon, who are all sitting around the corner of the pool, letting their legs sink into the cool water.

"You are quite adorable," Devon adds.

"I am not—" I begin to protest again, but then I remember what I'm supposed to be focusing on today. *If people want to say nice things about me, why shouldn't I let them?* I'm lucky to have friends who say such lovely things. Even though my hair is too short for it, I make a motion like I'm flipping it over my shoulder. "Okay, I *am* adorable."

Bea dips her oversized sunglasses down her nose. "You're

even cuter when you accept compliments," she adds.

Did she just compliment my ability to take a compliment? Surely, I'm allowed to deny that. Right?

Before I can object, Cam, Luke, Rhett, and all three dogs emerge from the brand-new house. It's a modern design dream, built on a stunning desert property between Palm Springs and Joshua Tree that Devon and Rhett built together. They just finished construction, and we're all staying with them for the weekend to celebrate.

When the guys approach us, Betty follows close behind, plopping onto the shaded concrete near Allie, while Dandy and Spaghetti chase each other around the yard.

Cam—who still hasn't stopped bringing me coffee during my morning meetings every day—sets down a tray filled with cookies and drinks on a low table.

"You ladies need anything other than this before we disappear to the workshop for a while?" Rhett asks, pointing toward the tray.

"Looks like we'll be pretty well covered for a while," Devon answers.

"Later, sunshine," Cam says, tucking his hands into his pockets as he follows Luke and Rhett.

"I think I really like him," I sigh, once they've disappeared around the house.

Bea chuckles. "That's probably for the best, since you two are together."

Something true. Say something true. "Just feels extra poignant today, I guess."

"I was skeptical at first," Devon comments, sipping one of the rum and peach cocktails from the tray.

"Oh, you *were?*" Allie presses both hands to her collarbones in mock shock.

Devon arches a brow. "Obviously. He's the *Race Naked* guy."

"He's more than that," I jump to defend him.

Devon dips her chin in a single nod. "Clearly, I see that now."

"Even if he was just the *Race Naked* guy," Bea says, sipping an orange-hued drink from the tray. "I think that's good for you. You needed someone wild."

Someone wild? Is that what I need? I've wanted to share with my friends what's happening with Cam, but we're in so deep already. *How would they respond if they found out I've been lying to them about him for months?*

"What makes you say that?" I ask, relieved to at least ask for advice.

Bea slides her glasses up to balance on her head, looking me in the eye when she answers. "You've had such an incredible amount of change in your life lately, and I know that doesn't settle easily in your spirit. You like when things are steady. I think a wild man—specifically that gorgeous one with the red hair and all the tattoos—helps you realize you can still be okay when things aren't steady. He's comfortable with change and chaos, so he can help you through."

This is why I have to talk to my friends. "I don't think I ever would have put that together myself, but you might be on to something," I say. *His wildness is good for me, but it's also the thing that's keeping me from actually falling for him. How do I bring that up?*

Turns out I don't have to, because Devon does. "I am still not convinced that dating a motorcycle racer is the best thing for you."

I jump to answer before Allie can interject, like I know she wants to. "That part is hard for me still," I say, wading through my thoughts until I find the right words. "It's really, really scary to think how easily I could lose him."

Devon's tone softens. "Have you talked to him about any of that yet?"

"A bit," I nod. "It's hard because I'm not entirely sure how I feel about it all."

"It's still new," Bea says. "You don't have to have it all figured out yet."

She's someone who seems much more comfortable with change and chaos than I am, but I try to commit her words to memory. *I don't have to have it all figured out yet.*

Allie lifts a cookie in the air, turning it one way and then the other. "I'm not complaining, but can I ask why we're eating gingerbread in April?"

"They're Cam's favorite," I say, scooping a little gingerbread dude off the tray for myself. "Also, I think I might get a tattoo of one soon."

That admission sparks a conversation about the tattoo appointment Cam booked for us next month. It's been a couple of weeks since we had our late-night tattoo conversation and make-out. Neither of us has said a word about the kissing, but we did agree the next day to book a tattoo appointment. I don't confess that he's also considering a gingerbread tattoo because I know exactly what the advice about getting a tattoo with my *boyfriend* of two months would be. It's one secret I don't mind keeping.

Having a moment of openness with them eases some of the

anxiety I've felt these past couple of months, and it makes me want to share something else with them. I glance around the yard. Spaghetti and Dandy are on their way back to us now, but the guys haven't returned.

"Do you want to know a secret?" I ask.

Wrangling Spaghetti to lie down next to Betty in the shade, Allie says, "More than *anything*," like she's been waiting all day for something juicy.

"And you cannot tell anyone, especially not your boyfriend," I insist.

"Why am I the only one getting warned?" she asks, looking between Bea and Devon.

"Because Bea's a vault, and even if Devon told Rhett, he wouldn't care," I answer.

"So, this is a secret Luke can't know?" Allie nods, nibbling the foot off another cookie. "Got it."

"I think Cam has a tattoo of me," I whisper.

Bea's mouth drops open in shock—her eyes glittering with excitement.

Allie gasps a scandalized *"What?"*

When I look to Devon, her eyes are narrowed, but she says nothing, *holding her judgment for later.*

"He already got a tattoo for you?" Bea whispers, sounding more intrigued than anything.

"No, no. I think he's had it for years, before he ever met me or knew who I was." Hearing the words out loud, I realize just how unrealistic this sounds.

"What the fuck?" Allie whispers, petting Spaghetti's curly brown head.

"I'm not even *sure* it's me, but she's dressed like me, and she has dimples," I say. "I don't think *he* even realizes it's me."

No one says anything, but I get a trio of matching *oh-sweetheart-that's-not-what-you-think-it-is* faces.

"I'm not explaining this well," I say, pulling on the wide brim of my hat.

"You're really not," Bea says, in the most soothing voice imaginable. "But we're along for the ride. Try again."

I snort a laugh at her gentle tone. "The tattoo is a pin-up girl in a pink *Race Naked* t-shirt."

"I've never seen that one," Allie comments.

My cheeks flush at the memory of the time *I* saw it. My first thought is to not let my friends know what happened between us, *but I can't talk to them about that anyway.* We've already told them we're together, so now I can't tell them about the first time he kissed me only two weeks ago. *I suppose I could tell it as if it happened sooner, but how do I keep the details straight? What if I mess it up?* The lines between truth and lie tangle further. *What point was I trying to make?*

"Where is it?" Allie asks, reminding me where we left off.

"It's on the side of his thigh, but way up here." I lean back, tapping the area on my body to show them.

"And you feel like the tattoo can represent you now that you're together?" Bea graciously suggests.

"No, I think he used a photo of me as reference." Scrolling my phone for the photo in question, I explain what he told me about the tattoo. "Here," I say, holding it out for them to inspect when I find it.

"I remember that night. I took that photo," Devon says. We exchange a glance, silently agreeing not to mention it also happened to be the night I met Jared.

"That's positively precious," Bea says. "You two were connected already such a long time ago. You're meant to be." *Meant to be. Cameron Hacker and I meant for each other.* The thought rattles something in my heart that I'm trying desperately not to let loose.

"I think we're going to have to see this tattoo to be sure," Allie says, "But if it's true, that's the cutest shit I've ever heard."

"It honestly might be," Devon agrees, a small curve to her lips.

As we lounge by the pool, I'm struck by how different my life is now compared to when I came to visit a little over a year ago. Back then, Allie, Devon, and I had a pool day, too, and it was the happiest I'd felt in months. I was in a rough place—knew I needed big changes, but was too scared to make them. So, I spent the whole weekend imagining I *had* already made those changes.

When I pictured a happier version of myself, I wasn't with Jared anymore. I lived close to good friends, and I made time for things that made me feel fulfilled. And now that I have all of those things, I'm happy.

What I *hadn't* imagined was a different man. *But there's one here now.* He's larger than life, treats me better than I deserve, and it's getting harder and harder to picture life without him.

When the guys come back, Allie manages to keep her mouth shut about the pinup tattoo, but I'll be shocked if it hasn't made its way to Cam by morning.

He steps around sleeping dogs to reach our spot by the edge of the pool. "You are absolutely gorgeous today. Sunshine looks good on you, sunshine."

I have to physically bite my tongue to keep from shooting him down.

Realizing he won't get a response, he asks, "Still good? Anyone need new drinks? Snacks?" When we all answer no, a devious look takes over his face, and he backflips into the water, splashing Allie and me.

"He's such a *boy*," Allie laughs, wiping water from her face.

When he comes to the surface, his oversized smile is out in full force as he swims straight for me.

"You got me all wet," Allie complains, splashing water at him.

He folds his arms on the pool's edge, his elbow brushing against the scarred side of my leg. In the direct sunlight, the scars are more visible than usual, but fortunately, he doesn't seem to notice. "Yeah, I have that effect on women," he says, leaning over to kiss my knee. "This one, anyway."

He does have that effect on me, and it's a problem because it's getting harder to know what's for show and what's real with him.

"Ew," Allie says. "You guys are cute."

Cam pushes off the wall and starts tugging lightly on my calves. "You gonna come play with me? Or do I have to play with myself all day?"

"Ew," Allie repeats.

But I snort a laugh. "Sometimes I wonder if you hear the things that come out of your mouth."

"Oh, I hear them," he says, flashing me a giant smile.

"I'll come *swim* with you in a little bit," I say.

He comes toward me again, and I think he's about to pull me into the water, but he braces his hands on either side of my legs and launches himself up until his elbows are locked, our faces level. "Don't take too long," he says, leaning in to give me a kiss. It's only the second time he's kissed me, and it's sweet and simple, but my blood heats just the same.

It's been two weeks since the first time he kissed me—*the only time he's kissed me*. Since then, it's like he's turned up the charm—something I didn't even know was possible. I've always figured he probably flirts with every woman—*although I struggle to think of examples of him making teasing remarks or rubbing his hand across the lower back of anyone else.* But it's getting harder to believe this is all fake for him.

As he swims away, I turn to Allie with a bewildered laugh. "*All* of that works for me."

"Perfect for each other," she shrugs. "Totally called it."

After a day spent in the pool and sunshine, everyone's quick to split off to their rooms for bed. Even though my body carries the bone-tired feeling a day like this demands, the second Cam and I are both in bed, my brain refuses to shut down.

I don't think he's asleep yet, but he's lying flat on his back with his arms propped behind his head. *Who sleeps like that? Is he actually comfortable? Is he sleeping?* Rolling onto my side, I adjust my pillow. *Maybe that'll help.*

"Trouble sleeping?" Cam asks, without opening his eyes.

Even though he didn't whisper, I do. "I'm sorry. Am I keeping you awake?"

"You're great, don't worry," he answers—but doesn't answer my question.

So, I am keeping him awake? Doing my best to lie still, my eyes catch on a tattoo I haven't asked about yet. Maybe it's because this is what we did the one other time we shared a bed, but I can't help myself from asking, "Is that a *Hot Wheels* car?"

He's still for a moment, then a smirk curves his lips, and his blue-green eyes open as he turns onto his side so he's facing me. "It is," he says, holding his arm out for me to analyze the tattoo.

On the upper half of his forearm, just below his elbow, there's a little black and yellow sports car with flames coming out the back.

"You gonna tell me about it?" I ask, tracing the ink with my fingertip.

"Sure. I saw something similar on a flash sheet and decided to get it as a '69 Camaro because I had this toy as a kid." His chuckle is low. "And also, I like that there's a sixty-nine-joke hidden in there." It's a less meaningful answer than any of the others he's given me, but it still suits him. "Honestly, sixty-nine's not even my favorite thing, but I love a dirty joke."

"Not your favorite?" The words slip out before I've thought about them. *Why would I ask him that?*

The smirk that hasn't left his lips lifts a little higher. "I prefer being able to focus all my attention on my partner when I'm going down, let her revel in it without having to worry about me. But sometimes the moment calls for something different. You know?"

I do *not* know, *but can I tell him that? Will he judge me?* His sincere eyes hold mine, and I can't imagine he would. *Keeping a secret* is on my list, but I don't want it to be this one. "I actually haven't ever done that." My heart races with the admission.

"Never came up, huh?" His response is more confusion than anything, but there's no hint of judgment. "Not even just to see what it's like to go down on someone at the same time?

Have a little race—see who can get the other one off first?"

The way he talks about sex is so casual. *Have a little race?* Like sex is a light, playful experience. It was never like that for me. I was always self-conscious, and eventually, I only slept with my ex because it seemed like something I *should* do. I rarely got anything out of it. Shaking my head, I say, "No, never."

His brow furrows.

Before he can ask more questions, I decide to unload the whole secret—something I've always been too ashamed to admit to my friends. "Jared never went down on me at all."

Cam's jaw clenches, and I swear he looks *angry*. "That fucking idiot," he breathes.

"He's the only person I've ever been with. So—" I take a steadying breath. "I've never experienced that, *ever*."

Cam's silent for long enough that I wonder if something's wrong.

Maybe he is judging me after all?

"I know, it's embarrassing," I start to fill the silence, staring at my hands as I wring them together. "I probably shouldn't have told you—"

His fingertips dip under my chin, gently lifting my face toward his. "First, there is *nothing* for you to be ashamed of. Him, on the other hand—I didn't think it was possible to lose even more respect for that asshole, but..." he lets his words trail off, shaking his head.

"Secondly," he says, releasing my chin as he stands up from the bed and walks around to my side. His broad hands reach under the blanket and flip me around until I'm sitting with my legs dangling off the side of the bed. He drops to his knees, placing himself between my legs. If he wasn't staring intently into my eyes, he'd be looking right at the crotch of my tiny pajama shorts. His hands grip my knees. "Will you *please* let me do this for you?"

"*What?* Cam, you can't—"

He lifts a finger to my lips and *shushes* me. "Let me finish."

Too stunned to speak, I nod my agreement.

"Please, Sadie." He blows out a breath, shaking his head from side to side before fixing me with an intense, *for-the-love-of-everything* stare. "This is an experience you need. You deserve. And I—" he takes a deep breath. "I *want* to give this to you. I want to do this for you. I want to show you why this is something you should never allow yourself to go without again. Let me show you why you should *never* tolerate a man who doesn't bury his face between your legs and worship."

Worship? He wants to worship me? How did we get here? Do I want him to—who am I kidding? Of course I want him to. But it's not a good idea. We can't—

"Talk to me," he interrupts my thoughts, holding my gaze. His hands grip my spread legs as he kneels before me, wearing nothing but a pair of boxer-briefs.

Is he offering to do this right now?

I release a shaky breath. "On the ground like that, it looks like you're begging."

His eyes narrow, and his head tilts. "Not sure how I could be clearer," he says, letting go of my legs and folding his arms, elbows propped on the bed. "I *am* begging you."

"Cam, you don't—you can't—" I start to protest, because denying him feels like the right thing to do—even though I want exactly what he's offering.

His pleading eyes search mine. "It doesn't matter who I am to you—friend, boyfriend, *pretend* boyfriend, roommate. It doesn't matter. I'm *begging* you as one human being to another. Please, let me do this for you."

My heart races. Where, normally, my mind would be cluttered with a thousand thoughts, all I can think now is *I want it to be him.*

He sits there, silent and yearning, watching me. Earnest. Kind. And he looks at me in a way no one else has. If I allowed myself to acknowledge any of the thoughts I've had about him today, I'd already admit it: I want him. *I want him.*

Why can't I say yes? Why can't we do this?

"Tell me what you're thinking?" he asks after a long silence.

I should just say yes. But he would have to *do* it. He would see me. Taste me. Know me in a way no one else has. *That's the point, right? But what if he doesn't—what if I don't—what would it do to us—*

"Sadie." His hands drop to the outsides of my knees as he pushes to his feet.

Did I take too long to decide? Does he not want me anymore? Should I have—

"I don't want to stress you out." He cups my face, pulling me forward to press a soft kiss to my forehead. "You don't have to say yes now, but it's always on the table."

Chapter 15
Cam

Delicious - *caption from Cam's social media post - a picture of him eating one of Sadie's race-themed cookies, May 1st*

"Where did this come from?" I ask, pointing at the cat dish in our backyard filled with kibble.

"From the pet store." Sadie smiles, walking past me into the house.

I tilt my head. "But we don't have a pet?"

"He could *hear* you." She holds a finger up to her lips. "It's for Boo. What if he's hungry?"

The cat is clearly well-fed. I doubt we're the only house in the neighborhood he visits, *but she looks so excited.* "Good for him," I say, following her into the kitchen, where there are a few dozen sugar cookies cooling on the counter.

"I feel like I'm getting in on this during the fun part," I say.

"You won't be saying that after your hands ache from

squeezing these damn piping bags," she giggles.

She's been learning how to decorate with this kind of icing and offered to make another set of race-themed cookies for me to use for content.

"Have you ever thought of starting your own business?" I ask. "You could have a bakery, or you could make baking videos if you wanted."

"I have thought about it. Devon suggested it a few times, and Allie has said she'll sell my stuff at *Turbine Café* if I decide to open a bakery. But I like that it's a hobby. I don't want to monetize it. I don't want baking to be a job," she says, pulling a bowl full of frosting out of the refrigerator. "They both like running businesses, but I like having a job I just do and then don't have to think about later. I play with spreadsheets and analyze data, and then *I don't*. It's perfect."

"That does sound perfect for you. When you explain it that way, I'd hate to see you lose any of the joy you get from baking," I say, watching as she begins to prep piping bags. "Are you going to let me help with this?"

"Not yet," she says, her eyes dropping to my lips.

She keeps doing that. And I'm sure I do, too.

We just got back from Devon and Rhett's place this morning. It's been less than a day since she told me her secret, and it's all I can think about.

How the hell someone was with this gorgeous woman for nine years and never once tasted her blows my mind.

I don't want to push her, but I know she's interested. Her mind was racing, so I dropped it. But now I'm second-guessing myself. *If I'd waited for her to answer, would she have said yes?*

"Cam," Sadie's voice cuts into my thoughts. I realize I've

stepped in closer to her, and now I'm the one staring at her lips.

"Yes?"

"What are you—" she swallows, pulling her shoulders back. "What are you thinking about?"

It doesn't really count as her bringing it up, but I might go absolutely mad if I don't ask her just one more time.

"You sure you want to know?" I ask, lowering my voice.

She nods. "Please tell me."

"Same thing I've been thinking about since last night," I say, wanting to touch her but making sure I keep my hands to myself.

"Oh?" She swallows again.

My eyes scan her face. "You are absolutely stunning. Your freckles, those dimples, your lips. Do you know I'm *obsessed* with your lips?"

"I didn't know that," she says, her voice almost a whisper.

"I am," I nod. "I've been thinking about them, and I've been thinking about what I offered you."

"I've been thinking about that too," she says.

Good.

"Any chance you're ready?" I ask, like it's an idea of when, not if.

She holds my stare for a long moment, but this time I stay with her, watching as the wheels turn in her mind, and she decides if she—

"Yes."

She said yes.

It was a long shot, but I had to take it. *A second time. No risk, no story.* But this isn't about a story I'll tell, it's about the story that's been unfolding between Sadie and me long before either of us ever realized it.

My hands bracket her hips, and I lift her onto the one area of marble counter that isn't covered in cookies and drop to my knees.

"Right now?" she asks, pressing her hands to the counter's edge between her legs.

"Did you have another time in mind?" I ask.

"I guess not. I just—" she takes a shallow breath. "It makes me nervous."

"That's okay. You can trust me, and I'll take it slow."

I wait for another long moment to pass, and she finally moves her hands, bracing them outside her legs. "Okay."

Still on my knees between her legs, I grip them, running my fingers up her calves to her knees. I dip my head and place a soft kiss on the inside of her right thigh, easing her into the feeling of having me down there. When I turn my head to do the same on the other leg, her muscles tense under my fingers. Looking up, I see she's digging her teeth into her bottom lip as her chest rises and falls on tight breaths.

It's gonna take a lot more than a few soft kisses between her knees to make her comfortable.

When I stand up, her mouth turns down. "Wait? Why did you stop? Did I—"

The insecurity dripping off her words breaks my heart.

"I'm not stopping, love. Don't worry." I say, scooping her off the counter and carrying her into the living room. I lean her back onto the pillowy couch until I can cage her in with an arm on either side of her head. "Why don't we start with something else?" I ask, dipping down to kiss her.

The tension in her body shifts the moment our lips touch.

Instead of fear, her body buzzes with anticipation, her fingers grasping onto my shoulders as her lips meet mine. We've been here before, and she knows what to expect—what to do. *And she does it so well.*

I've been dying to kiss her again—properly—for weeks. Taking my time, I bask in slow, searching presses of our lips and seeking tongues.

"You are gorgeous when you kiss me," I tell her between kisses.

"Your eyes are closed, Cameron," she giggles, pressing another kiss to my lips. "You can't know that."

With a hand at her waist, I roll us so we're both lying on our sides, facing each other. "I assure you, I *can* know that."

Her eyes sparkle with anticipation, a sly smile on her lips, as I tuck my fingers into the waistband of her shorts and draw them down her legs.

Taking my time, I let my hand drift up her leg, paying extra attention to the scars there. When my fingers graze the edge of the longest one, she flinches. My eyes snap to hers as I run my hand over her thigh again, my palm covering an expanse of scars.

She flinches again. "You don't have to touch them."

That fucking asshole. I don't have to ask to know what's making her insecure. "I *want* to touch them."

"But my scars aren't part of," she lowers her voice to a whisper, "going down on me."

My lips pull into a smirk as I tap the tip of her nose.

As expected, she giggles, loosening up a little again.

"It's cute that you're too shy to say that out loud, but you're okay with me doing it."

I kiss her nose in the same place, then move down her body to her beautiful, scarred leg. My lips find the lowest scar, all the way down on her calf. "And the point isn't only for me to go down on you." I kiss the next one higher. "It's to worship you." My hand turns her leg, giving me access to kiss another scar. "I want all of you." and another. "Every single inch."

"They're just *ugly*. I hate them. You shouldn't—"

"No, *you* shouldn't." I continue kissing up her leg, covering every bit—scarred or otherwise—with my lips. "Every part of you is just as beautiful as the next. If it takes the rest of my life to erase the ugly comments some useless asshole put in your head, then so be it." She begins to soften again, sliding her leg under my hands to help me reach the best angle for a scar high up her leg. "I'm happy to cover you in kisses every night until it clicks, but I will not let you talk about yourself like that—not while you're with me."

She doesn't admit that they're beautiful like the rest of her. I knew it would take more than one afternoon to change her mind about something so deeply rooted, but she stays loose and comfortable in my hands as I do my best to convince her with my kisses.

When I reach the top, I kiss the soft curve of her ass, my fingers sinking into her flesh as I breathe out a curse. "I've been dying to do that ever since I saw you in that tiny bikini bottom yesterday morning."

"Grab my ass?" she giggles.

The underwear she's wearing now covers even less than the bikini did, leaving plenty of skin for my hand to explore. "This is magnificent," I groan, bringing my face up to hers again.

"It is *not*," she says, using the same tone she does when she thinks I'm being ridiculous. "It's just an ass."

"What did I *just* say? Every part of you is beautiful, and you will not deny that when you're with me." I drag my teeth along her lip. "You aren't allowed to argue compliments about your ass. It's perfect."

"It is n—"

I interrupt her. "I'm serious."

Her cheeks flush, and she buries her face in my chest. "Fine."

"You're doing great," I reassure her.

I dip two fingers under the hem of her tiny lace panties, running them from the curve of her ass cheek, over her hip, and forward, pausing when I reach the front of her pelvis.

Her eyes meet mine, and she nods in silent approval. This is new territory for *us*, but not for her, so I'm hoping it will help her trust me with the rest. When my fingers find her wet center, her hand drops to my cock, gripping me through my pants.

I breathe out another curse, undone by the simple touch. I need her in every way, but today, I want to take care of her, guide her through something new—not use her for my own pleasure. As my fingers trace a slick line to her clit and back, she begins to unbutton my pants.

"Does it make you more comfortable if you're touching me too?" I ask, my movements slow and deliberate.

"More comfortable?" she asks, her hands stilling. "Not necessarily, but shouldn't I?"

"*Shouldn't* you?" I ask, raising an eyebrow. "No, you shouldn't unless that's what you need. Remember what I said last night? I want to focus on you, make you feel good."

Her face twists between pleasure and concern as I begin

slow circles on her clit. "Do you not like—"

"I *love* every way you touch me," I interrupt her. "But I don't want you thinking about me right now. I want you to try to be selfish." Adding the smallest amount of pressure, I ask, "Do you think you could do that for me?"

Her hand leaves my cock, and she digs her fingertips into my biceps. "I can try," she breathes.

My fingers trail down, slipping into her entrance. "I'll help you."

She closes her eyes, holding tightly onto me. But her features soften as I sink my fingers deeper, letting soft moans slip from her lips.

"You're going to help me be selfish?" she asks, her voice breathy as I ease her onto her back.

I drop my lips to her collarbone. "Yes, sunshine. All you need to think about is what feels good for you. If I do something you like, will you tell me?" I increase the speed with my hand.

"Like that?" she asks, tightening around my fingers. "I like *that*."

"Exactly like that," I say, maintaining the pace. "But I also need you to tell me if you don't like something."

When she doesn't respond, I start to pull my fingers away from her wet heat.

"Hey, I didn't like *that*," she breathes, almost frantic. "Don't stop."

I resume my movements, kissing the mound of her breast exposed by her low tank top. "You promise to tell me if you want me to stop?"

"Fine," she sighs.

Needing her panties gone, I reach to her hips to pull them down. Immediately, her hands fly to the hem of her tank top to help me undress her. "Will you let me?" I ask. *She's not very good at being taken care of, but I can teach her.*

Her voice is breathy when she responds, "Let you what?" She pulls the shirt over her head, revealing her peaked pink nipples and soft, rounded breasts. The sight of her is enough to derail my thoughts.

"You are gorgeous. Have I told you that lately?" I ask, tugging her panties past her feet.

"Like three minutes ago," she giggles, leaning back and crossing her arms over her middle.

"Mm, still true," I hum, uncrossing her arms. "Maybe even more so."

Bringing myself to lay over her, I tilt her head to mine for another deep kiss. "Next time, I want to undress you myself."

Her brows furrow briefly, but she agrees. "Sure, but Cam?"

"Yes, sunshine?" I ask, moving down her body, leaving kisses every few inches.

"Can you—I know you don't want me to touch you, but— would you, so I'm not the only one?"

Sitting up, I see that she's gesturing to my cock. *Of course, she doesn't want to be the only one naked.* Standing, I peel off my shirt, pants, and boxer briefs.

I make sure she understands, "I always want you to touch me, in any and every way you'd like. But today isn't about what I want. You understand how much I want you, don't you?" I ask.

It's no small pleasure I get from seeing her eyeing my naked cock, thick and throbbing for her.

"I understand," she answers with a thick swallow.

It's the middle of the day, and light pours into the living room through the glass doors leading to the backyard, giving me a clear view of her smooth breasts, stomach, and thighs, as I kneel before her on the couch. My hands glide over her calves, into the folds of her knees and higher, until I'm between her legs. When I grip the back of her thighs to open them wider, she resists. *Being bared like this might be too much for her.* Instead, I kiss the inside of one knee, moving up her thigh until I can use my shoulders for the same purpose. As my mouth reaches the crease where her leg meets her body, she opens wider for me.

I stare at her glistening pink sex, marveling at the luck that makes me the first man to experience her this way.

"Please don't tease me, Cam," she whispers.

Immediately, I lower my face for my first taste of her, starting with simple, tender kisses—letting her learn the feel of my lips in her most sensitive area. Her legs remain tense, so I hold them steady, grounding her to me as I soothe my thumbs over the base of her ass cheeks.

When I add my tongue to the kisses, she gasps, rocking her hips into me.

Looking up, I see her watching me, hands gripping the cushions of the couch.

"You *can* touch me," I say, kissing my way down until I reach her entrance. "Hold my shoulders, squeeze me with your legs, dig your fingers into my hair."

The second I suggest it, she does just that, curling her fingers through my hair as I dip my tongue inside her. She holds on tight as I delve deeper, slowly building the intensity until I think she's ready for me to move to her clit.

I start with another simple kiss, then a swipe of my tongue. Her hips rock again, and she moans loud enough that she gasps afterward—*embarrassed by the sound?*

"You can make noise if you want," I tell her between swipes of my tongue.

"But what if—I mean, I'm sure no one can hear, but you don't mind?"

"Mind? I don't mind," I shrug, my shoulders tipping into the soft undersides of her thighs. "I love it."

The urge to devour her quickly rises, but it's not what she needs, and it's not what I want. I want to stay here, my face buried in her slick arousal, her hips rocking against me, tiny gasps slipping from her mouth with every pass of my tongue.

When her fingers tug at my hair, it takes a moment to realize she's not pulling me in pleasure but trying to pull me back. I release her, looking up. "You okay?"

"Yeah," she nods, her brow drawn tight with concern.

"Did I do something you didn't like?" I ask, smoothing my hand across her belly.

"No, no. That was all—I liked *all* of that," she says with a shy smile.

Pride flares in my chest. "Then why did you stop me?" I ask.

"I just figured you probably didn't want to keep going."

Those words come from somewhere deeper than a passing thought, so I draw her legs off my shoulders and move forward, crossing my arms over her belly so I can look into her eyes. "I was having an amazing time, actually. Why did you think I wasn't?" I ask.

She holds my stare for a while, searching for words. "I

just—he used to—" she sighs. "I'm sorry."

I don't completely grasp her meaning, but it makes sense that he's the source of her anxiety right now. "You have nothing to apologize for."

Her fingers return to my hair as her peaked breasts rise and fall with a shaky breath. "I'm taking too long to come, aren't I?" she asks.

Once again, her insecurity tugs at something deep in my chest. How could anyone let her feel this way? "Not at all. I was just getting started."

"Really?" Her eyes widen. "But you don't know how long it takes me to get there."

I lower my voice, holding her gaze. "I don't care how long it takes you."

"You'll care eventually," she says, nails twirling against my scalp.

"I loved every second of that." *Doesn't she understand?* "You seem to think this is a chore for me, but it's not."

Her brows lift in surprise. "*I* loved every second of that, but I can't expect you to spend your whole day licking my pussy."

"That was barely ten minutes," I chuckle, dropping a kiss to her sternum. "Licking your pussy all day would be an ideal outcome for me."

"You cannot be serious," she laughs.

She still doesn't believe me. "You are delicious, and feeling you move around me—feeling how you react to my touch, learning what your body needs—it's a gift."

Her face tightens as a denial forms behind her lips. "It's fine. I don't really want to come."

"That's the *least* adorable lie you've ever told me."

"Okay, you're right," she admits. "I just feel bad."

There it is. She feels guilty that I'm putting in effort for her pleasure. "Have you ever tasted yourself?" I ask.

"No," she shakes her head.

"I think you should." Even though her taste still lingers in my mouth, I dip down, quickly swiping my tongue through her wetness for the full effect.

She gasps, a laugh escaping her—an entirely new sound. One I want to hear again and again.

Coming up, I hold her face in both hands and pull her in for a kiss. She swipes into my mouth with her tongue, but it's different this time. She's tasting herself for the first time—on my tongue. My cock throbs at the realization.

"It's not bad," she comments, licking her lip. "Kind of salty and sweet."

"*Not bad?* I believe I said delicious."

She giggles. "If you say so."

"Do you still want me to do this?" I ask.

After a few breaths, a shy smile curves her lips as she nods.

"Try to relax," I say, moving down her body again. "Let me get lost in you." Kissing across her hips and then over her sex, I begin with tender kisses once more. "I'm not going anywhere. I literally *do* have all day."

Her response is a hum and a slight lift of her hips to meet me. Fingers twine in my hair as I drape her legs over my shoulders again. Taking my time, I savor long, searching swipes of my tongue, pulling with my lips until she feels soft and yielding beneath me.

When I glance up, her limbs are lax, her peaked nipples rising and falling with each heavy breath as she watches me with eyes heavy with desire.

She is beautiful as she takes her pleasure. She is everything.

Concentrating on her clit, I bring my fingers to her entrance. She's slick and ready, accepting me eagerly as I push inside. I pay attention to every moan, every rock of her hips, the way she clenches around my fingers, and the pull of my hair, finding the rhythm and pressure she needs.

As she nears release, she whispers my name over and over until I swipe my fingertips against her g-spot, and she switches to a full, "*Cameron,*" on a moan.

Her legs shake, tightening around my head, pressing me in with her hand until she reaches her climax. Her sensual moan is cut off with a muffled sound as she buries her face in a pillow. *Next time, I'll make sure she knows it's okay to be loud.* I stay with her, continuing every movement with my lips, tongue, and fingers, until she pulls away.

She's sated, eyes sparkling as she stares at me—a level of wonder I've never seen before.

"Cameron," she says again, this time with a satisfied smile.

I move to sit next to her, wrapping my arms around her and pulling her in for a kiss. "Oh, you liked that?" I ask with a low chuckle.

"I did," she says, resting her head on my shoulder.

"You ready to go again?" I ask.

"*Again?*" she says, incredulous.

"Trying not to be offended by the shock in your voice, Winslow," I say, sliding down so I'm lying on my back. "Did I not tell you all day?"

"You did, but—*Cam!*" Her objection is cut off in a squeal as I grab her hips and drag her to me.

"Do you want more?" I ask.

"You don't have to—" she cuts off her own denial, "You know what? I do want more."

"Good. So do I," I say, pulling her over until she straddles my face.

She makes that gasp-laugh sound again as I start moving my tongue over her clit.

Using my grip on her hips, I pull her down against my face, rocking her hips in time with my tongue. She's ready for me now, softening and letting her weight settle.

"Like you stole it, baby," I say between swipes of my tongue.

"*Cameron*," she squeals. "Oh, my word. I cannot *ride* your face."

My hands grip her hips more firmly, rocking her in time with my movements—showing her that she *can* ride me. It only takes a few seconds before she gets the movement, bracing herself with her hands on the back of the couch as she rolls her body, pressing into me more firmly. And exactly as I wanted—as I've been craving—she uses me for her pleasure, crying out when she reaches her peak.

Breathless, she shifts back, resting her weight on my chest. From this angle, her hair looks completely pink as she leans over me, a smile that's both giddy and sensual spread across her lips.

"Just *beautiful*," I say.

"Maybe," she says, looking off to the side.

"Absolutely," I insist, squeezing her full ass cheeks. "You ready for more?"

Chapter 16
Sadie

Make a new friend in Palm Springs - *from*
Sadie's list of things she's never done

After about thirty selfies, I finally settle on one where my hair
falls just right, my face doesn't look weird, and the *207* on my
shirt is legible. I post it with the caption *Supporting my guy from*
afar today. My phone buzzes a moment later.

Cam: You look gorgeous.

A month ago, he kissed me—really kissed me. Three weeks
later, he offered to go down on me. Then, two days ago—he
did. He went down on me—that's an understatement. He ate
my pussy like he was starving. But it was deeper than that, too.
I told him things I've never told anyone. We did things I've
never done. He stuck with me when I got emotional and scared,
reminding me that my pleasure isn't an imposition.

At this point, it would be impossible to believe he's not into me.

Cam Hacker is into me.

I'm not sure how to feel about it. He's a dangerous man—not necessarily to me, but to himself. He races motorcycles for a living, and something tells me even when he's not racing professionally, he won't give it up. If I let myself feel for a man like that, fall for him—I could lose him too quickly. Too easily. Too permanently. Loving Cam Hacker would be like begging for a shattered heart.

But on the other hand, the idea that he would pick me, that we could be together—that someone so caring, patient, funny, and an exceptionally good kisser would even be an option for me—is hard to ignore. How could I ignore him? He's taking up more space in my mind these days than he is in my home.

Me: Sorry I'm not there for this one.

He's had three weekends of racing—making a total of six races—since the one I attended. I buried my head in the sand about him racing the first weekend and looked up the placements and points during the second and third. Today, Bea is coming over for moral support so I can hopefully watch one from home.

He's been incredibly supportive of me, and I desperately want to be supportive of him too.

Cam: Please don't worry about it.
Me: But I should be there to support you.
Cam: It's really okay. I understand it's a lot for you.

Me: I'm at least going to watch it from here.

Cam: You are?

Me: Yup! Bea's coming over to watch it with me.

Cam: What'd you bake her?

Me: Sausage rolls and pistachio macarons. You're missing out.

Cam: Kind of wishing I wasn't out of town now.

Me: I'll make something just for you when you get back. Any requests?

Cam: I'll eat any of your cookies any time.

We haven't talked about what happened between us directly yet, but he's made plenty of indirect comments like this one in the days since. I never know how to respond. *He was right. It was an experience I needed. And I want it again—immediately—with him. But is that a good idea?*

Cam: I've got to get ready. Talk to you after, love.

Me: Remember, rubber side down! And don't forget your SPF!

SPF would be redundant. He's covered head-to-toe, but I still tell him about it every race. I get to remind him to be safe without actually saying *don't crash.*

Me: And don't get too cocky. Find your balance between the tortoise and the hare.

Cam: You got it, sunshine.

Bea shows up an hour before the race's official start, wearing a classic *Nirvana* t-shirt—black with a yellow smiley face that has *X*s for eyes and a tongue sticking out.

"Look at you, wearing the right colors and everything," I say, pulling her in for a hug.

"I'm here to support," she answers with a warm smile.

We take Dandy to the backyard to throw a ball and get some of her energy out before she's expected to sit still for an hour and watch the race with us. Bea and I smoke a bowl to get some of *my* nervous energy out before we move back inside and dig into the baked snacks I prepared.

Bea adjusts her position on the couch, facing me. "How are you feeling about the race?" she asks.

"A little nervous," I admit, releasing a heavy breath. "I get nervous every time, thinking he's going to *crash*." Even though he isn't here, I still whisper the last word.

Nodding, she hums a response, giving me a *tell-me-more* look.

"He doesn't *crash* often, but at least a couple people go down during every race. They almost always get right back up, but every time I see it—" I take a tight breath. "It's terrifying."

"I bet it is," she affirms.

Bea's presence is a steady comfort. Moments ago, we were laughing, snacking, and smoking. Now, I'm pouring out my heart about Cam, and I haven't even decided how I feel about him yet. She has a way of disarming me, letting me feel safe sharing raw emotions.

She already knows the story about my crash from high school—the whole reason I find Cam's racing so unsettling, so I skip over those details.

"It's hard to shake the images of people I cared about being bloodied and wrecked by motorcycles. I can even still see Cam lying eerily still on the racetrack when he broke his leg. I didn't even know him then, but that crash is one of the reasons I fear for him.”

“He survived that, though—came back stronger,” she points out. “Would it help to focus on that? It wasn’t enough to make him fearful of racing.”

My shoulders shake on a defeated laugh. “That’s kind of the issue. Breaking his damn femur wasn’t enough to make him fearful. It made him more determined. There’s no level of injury that could stop him. I don’t think *anything* would be enough to make him quit.”

She tilts her head curiously, thick dark hair momentarily falling over her face before a silver-and gold ring-stacked hand pushes it back. “Is that what you need from him?”

She doesn’t ask if it’s what I *want*, but if it’s what I *need*, as in—what do I need from my partner in my relationship? She’s only operating with the information I’ve given her. She believes he’s actually my boyfriend—*not just my friend*—because that’s what I’ve told her. There’s a layer of complication to this that I can’t unfold with anyone. Although, something tells me Bea would keep our secret if I asked her to. She’s patient, petting Dandy’s white fluff as she waits for me to respond.

“I want so badly to be supportive,” I finally say. “I know it’s important to him—important isn’t even the right word. Racing is integral to his being. I *want* to be supportive, but I don’t want…”

When Bea sees I can’t bring myself to finish the sentence, she offers, “You don’t want to see Cam hurt or worse.”

“I don’t want to lose him,” I admit, although I haven’t shared enough for her to fully comprehend what an admission it is. He’s important, and even though he’s not my boyfriend, and I can’t love him, the idea of losing him terrifies me.

Bea hums a response again, rolling over my words before saying, "That's a very reasonable desire. It's obvious he doesn't want to lose you either. I'm sure that's on his mind while he's out there."

Obvious? Maybe he's just a good actor, good at pretending to be my boyfriend. Or maybe, she's right. Maybe his charm and flirtation with me isn't just for show. His going down on me until I came multiple times certainly wasn't.

"Today, I want to focus on being excited for him," I say. "I want to cheer him on like a normal girlfriend and not worry about anything else."

Bea's eyes narrow, and a knowing smile curves her lips. "Okay, angel. I'm here to help."

The broadcast starts with two announcers sitting at a table in front of a *USMoto* sign.

Announcer One: We're about halfway into the season here, and things seem to be shaking out well for both Ryan Ludlow and Cameron Hacker. We don't have a clear frontrunner yet this season.

Announcer Two: I'd say we do have a clear frontrunner. Things are looking better for Ludlow. Hacker has been on his tail all season. He's only ten points behind, but he has yet to pull into a points lead.

Then they go into a detailed breakdown of points and placements leading up to this point in the season, followed by a conversation about tire pressure decisions that almost puts me to sleep, and then on to interviews with racers.

"The pre-race stuff is a little dry, isn't it?" Bea jokes.

"This part kind of sucks," I agree. "Hate to admit it, but the actual race is really fun."

"You think you'll end up traveling to any of them?" she asks.

"I'd like to. Or at least, I'd *like* to *want* to," I admit, offering Bea more than I've shared with anyone in a long time. "I wish I didn't get so anxious about it. If I can get through this race from the couch, maybe...?"

"I'll go with you, if you want," she says.

"Really?" I ask, surprised.

"Fuck, yeah. You're my friend. He's my friend," she says, tugging on her shirt to show off the black and yellow. "Why wouldn't I?"

It's been a while since I had a new friend. The last ones I made were more interested in helping my ex cheat than actually caring about me. Bea's willingness to jump into my life is a refreshing gift. "I think I love you," I giggle.

"You do." She nods. "We're besties now. Don't worry about it."

When the interviewer reaches Cam, he's already straddling his bike at his mark on the track.

"Qualifiers were close for this race. You were only a quarter-second from first," the tall, dark-haired woman says. "Were you disappointed you didn't grab pole position?"

"I'm pretty sure pole position means starting the race first," I whisper to Bea.

"Disappointed?" Cam laughs. "You know me. I've won more races from second on the grid than from first. I like having someone to chase, and no one's more fun to chase than Ludlow." I try not to get hung up on the *"you know me"* part. *He probably only knows her in a professional capacity.*

"Tell me about the adjustments you've made to your bike

and tire pressure based on today's heat," she asks.

"We've taken everything into account. Don't worry," he answers with a chuckle. When she leaves, I remember him saying this is his least favorite part. *I wish I could be there with him, standing by until the race starts.*

When the racers take off, Bea comments, "This feels awfully chill for a race."

"I *wish* they raced like this, but it's just a warm-up lap."

As Cam rounds the halfway point of the track, my heart rate speeds up. *It's almost time. Almost time for the race. For the risk.* The tattoo across his chest that reads '*No Risk No Story*' flashes in my mind. *Is a story really that important, Cameron? What if the story is: today I raced zero motorcycles, got in zero crashes, and lived happily ever after? Sounds like a good one to me.*

Dandy's wet nose bumps my hand.

"Hi, sweet girl," I greet her, reaching through her fluffy fur to rub her head.

She's crawled off Bea's lap and is now walking circles on mine. After seven or eight turns, she settles with a plop and a heavy dog-sigh. Dandy may not look anything like her owner, but their energy matches—comforting, steady, and insistent that no one should have to handle anything alone.

Doing my best not to lose my shit, I go through a calming breath exercise I found online this morning, petting Dandy in time with each exhale.

"He'll be okay," Bea reassures me, resting her hand over mine where it sits in Dandy's fur. "And no matter what, *you* will be okay."

I look down at the pile of encouragement in my lap and spot the tattoo on the inside of Bea's forearm: *No Matter What.*

"What's this tattoo for?" I ask.

Bea turns her arm up, running her thumb over the ink. "I got it with my childhood best friend. He has one that says *No Matter Where.*"

"I don't think I've heard you mention him before," I say, taking in the details of the script. "What's his name?"

"Teddy," she says, her voice softening. "He's a doll, but we don't really talk anymore."

Feeling a twinge in my chest at the rare sadness pulling her features, I say, "If you ever want to talk about him, I'm here to listen."

"Thanks, bestie," she says, squeezing my hand but offering no more about whatever happened with Teddy.

The green flag waves, and the motorcycles rip away from their starting marks—thirty or more racers going over one hundred fifty miles an hour as they head into the first turn in a terrifying mass of engines and leather. Cam and Ludlow are out front, and by turn four, there's enough distance between them and the pack that I can breathe a little easier.

"This isn't so bad," I admit as Cam crosses into his third lap. When my petting slows, Dandy presses her little head into my palm. "Okay, that's fair," I say, resuming the motion.

Announcer One: Hacker is ripping around these turns.

Announcer Two: What he said to Jolie at the beginning is true. He thrives on the chase, and Ludlow is giving him a good one.

The camera zooms in, showing Cam's front tire lifting off the track as he comes out of a turn.

"That is not—no, no," I whisper. "All tires *down*, all the

time, please."

"He's alright," Bea reassures me. "He's not the only one who does that. It's okay."

I've seen it before. I know it's common, but it's like I've forgotten everything I know about the sport. *I just want him to pull over and be done. It was just a little air, but I hate it.* Anxiety tightens my chest, then moves to my throat. *He still has seven laps left. Anything can happen in seven laps. Bad things—*

"What do you suppose he's thinking about right now?" Bea asks, clearly aware I'm freaking out but graciously not making me address it.

"I have no idea," I snap, my words sharper than they should be. I apologize immediately.

Always understanding, Bea answers, "It's okay. This is a lot for you. Try to imagine it, though. He does this for a reason. What do you think he focuses on while he's out there?"

After forcing a few steadying breaths, I consider her question. He loves this. Allie's words from his first race of the season come to me. *"Cam is the happiest he's ever been. This is what he lives for."* He's told me how important the freedom of speed is, how that feeds his soul. I doubt he's thinking about speed, though. That part's built in.

Giving myself a break from the race, I look at Bea. "He's probably somewhere between the thinking equivalent of yelling *'woo hoo'* at the top of his lungs and trying to figure out how to pass this guy. Cam wants to win. He *needs* to win, so I bet that's what he's thinking about—how does he get first?"

"He's getting close," Bea says as Cam slides out around Ludlow going into the next turn. He pulls ahead for just a moment but loses the lead as they come out of it.

Announcer One: Hacker will not back down today.

Announcer Two: And he shouldn't. He needs these points today if he wants a shot at signing with Incite Energy next season.

On the next turn, the camera zooms in on Cam's front tire again. This time there's chatter—his tire skipping on the track, and a bit of a wobble, but he recovers it. My natural inclination is to draw my knees in close to my chest, but Dandy's still heavy in my lap, so I pick her up and hold her tight to my chest instead. She nuzzles in, appreciating the affection.

"She's a sweet little snuggle angel, isn't she?" Bea comments.

"She's helping me a lot," I say. "Thank you for bringing her. And for being here."

"Of course. I'll come over for every race if you need the company," Bea says, offering me the kind of support an old friend gives, even though we've only just gotten to know each other this year.

"He has a race tomorrow, too," I say. "Maybe we can do our run before to help me calm down, but I want to try watching one on my own."

Announcer Two: Looks like we have a crash on the track.

No, no, no, no.

The racer on the screen is holding his motorcycle's handlebars as he and his bike slide across the racetrack. *I can't look.* I bury my face behind my hands, holding Dandy tight.

"It's not Cam," Bea reassures me.

"But it's *someone*. What if they—" I can't finish the thought.

"Watch," Bea says. "I know it's hard, but the guy's okay. Look, he's standing right up."

I brave a look back at the screen, and she's right. The racer is standing, leveraging the bike to lift it into an upright position. He climbs back on and rejoins the race like nothing happened. *Like nothing happened. How the—*

"That bike looks heavy," Bea comments, not letting me dwell or spiral.

"We probably have a few in the garage if you want to check," I joke, the lighthearted interaction taking some of the pressure off my speeding heart.

Cam gets so close to Ludlow as he tries to pass him that I swear they must be touching. I swallow a thick lump in my throat when my heart races again. *At this point, I'm irritated with myself. Every scary, anxious thought is also an annoying one. Why can't I just ignore it and be happy for him?*

Normally, I'd try to calm myself with rational reasons why my anxiety is unfounded. But being anxious about this *is* the rational response, or at least it feels that way to me.

Announcer One: Whew, a lot of trust there. See how close Hacker's getting to Ludlow?

Announcer Two: Absolutely. These guys have been racing each other for years. I know they're friends off the track.

"Do you know him too?" Bea asks.

"Nope," I answer without thinking. *Shit. Shouldn't I know his friends? Say something true. Say something true.* "He's mentioned him, but we haven't met."

Announcer One: I think this might be the one. Cam's lined up perfectly for the pass on this turn.

Announcer Two: If it's not this turn, it probably won't happen. There's only one lap after this, and Ludlow has maintained his lead the whole time. It's been tight, but Hacker has yet to pull off a pass.

Letting Dandy down from her place cuddled against my chest, I lean forward. *Pass him. Pass him. Pass him. Don't crash. Don't crash. Don't crash.*

"Now *I'm* nervous," Bea—who's also leaned toward the screen—says.

"Me too. I mean—nervous for two reasons now."

My adrenaline spikes as Cam pulls up right next to Ludlow again—so close I'm worried they'll both crash. *When I was in a motorcycle crash, it was on a turn, and seeing them so close together—*

Announcer One: And he pulls it off!

Announcer Two: That was close. Almost looks like they had a little contact there.

A little contact? What the fuck?
As Cam pulls away, he briefly lifts one hand from his handlebars. My stomach drops. *Don't let go!*

Announcer Two: Definitely contact. See that wave from Hacker? He's apologizing for getting too close.

Not going to dwell on that. He's winning. He's going to win. Cam's words from our discussion about his tortoise and hare tattoo come back to me. *It's not over 'til it's over. Never get too cocky.*

"Now he just has to keep the lead," I breathe.

"He can do it," Bea says.

Ludlow tries to regain his position on the next few turns, but doesn't manage to close the distance between him and Cam in the short time left. Still, I know it's not over 'til it's over, and I don't take an easy breath until the checkered flag flies and Cam crosses the finish line first.

"He won!" I yell, startling poor Dandy. I quickly apologize and set her down, then Bea and I jump up and down, cheering for Cam. *He did it. He's safe. He's alive. None of his bones are broken,* and *he won.*

Wishing I was there to celebrate with him, I send him a quick text.

Me: You did it!

"You got through it," Bea says as we settle back onto the couch. "Did that feel any better than last time?"

"A lot better. I even enjoyed it a little bit," I admit. I consider the reasons. "Could be because we aren't actually there."

"I bet. Probably helps that he won, too."

We keep the live broadcast up, waiting for Cam's interview. When they reach him, he's standing next to his bike, typing on his phone.

"Sorry," he says, still looking down. My phone buzzes as he looks up. "My girl's celebrating at home. Didn't want to leave her hanging."

Bea makes a *aww-that's-the-sweetest-thing-I've-ever-heard* face. "Check your phone!"

As I read it, my face softens into the same.

Cam: Feels amazing! Wish I could hug you.

Half an hour later, when the broadcast is over and Bea's gone back home, another text comes through.

Cam: Thank you for watching. I know it's hard for you. Means more than you know.

Chapter 17
Cam

Think they'll give me points for this? –
caption from Cam's social media post – a video of
him doing donuts in a go-kart, May 7ᵗʰ

"Nervous?" I ask, pulling off the highway toward the go-kart track.

"No," Sadie answers, looking away.

"Why do you bother lying to me?" I ask.

Her voice is somewhere between a laugh and a curse when she responds, "Why do you ask questions if you already know the answers?"

"Alright, I won't make you talk—"

She cuts me off. "I'm not worried about anyone *crashing*," she whispers the last word, the way she always does. "No one will get hurt. *Right?*" She looks at me for confirmation.

"No one will get hurt," I promise.

"So that part, I'm not nervous about," she says on a shaky

breath.

I give her a sidelong glance. "You sure, Winslow?"

"Okay, I'm a little teeny tiny bit nervous about that part. Just the idea of being at a track, of racing *anything*, makes my heart all flittery," she admits, wiggling her fingers and hands frantically in front of her chest.

The *braaap, braaap, braaap* of revving motorcycle engines carries over our conversation as I turn into a parking space. The sound lights me up inside in the best way, but at the same time, I worry about her.

We're at a smaller track today—one I raced on countless times when I was in the 600 class. It has a go-kart track adjacent to the motorcycle track. One of my buddies who works here hooked us up for the afternoon, along with seven go-karts. But I hadn't thought about how hearing the motorcycle engines while she's racing go-karts might affect Sadie.

"Is it going to bother you that there are motorcycles here too?" I ask. When her eyes go wide, I realize my mistake. "They're on a different track. You'll only hear them."

"Oh," she sighs in relief. "In that case, I think it'll be okay." Unbuckling her seatbelt, she turns to face me. "I think I'm actually going to have a lot of fun."

I squeeze her hand. "I think you will too."

A dimpled smile fills her face. "Sometimes I'm just nervous. Like my body has nerves that haven't met my brain yet. Does that make sense?"

"Sort of," I answer, trying to place the feeling. "It's not an experience I've had, but it sounds exhausting."

She shrugs. "You get it."

I make her promise to tell me if she needs a break or if there's anything I can do to help her feel safer as we gather up helmets and head out to the track. She surprises me by lacing her fingers with mine as we walk.

I've held her hand before, but I can't remember a time she initiated it, or a time we did it when no one else was around. At this point, we've done a hell of a lot more than hold hands, but it still sends a rush through me when she intertwines her fingers with mine.

Squeezing tightly as we pass the motorcycle track, she leans her head into my shoulder. "It's like exposure therapy," she says, watching the motorcycles. "I have to get used to it at some point."

Has to get used to it at some point. Even if she was truly my girlfriend, I wouldn't force her to be around something that upsets her so much. "You don't have to," I say.

She smiles brightly at me, dropping my hand as we reach the go-karts. "I guess not, but I want to."

We start out with the most in-depth safety talk anyone's ever made about go-karts. It's been years since I drove one, and I spent hours last night researching everything I thought she'd need. Knowing she would ask, I even memorized statistics about how rare deaths and injuries are. It's not that no one ever gets hurt on go-karts—there are precautions to take—but it's nothing compared to racing motorcycles.

Toward the end of my talk, she starts to get antsy, bouncing on her toes and glancing back and forth at the karts.

"You ready to try?" I ask.

She nods. "I thought you'd never ask!"

"You want to follow me the first few laps to get a feel for

it?" I ask.

"No," she answers, a sliver of her competitive streak showing through. "I know how to drive."

She picks a black-and-yellow kart, number seven, and I take my time helping her get buckled into the four-point seatbelt.

"Is this necessary?" she giggles, as I run my fingers under the straps that go from her shoulders to the connection point at her waist.

"Of course," I answer.

"For safety?" she asks, narrowing her eyes.

"Not at all," I answer with a low chuckle. "That was necessary because I wanted to touch you."

Her cheeks flush, but her lips turn into the same teasing smirk I'm beginning to yearn for. Giving her buckle a firm tug—that actually is for her safety—I reach down and pull the starter on her kart. "Rubber side down," I say, kissing her helmet in the same place she once kissed mine—right underneath the visor's opening.

She giggles and smiles as I fold myself into the one next to hers. These karts are low to the ground, with a metal frame, bucket seat, and not much else. They're so small, my knees stick up comically close to my ears.

"You look ridiculous," she laughs.

"Won't affect my ability to win a race. Don't worry," I say with all the seriousness a man who's folded himself into a pretzel to race a go-kart can.

"I thought *I* was supposed to win," she says.

"It doesn't count as winning if I *let* you—"

She slams on the gas, pulling away before I've finished my

sentence or buckled my seatbelt. *Smart girl.*

The tiniest ball of anxiety appears in my chest when I see her out on the track by herself. It *is* safe, but I wanted to be there to help her. I'm sure it's only a small fraction of what she feels every time I race, but it's good for me to experience it.

I make it onto the track as she disappears around turn one, tires screeching loudly enough I'm surprised she doesn't hit the rubber barriers that define the track. Letting her experience the joy of an empty track, I keep some distance. She doesn't take turn two quite as fast, but her tires are still screeching— slowing all the momentum she built on the straightaway. In the next few turns, she starts to find the rhythm of entering a turn slow and exiting it fast. By the time she's finished her first lap, she's even racing the most efficient line of the track.

I come up close, letting her feel what it's like when someone's trying to pass. She looks over her shoulder at me, and I throw my fingers up—pointing first to my eyes, then to the track ahead. *No girlfriend of mine—pretend or otherwise—is going to make the mistake of not watching where she's going.* Sadie's head snaps forward just in time to save herself from hitting the rubber barrier.

The ball of anxiety appears again. *Even if she had hit it, she wouldn't have been hurt, but I don't want that for her.*

She needs to be comfortable with other racers getting close and trying to pass, so I nose into the opening she leaves on the next turn but hang back instead of passing. I keep that up, giving her a break on a few turns, since having me that close likely made her anxious. One time, she actually blocks me herself, so I *can't* pass her. *It's pretty hot.*

During our third lap, I take the opening and move past

her into the lead. Giving the *go* pedal everything I've got, I take the kart to its sixty-five-mile-an-hour limit. Sadie does an impressive job of following my race line and staying reasonably close to me—usually no more than two or three turns behind.

We pull over after a few more practice laps, and she barely has her visor open before she cheers, "That was *so* fun! And— *oh, my word*—how dare you be so much better at that than I am?"

"I'd be in a lot of trouble if your first time on a track, you beat me in a race," I say, unbuckling the strap under her helmet and helping her lift it off.

"I guess." She stands up from her kart and shakes out her legs. "But I had a good lead on you in the beginning."

Unable to resist, I tease, "Because you cheated."

"I did not cheat," she denies with a scandalized gasp.

"You started before the green flag."

"What green flag? It's just the two of us." She puts her hands on her hips.

"Alright, you didn't cheat," I give in, stepping closer. "You were amazing out there."

"I was, wasn't I?" she beams, in a rare moment of accepting my compliment.

I run through some quick advice to help her with speed before we head back out on the track for more practice. By the time our friends arrive, her nerves seem to have settled, and she's ready to race.

When Bea, Allie, and Devon rush her with hugs, I step back to give her space with her friends. But she cuts through the little crowd past Luke and Rhett, grabbing my hand and stepping in front of me with her back to my chest. Excitement rolls off her as she gives everyone an abridged version of the safety talk we went through an hour ago.

"When you go around the turns, you don't want your tires screeching, but a little chirp is okay." Sadie moves on to racing advice. *I'm not sure if she's ever been cuter.* "If your tires are screeching in a go-kart, you're losing all the momentum you built on the straightaways. Not worth it."

"Did you just teach her that?" Luke's voice is quiet at my shoulder, careful not to talk over Sadie.

"Sure did," I nod, rubbing my thumb at her hip. "I think she might like it enough that we'll get to build her a custom kart."

"I bet Allie loves it, too," Luke says, likely already imagining the specs of the racer he'd build for her.

Devon's eyes are trained on Sadie, like she's mentally taking notes. *Something tells me she's the most competitive person in this group.*

Rhett steps in close to Luke and me. "How much trouble you think I'll get in if I beat Devon out there?"

"You ever raced anything before?" I ask.

"Never," he answers.

Taking in the set of Devon's jaw, narrowed eyes, and the stance that looks like she's ready to pounce, I laugh. "Don't think that's gonna be your problem, boss. I'm half worried she'll beat *me*."

"How do we determine the starting positions?" Devon asks after Luke and I have lined up the karts on the track. "Are there qualifying laps we need to do?"

Shaking my head, I answer, "We'll put the experienced racers in the back. The third and fourth kart already have warm tires, so that should help even it out between who starts out front."

"So damn precious with your tire temperatures," Allie laughs as she walks up to the second kart.

Devon's eyes narrow, not liking my answer. I've never been Devon's favorite, and I know she's still skeptical about Sadie and me. She doesn't doubt if we're truly dating, but I'm sure she questions if I deserve her. *We have that in common.* "Okay," she agrees, and I honestly cannot tell if she's unhappy about it or not.

Bea ends up with the first kart, followed by Allie, then Devon, then Sadie—who insisted she'd have more fun if she got to pass some people. *My racer girl.* Rhett, Luke, and I fill up the back three.

Once my buddy from the track waves the green flag to indicate the start of the race, Sadie does an impressive job of laying into the turns exactly how we practiced, immediately gaining on Devon.

Luke and I both pass Rhett fairly quickly, bringing Bea into focus—meaning Devon and Sadie have passed her already. *I wonder which turn Sadie used.* Part of me wishes I wasn't racing, just so I could watch her the entire time.

Before long, Luke and I are at Allie's tail. But he hesitates to pass his girlfriend. *Coward.* We're close enough to the front now to see that Sadie is holding on to the lead, but just barely. Devon—who's presumably never raced a kart in her life—is all over her, nosing in on every turn.

I hate it. I want to get in there and dice it up with Devon to keep her out of Sadie's way. I'd be up there already, but Luke is pulling out on every turn next to Allie, leaving no room for me to pass, but also not passing her. *Again, coward.*

He's a tough challenger on a racetrack. Professionally, it's lucky for me he enjoys the mechanic side more and gave up racing before we even got out of high school. This is the first time I've raced him in years, and it's time to show him what's changed.

On the next turn, he pulls to Allie's outside, and I begin nosing in on the inside. Poor Allie has no clue how to handle it and slams her brakes, letting Luke and I both fly by, putting Luke in third and me in fourth. Which is absurd, considering the race is almost over and we're the only two people on this track who have any experience racing.

I can't take him yet, so I give him a little love-tap, letting him know I'm here.

Racing is rubbin'. It's a racing phrase I specifically have not shared with Sadie because I'm sure it would scare the shit out of her. But it *is* fairly common—even in motorcycles—to make a little contact with other racers on the track. *In go-karts, when we have rubber barriers framing the entire track? It would almost be rude not to.*

As Luke and I continue to battle it out, we end up right on top of Sadie, who is now just behind Devon. *I want Sadie to win this, but I can't hand it to her.* He's holding his line like a pro, but I manage to squeak by him with minimal contact, using the momentum to rocket past Sadie.

On the next turn, Sadie starts gaining on me. *Good girl. Come and get me.*

The first turn I'm close enough to Devon to pass, I grab it—shooting past her. We're on the last lap, and I'm in first. *But that's not what I want for Sadie.* Breaking my own rules, I glance over my shoulder and see that Luke has passed her, and he's gaining on me. When we only have two turns left, he's too close to pass without clipping me. I brace for it, thinking it'll be a love-tap, but he gets me at just the right—or wrong— angle.

As we both spin out, my first thought is how this will register to Sadie as a crash. *She's doing so well, and I don't want her to lose her edge. We're fine, but will she know that?*

My kart slides well enough out of the way, but Luke is an obstruction on the track. Devon's coming too fast, and slams her brakes, barely missing his kart and losing all of her momentum.

The track is different now with three karts in the way, but Sadie maneuvers it perfectly, adjusting her speed and braking for the tighter turn. No one has enough time to catch her after that, and she crosses the finish line first.

She did it. She beat every single one of us.

She has her helmet off immediately, and I'm unsure if I'm about to get yelled at for crashing or—

"Did you see that?" she yells.

"Hell yeah, Winslow! You won!" I yell, rushing to her.

Seeing her race lights me up inside. The fact that she's willing to overcome her fears in order to let me share something I care so deeply about is overwhelming in an incredible way.

For what feels like the thousandth time, I'm blown away that her ex didn't see how amazing she is. He's still in my DMs talking shit and saying she wasted his time, but he's the one who wasted his opportunity with her. He had her for *so long. How could anyone know her, be loved by her, and not be completely taken to their knees in awe?*

"Does it still count even though some of you guys got stuck

back there?" she asks when I reach her. *Got stuck. She doesn't even call it a crash.*

"*Yes.* Yes, it counts. You won. You're a badass little go-kart racer," I say, scooping her up in my arms.

She wraps her legs around my waist and rests her forehead on mine, whispering, "That was *so* fun. I want to do it again right now."

Shifting so I'm supporting her with one arm, I use the other to hold her chin and tilt her face toward mine. "You were amazing out there," I say, drawing her close and bringing her lips to mine. It's the first time we've kissed since the day she let me taste her, but even if no one else was around to witness—to corroborate our relationship—I would still be kissing her right now. *Nothing has ever felt better than celebrating her after she won her first race.*

Resting my forehead on hers again, I whisper, "*You* are amazing."

Chapter 18
Sadie

Get two tattoos – *from Sadie's list of things she's never done*

"Nervous?" Cam asks, grabbing my hand.

"No," I answer, squeezing his as we dash across the PCH toward a white stucco tattoo shop with black window frames and a sign that reads *Shadow's Ink*.

When we reach the sidewalk, he uses our connected hands to pull me in front of him, tilting his head and lowering his brows.

"Okay, a *little* nervous," I admit. "But I'm not scared. I'm okay with a little pain. It's just new. Kinda intimidating," I whisper, nodding toward the shop.

"You're getting better at doing things that make you nervous," he says, kissing my forehead and pinching my ass cheek at the same time. "You'll be great."

Today is the first day we've been together since he got

back from his latest race. It was a charity invitational, so even though he won, it didn't count toward the championship. All the prize money went to a children's hospital, *and I managed to watch the whole thing on TV without freaking out.*

Neither of us has mentioned our arrangement or our actual relationship. Physically, we've kissed a handful of times, and we hooked up once. But it's deeper than that. He's one of my best friends. He's the first person I want to talk to when something new happens—good or bad. I want him there when I cross things off my list. I miss him terribly when he's away at races. I'd be delusional at this point to think what's happening between us is still pretend.

So, obviously, the healthiest thing to do is get tattoos together. I snort out a laugh at the absurdity of the situation.

"What's up, Winslow?" he asks, pushing open the door to the tattoo shop.

"Just excited, that's all," I answer, though we both know it's a lie.

If any of my friends asked me if they should get matching tattoos with the person they're dating after a few months, I'd say *no.* And yet, here I am, about to get matching tattoos with a man who I'm not *technically* even dating, who I cannot allow myself to love, and who I can't get off my mind.

When Cam opens the door, there's no one at the front desk, but he doesn't seem concerned.

"Is it weird that I brought cookies?" I whisper.

"Not at all," he answers in his normal volume. "They're human. They'll love them."

"What are we supposed to love?" a woman calls from the back room. She's short, with medium brown skin, dark hair twisted into a wild bun, and ear gauges. She must be Inez, the woman who did his Betty tattoo and is about to do mine.

"Sadie made you cookies," Cam says, nodding to the container in my hands.

"I already knew I'd like you, since you're attached to this giant sweetheart," she says, taking the container from me. "But with cookies? Now I think I might like you even more than him."

"You want me to go first?" Cam offers, sliding my hand back into his. "So you can see what it's like?"

Anticipation buzzes in my veins. "Nope, I just want to do it. Get the nerves out."

"Send it," he says, squeezing my hand.

"Send it," I agree, nodding.

Inez is incredibly sweet, explaining *in what may be excessive detail* everything I need to know. The drawing she prepared for me is even prettier than I imagined—a whisk crisscrossed over a rolling pin, with a pink banner that reads *Life is Sweet*.

Cam waits in a nearby chair, not speaking up until I ask his opinion about the exact placement. Then he and Inez help me decide on the inside of my upper arm.

He reminds me to breathe when she brings the tattoo machine to my arm. It's okay—a little sharp and unpleasant—but it's doable. They've known each other for years, so time passes quickly with stories and updates about his race season. *He's tied for first place in points with Ludlow.*

When she asks how we met, I tell her about Allie and Luke—that Cam and I met at the opening of their bar and shared a drink in the back parking lot.

"That's not *really* the first time we met, though," he says.

For a moment, I think he's realized he has a tattoo of me on his thigh. But then he continues, "Six or seven years ago, I was in Portland for the invitational race I do up there every year."

"I used to live in Portland," I explain.

"I had a meeting with my agent after the race at some pretentious steakhouse, and this absolutely stunning blonde was standing in front of the restaurant by herself." *I didn't know that's why he was there.* "It made me late, talking to her, but I couldn't help myself. She looked like she needed a little cheering up—"

"And you're just the right person for that," Inez adds, dipping her needle back into the little yellow container of ink.

He continues, "Once I made her smile, I wanted to keep seeing her smile. Still do."

At those words, I can't help but do exactly that.

"See?" he lifts a hand toward my face. "The dimples? She's fucking gorgeous."

None of that was pretend. It's all true. That's how we met, and apparently, that's how he felt about it. *How much of the rest of this between us has been true?*

When the tattoo is finished, I go over to the mirror to check it out, turning my arm one way, then the other.

Leaning over, he whispers, "Looks good on you."

"You feel up for doing the other one?" Inez asks. "It'll be a lot quicker than the first, but we can definitely do it another day if you're tapped." The *Life is Sweet* tattoo took a couple hours, and by the end, I was ready for it to be over. But I want the matching one with Cam, so I agree.

This one is a different style, much simpler. It's all black— the outline of sunrays behind a palm tree and a cactus, to represent Palm Springs. We put it inside my other arm, just above my elbow. It hurts a bit more, but it's over in fifteen minutes. *And now I have two tattoos.*

"Not too bad for one afternoon," I say, admiring my arms in the mirror.

He gets the same tattoo, but since he's pretty much out of arm real estate, it goes a few inches above one of his knees.

After we pose together for a picture that Inez snaps, I ask, "Can I just make another appointment with you right now? I have this gingerbread idea, and also this cat friend I kind of want a tattoo of."

She and Cam share a laugh. "You sure can, babe," she says, then asks Cam if he's coming too.

"Of course."

"Do you even know what you want?" I ask.

His eyes settle on me, and he brushes an errant strand of hair behind my ear. "I know exactly what I want," he says.

"You two are so cute, it's *almost* sickening," she laughs.

"Do you think your mom would like the *Life is Sweet* tattoo?" Cam asks, as we step outside.

"That's exactly what I was just thinking about, actually. I think she'd love it. I wish she could see it."

Cam tucks his hands into his front pockets. "If you're up for it, you could send her a picture."

"I could," I admit, watching my toes drag an arc on the sidewalk below.

"Or, you could call her. Cross two things off your list today."

It's overdue. It's *so far* overdue. She hasn't called me in over a year either, and part of me wants to leave it to her. *She's the parent. Shouldn't she have to be the bigger person by default?* But I miss her. And I'm not even mad at her anymore.

"I'm gonna do it," I say. "Right now, before I lose my nerve."

"Proud of you," he says, turning back toward *Shadow's Ink's* door. "I'll hang with Inez until you're done."

And then I'm standing on a sidewalk off the PCH, staring at my phone. *I have to do this. I want to do this.* I can *do this. I can* do *this.*

I dial her number and hold the phone to my ear.

She picks up halfway through the second ring. "Sadie? Are you okay?"

Of course she asked that. I haven't talked to her in forever.

"Hi, Mom. Everything's great. Really great actually, um…" *Should I apologize? Should I explain why I haven't called?* "I did something today I thought you'd be excited about."

"Oh yeah?" she asks, and I hear the familiar squeak of her favorite chair as she sits down. "I'd love to hear about it."

"I got my first tattoo. I'm gonna text you a picture right now. It's so cute, and it's about baking, and I just thought…"

"Oh, Sadie," she squeals when the picture comes through. "I love it. Now I kind of want one too. Tell me *everything.*"

"Okay, so, obviously I love baking. You taught me that." I walk to the side of the building where the noise from the cars rushing by on the busy freeway isn't quite so persistent. "Life has been so good, and I'm realizing that whether or not *life is sweet* is within my control. And I wanted that to be my first tattoo. Baking makes me happy on sad days, happier on happy days, and it reminds me of you."

I hadn't realized until I started explaining just how much

I connected this tattoo to my mom. It's a reminder of her, of my connection with her, and the fact that she taught me how to do one of my very favorite things. We fall into an easy conversation—the way it feels when you catch up with an old friend without missing a beat. But it's a thousand times stronger because *it's my mom*. We only stay on the phone for about twenty minutes, and we don't address any of the reasons we hadn't been talking. But the door between us is open again.

Chapter 19
Cam

Send it — *caption from Cam's social media post — a video of him passing two other racers during his latest race,* May 18*th*

"You're sitting in second place on the grid behind Ludlow for the fifth time this season," Jolie says, holding the microphone between us. "How are you feeling going into this weekend?"

We're lined up for the first of two races this weekend, and I'm grateful for the distraction of the interview to pass the time.

"You know, I wouldn't hate a pole position coming out of qualifiers one of these weekends," I laugh. "But I'm feeling good. How could I not? I get to race this beast," I say, patting a gloved hand on the gas tank between my legs.

"We're getting to the end of the season, and you're tied up with Ludlow. It's been neck and neck between you two, but you've yet to pull into the lead. What do you think it'll take today for you to get that edge?" she asks.

"We both know it's not over 'til it's over, but if I stick to—" My words cut off when I catch sight of pink hair in my pit.

Sadie hasn't been to one of my races since the first one of the season. She's only recently started watching them on TV. I'd given up on seeing her at the track again after she explained why it's so hard for her to be here. *But she is here*—in Austin.

"She's here," I breathe out.

Following my gaze, Jolie spots my girl too. She gives me some well wishes for the race and ushers the cameras away to another racer.

Wearing a tiny, pale yellow sundress, Sadie steps over the divider and rushes to my side. *She's here.*

"Look at you," I say, awe filling my voice as I use a hand at her waist to pull her in close.

Her face is bright with a full, dimpled smile as she braces herself with a hand on my thigh and lifts on her toes to kiss me. "Surprise," she says, bouncing back down on her toes. "Figured it was about time I made it to another one of your races."

"Have I told you how good you look on a racetrack?" I ask.

"Yeah, but you can do it again," she giggles, the loose set of her shoulders showing she isn't carrying her usual nerves about motorcycles.

I let my eyes run over her figure. "You look hot as hell on a racetrack."

Her hands trace over the leather arm of my suit. "Might have to make a habit of spending time on them, then."

"Did anyone come out here with you?" I ask, worried about how she'll manage on her own for the whole race.

"Nope, but I'll be fine," she says, knowing what I'm getting at. "Besides—" She lifts on her toes to lean in close again. "I want you all to myself tonight."

"*Well, fuck me*," I chuckle, completely stunned by her presence, her casual attitude, and her words.

Her brows lift suggestively with a smirk. "Rubber side down, Hacker," she says, pointing toward the timer that indicates it's time for me to put my helmet on. "I'll be waiting for you."

When I pull my helmet on, she plants a kiss on it and rushes back to the pit.

She's here. How long has she been planning this? Is she really going to be okay?

As the timer continues to tick down, I push those thoughts aside. The only thing I can afford to focus on right now is the race. *A distracted racer is a dangerous racer.*

When they release us for the warm-up lap, the anticipation builds. When we grid up again, my nerves reach their peak. But when the green flag waves, I get an ideal start, keeping both tires down as I rip the accelerator and launch forward.

The closest I get to fear during a race is going into the first turn. It's the biggest group we'll have for the entire race, with everyone diving in and fighting for position—like riding in terrible traffic at top speed.

By turn four, I've settled into a groove, able to keep my line without all the other racers clogging the track. It's the hottest day we've had on the track yet this year, but I've gotten good at ignoring the sweat dripping into my eyes and the overwhelming heat inside my suit. *It doesn't matter.*

Each time I pass the pit, Sadie is standing at the edge,

smiling and cheering for me. *She's here.* I allow myself a moment to bask in her presence as I pass, then focus back on getting around Ludlow. We've been racing together since we were kids, so it's impossible to surprise him. I have to watch for my opening and take big chances.

After an entire lap working myself into his slipstream, I finally manage to launch past him and take the lead.

Racing is in my soul. The highlights of my life have all been on the track, but I don't think I've ever been happier than I am the moment I pass Sadie in the pits on the final lap and cross the finish line first.

Ludlow pulls up next to me on the cool-down lap, extending his arm to pull me in for a hug across our bikes. "Hell of a run today," he yells over the sounds of our motors.

"*You* put up a hell of a fight, boss," I yell back.

The podium is made up of my favorites—me in first, Ludlow in second, and Hart in third. It's Hart's fifth podium of the season, and I'm thrilled to see her climbing the rankings. They invite me out to celebrate, but I have to pass.

Sadie's words from earlier repeat in my mind. *I want you all to myself tonight.*

We've been dancing around this thing—*around us*—for months now. I've been back and forth between wanting to be direct with her about how I feel and not wanting to scare her off. She's been hot and cold since the beginning. But lately, the cold moments are few and far between. *She wants this, and I'm not holding back anymore.*

The second we're alone in the hotel elevator, I have her pressed against the wall, grinding my hips against her as I take her mouth in mine. "Fuck, I need you." My hands glide up her thighs until I reach the exposed cheeks of her ass. *Does she own underwear that covers more than the bare minimum? I hope not.*

She squeals when I use my grip to lift her, bringing her thighs to wrap tightly around me. "I need *you*," she gasps between frantic kisses. The elevator door finally dings, and her lips burn feverish kisses down my neck as I carry her down the hall. She rocks against me while I fumble for the key card, uttering my name in a near desperate whine.

When we make it inside, I set her on her feet and tear off my shirt and pants. She starts toward the bed, but I grab her hand, pulling her over to stand before the floor-length mirror at the end of the bed. Locking an arm around her waist, I pull her back against my chest, into a position we've been in many times before—*but never quite like this.*

Her back presses to my chest, and my hard cock presses against the top of her ass. "Look at you," I whisper, nipping at her ear as I send one hand under her skirt and the other to the neckline of her dress. Buttons run from the low neckline to the short hem. I slide open the top ones, revealing the swell of her breasts and a white mesh bra that exposes her pink nipples.

Whatever it is that usually holds her back isn't here today. Her hands grip my arms, holding on as I delve my fingers into the front of her panties until I reach her wet center. She gasps when I use my other hand to toy with one of her exposed breasts, massaging the nipple through her mesh bra until it stands at attention.

Looking up to see her face in the mirror, I see that she isn't watching. Her eyes are closed, head tilted to the side. *This won't do.*

"You're missing a really beautiful show," I say, kissing

down the column of her neck.

"I'm not missing *anything*," she groans, rocking her hips against my searching fingers.

"Have you ever watched yourself come?" I ask, nipping at her shoulder.

"No," she says, pressing harder into me.

"Would you like to?" I ask, quickening the pace of my fingers inside her.

"I can't just—you can't just tell me to—I need—" Her words tumble out in a desperate ramble, and I realize I've made a mistake.

I don't slow my hand, continuing to push her closer to release. "You don't have to. You never *have to*. But you're beautiful when my fingers are inside you. I think you should see."

I flatten my other hand on her chest, sliding it up until I can grip her neck, just beneath her chin. I use the hold to turn her face toward the mirror. She gasps, tightening around me. My gaze locks on the tattooed horseshoe at her throat. *I really am a lucky motherfucker.*

"Open your eyes," I whisper, and because she seemed to like it when I begged, I add, "Please, baby," with a soft kiss where her shoulder meets her neck.

When I look up again, her eyes are open—but she's watching me now.

"I like the way *you* look," she says, her voice steady despite the trembling in her body.

I tighten my fingers around her throat, adding a third finger inside her.

She flushes, her skin glowing from her cheeks all the way

down to her exposed chest. "Do you see how prettily you blush for me? This delicious neck?" I draw out the words, pressing a kiss there to emphasize my point. "And the way your dress falls off your shoulders, exposing those perfect nipples?"

When she doesn't answer, I tighten my grip at her neck again. She gasps, her body responding, tightening around my fingers once more.

Finally, her eyes flicker to where I've kissed her neck and where her dress now rests at her waist. A sly smile tugs at her lips.

"You look good, don't you, baby?" I ask, picking up the pace with my fingers, kissing her neck and shoulders in rhythm.

She moans, clutching me tighter, her body sinking against mine as her release washes over her.

Once her breathing steadies, I pull my hands back, ensuring she stays steady in the aftermath. She locks eyes with me in the mirror, her caramel gaze intense. "You were right," she breathes. "I did look good."

I undo the last of her buttons and let the dress fall from her body, followed by her bra and panties. When I guide her to the edge of the bed, the sunlight pouring in through the windows paints her in the warm glow of the afternoon.

She's here.

Dropping to my knees, I slide her to the edge of the mattress, lifting her legs over my shoulders.

"Wait, how is it my turn again?" she asks, propping herself up on her elbows. Her face flickers with concern. "Are you going to let me touch you tonight?"

"Yes, I am, but I want to taste you first," I murmur, resting my palm over her swollen sex, peppering kisses up her thighs. I make sure to kiss the scars on her skin, my lips lingering over the marks she sometimes wishes to hide.

A brief flash of insecurity passes through her eyes, but it's gone in an instant. She allows herself to enjoy the indulgence of my touches, even where she's less confident.

Her legs twitch against my neck as I smooth my hand across her, applying gentle pressure to her clit.

Her sly smile returns as she watches me, propped up on her elbows. "That's probably a good idea."

I want her collapsed back on the bed in ecstasy, and that's the goal I keep in mind as I use my lips and tongue to pleasure her. She tastes even better than I remembered—salty, sweet, and all Sadie. She's braver now, bolder than last time. She doesn't shy away when I press forward, widening her legs, allowing herself the pleasure of crying out.

Before long, I get what I want—she falls back onto the bed, her legs trembling against my ears as she reaches her second release.

When I stand, she's done waiting. Running her hands up the back of my thighs, she draws me closer.

I breathe her name, my hands dropping to tip her face up toward mine. "You don't have to." It's clear she spent years giving without receiving, and I'm tempted to make up the difference here—never take anything from her.

But it's obvious that's not what she wants. She grips my cock at the base, guiding her hot mouth around the tip. Licking her lips, she looks up at me. "I want you," she says, then lowers her mouth back down, pressing her tongue to the underside as she rocks forward, filling her mouth with me.

My girl. I've allowed myself that indulgence—thinking of her as mine—thinking of *me* as hers, even though we only ever agreed to pretend. But that's not enough for me anymore, and as Sadie sucks and kisses around me, I don't think it's enough for her either.

I sink forward, my knees pressing into the mattress, my fingers threading into her hair as she continues to work me—both hands at my base and her mouth swallowing me deeper, each slide hitting the back of her throat.

She moans around me, bringing me closer to release I'm not ready for.

"Sadie, Sadie," I gasp, cursing. "You have to stop, or I'm going to come down your throat."

She leans back, pulling off with a wet smack of her lips. "Would that really be so bad?"

"No," I breathe, "I'm sure it would be amazing." Gripping her hips, I toss her back onto the bed, my body following, covering hers. "And I fully intend to take you up on that, but tonight, I want to come in here," I say, cupping her sex.

Her eyes sparkle as she lifts to kiss me. "You'd better."

Chapter 20
Sadie

Make it all the way through one of Cam's races without feeling anxious – *from Sadie's list of things she's never done*

Cam kisses my mouth the same way he kisses between my legs—like a man obsessed. *And I think he just might be.* Which would be a good thing, since *"obsessed"* would be an accurate way to describe how I feel about him lately.

I missed him so badly the last few times he was at races that I booked a last-minute flight to Austin to surprise him at this one.

My *possibly-not-so-fake-anymore* boyfriend rolls his hips, rubbing his cock against my wetness. Dropping his forehead to mine, he asks, "Any chance you brought condoms?"

Condoms? It never even crossed my mind. Shit, does that mean—

"I didn't bring any," he says, rolling his hips again, in a motion I can't wait to feel inside me. "Wasn't expecting you."

Wasn't expecting me. We never talked about dating other people, and I've assumed he wasn't seeing anyone else because it would have blown our cover. But the confirmation eases something in my chest I hadn't realized I was carrying.

"I'm okay without, if you are," I breathe.

He presses his lips to mine before I can finish the thought, teasing his fingers from my entrance to my clit and back.

I've already climaxed twice—because apparently, not being rushed is what I need to *actually* get off. Three weeks ago, I would have thought it's not possible for me to come a third time without a toy, but as he lines the tip of his cock up at my entrance, and I feel him slowly filling me, I think I'm about to learn how wrong that was.

His eyes lock with mine as he moves inside me, slow and shallow at first, but deeper with each rock of his hips. He kisses me in that obsessed way that makes me wild as he fills me more and more. "You good?" he asks once he's fully seated inside me.

"You're big," I giggle, rolling my eyes at him. He groans. "But it's not like that's a *bad* thing, Hacker."

"Alright, *Winslow*," he says, a determined set to his jaw. He hooks an arm under one of my legs, folding it up and opening me wider for him, so on his next thrust—*oh, fuck*—on his next thrust, he's deeper, hitting me at just the right angle that I can't help but cry out every time he comes forward.

My nails dig in, scratching down his shoulder blades— overwhelmed with the sensation of him filling me.

A cocky smirk tugs at his lips as I become jelly beneath him. "Still good, Winslow?"

"Uh-huh," I gasp out, my breath lost in pounding thrusts

that are steadily getting faster.

He rocks his hips, making the next thrust particularly poignant, and my head lolls back. "Oh, fuck you," I breathe.

"Is that not what I'm doing?" he laughs, the sound full and loud as he continues fucking me into oblivion.

But I'm laughing too, and even with the depth of meaning that having sex with Cam carries, the whole situation feels light and free. We're laughing and enjoying each other just like we always do—Cam gives me another poignant thrust, and I almost come on impact. *Okay, not like we always do.* But he's still Cam, and I'm still me, and I'm *having fun.* I giggle at the preposterous thought—*I've never had fun having sex before.*

"You know when you do that, you clench around me?" he asks, his voice breathy.

"What?" I force a laugh, and he groans. "That?"

He leans down to kiss me, then draws his teeth heavily against my lip as he lets go. "I'm gonna get you for that."

I'm too far gone to worry about who comes first or how, but I get a great deal of satisfaction at the look on his face when I come for a third time, clenching around him enough to stutter his pace. He follows soon after, making me wonder if he was holding back on my behalf.

When we're both sated, exhausted, and cleaned up, we lie in bed together—me wearing one of his shirts and him wearing pajama pants low enough for me to read his *Ride It Like You Stole It* tattoo.

"How was the race for you?" Cam asks, sitting up and drawing my head to his lap.

"It was magnificent," I nuzzle against his leg. "You won. I love it when you win."

"I love that too, but how did you feel being at the track?" he asks, brushing his fingers over the pink tips of my hair.

I blow out a breath. "I had a few moments that weren't *great*. I really don't like the chatter. Any way you could avoid that in the future?" I ask—half-joking, half-hopeful.

His brows furrow. "I hadn't thought about how that might look to you. It makes the bike tougher to control, but I can handle a tough bike." He must sense my concern because he adds, "We're doing our best to make sure it doesn't happen. That's something Luke is constantly tuning to avoid, but it's tough not to get *some* chatter if I'm riding hard enough."

I still don't like that, but it's better than a crash. "At least you're keeping your bike upright."

His fingers trace a soothing path along my scalp. "I've been lucky this season—only had two crashes. The first one—"

I cut off his explanation, sitting upright to face him. "What do you mean you crashed twice this season?" My heart pounds frantically. Even though I can see for myself that he's fine, I hate the thought.

"I'll tell you," he says, his voice soothing as he reaches for me. "But why don't you come here?"

When I move closer, he wraps his arm around my shoulders.

"I think both crashes happened between the first race you came to and when you started watching them on TV," he explains. "During the first one, I was able to get back up and jump back into the race immediately—still finished top five."

Of course, that's what he thinks about—how it impacted the race outcome, not his body or safety.

"The other one my bike got pretty mangled, and I had to

finish the race on my second bike, but I managed to pull some points that day too."

What do I even say? I hate it. I hate this. I hate that it's even a possibility. I don't want to lose him. I decide not to say anything, resting my head on his shoulder instead.

"Do you think you've gotten comfortable with the idea of me racing by pretending I can't get hurt?" he asks.

"Cutting right through the bullshit tonight, aren't you, Hacker?" I snort a laugh. *He called it when I hadn't even realized it myself.*

"The thing is, I *can* get hurt," he says. "It's rare, but it can happen."

My heart races again, but my mind doesn't. "Can I just say that I hate that, and I don't know what the fuck I'm supposed to do with it?"

"Yeah." He nods, then kisses me on the temple. "That's a good place to start. Did I tell you how happy I am that you're here?" he asks.

Grateful that he's shifting the conversation, I answer, "I don't think so, but you were a *little* busy."

"I was happier when I saw you than when I won that race," he says, giving me a soft kiss.

It sounds like a line, but I know he's being sincere.

"What about this one?" I ask, tapping the roaring cheetah tattoo on the side of his neck.

His chuckle is low. "Would you believe it has to do with speed?"

"I would." I smile. "They're the fastest land animal, aren't they?"

"Yup," he answers, turning so I can get a better look. "I

actually got this one with Ludlow, the guy I've been chasing for number one."

"Last I checked, you were in first place." After today's race, he's pulled ahead by ten points—his first lead of the season.

"Still a chase." He shakes his head, always balancing humility and arrogance. "We're both obsessed with speed, so we got the cheetahs. His is on his arm, though. I'll ask him to show you tomorrow if you want."

Tomorrow. Because I'll be back at the track tomorrow. For another race.

Remembering how many times I've heard announcers talk about their friendship and felt weird that I'd never met the guy, I agree.

And, first thing the next morning, he follows through.

"Ludlow!" Cam yells to his friend from across the pits. "Come meet my girl."

My girl. I don't think that'll ever get old.

The man jogs over with a welcoming smile, shaking my hand and introducing himself.

"So, you're the reason our boy's been distracted all season?" he asks.

Has he really been? That would be dangerous, wouldn't it? I don't let myself dwell on it. Instead, I ask, "Isn't he still winning, though?"

"Yes, he is. Yes, he is," Ludlow answers with a laugh.

"Season's not over," Cam adds, and I can tell he's trying not to jinx himself. He never wants to say he's winning, even when he is.

"Sadie!" someone calls from behind us. *No one here knows me,* but when I turn, I see her—*Shane Hart.* I only met her once, at the first race of the season, but she's running across the pits to greet me.

When she wraps me up in a hug, I feel the strength in her. She's tall like Devon, probably around six feet of lean muscle. "Thank fuck you're here. Sometimes I need a break from all the boys."

"We're not *so* bad, are we?" Ludlow asks, exchanging a mock-offended look with Cam.

"You two are tolerable," she says, but there's a friendly affection in her tone.

"She's having an amazing first season out," Cam explains, pulling me closer. "Made more than a few podiums."

"*You're* having an amazing first season," Shane laughs.

"That's just because I'm old," Cam says, rubbing his thumb at my hip. "Should've been my third. Don't worry. You'll be lapping me in no time."

Most of the racers spend the morning like it's just another day—eating foiled-wrapped breakfast burritos, scrolling on their phones, and messing with each other. It's not until about an hour before the race that the energy shifts, and they stop buzzing around to other pits.

My anxiety is lower than it was at the first race I attended, and even a little less than yesterday's. Each time he finishes a race without getting hurt, it's easier to quiet the ever-present fear of losing him and focus on the joy of watching him do what he loves.

"Any race advice for me?" Cam asks when I meet him on the grid.

"From me?" I laugh. "I don't know... go slower than you want to? Did you remember your sunscreen?"

His face softens, and he leans closer. He knows it's my way

of asking him to be careful—*not to crash.* "I can't promise to go slow, but I will make the safest choices I can, and I *always* wear my sunscreen."

It has to be enough.

Once the race starts, I stand by Luke, his presence a comfort. He loves the shit out of Cam. I have to believe he wouldn't support his racing if he thought it was too dangerous. It helps, too, that I've met so many more of the racers today—learned their names and faces, how friendly they are, and how much they all seem to care about Cam. It makes them look less intimidating as a unit—seeing them more as individuals who all want everyone to be safe.

Cam's qualifying for today's race had him starting in third, and by the fourth of twenty laps, he still hasn't managed to pass either of the front bikes—Ludlow in second, and another racer I met this morning in first. Shane Hart follows him close behind.

My gut twists when he gains enough on Ludlow to try moving in on the turns—looking to pass. The image of my high school friends laid out on the asphalt flashes in my mind again as his bike gets closer to Ludlow. *I don't know if that will ever go away, but this* is *different.* Cam's not an inexperienced teenager trying to impress a girl on the back of his bike. He's wearing protective gear. He's a professional. All of these racers are.

This is not the same.

On the next turn, his tire bounces with the chatter he doesn't seem to be worried about.

This is not the same.

"Got a little contact there," Luke comments as Cam makes it past Ludlow on the next lap.

This is not the same.

I lied to him yesterday when I said I only had a few moments of fear during the race, but today is better. I saw him race safely on this exact track. He *can* do this without getting hurt.

I run back and forth from the screens that stream the race to the edge of the pit to see him pass by each lap. He's getting close to the lead racer now. *He could really do this.* He could win this race. There are only two races left this season after today, and he's *still* in the lead. Cam is so close to getting exactly what he wants—a superbike championship and a spot on his dream team next year.

And I'm only two and a half races away from relief until next season. *Next season. Will we still be together next season? Are we even together now? I think so, but we—*

"Shit," Luke's low voice says from beside me. "*Shit*," he repeats, with an edge to his voice I don't want to believe is there.

My eyes scan the screens, finding the one he must be watching. *There is smoke coming from Cam's tailpipe.* Smoke can't be good, especially if Luke is concerned—*which he is*. His jaw is clenched, and he keeps stepping closer to the screens—as if it will show him something different if he gets close.

My breath catches in my throat, but I try to reason with myself. *Maybe this doesn't mean*—flames accompany the smoke. Occasionally, a small burst of flame will appear at the end of a tailpipe during a normal race, and it actually *isn't* something to be concerned about. *But that's not what this is.* This is fire. *His bike is on fire. And he's still racing.*

Chapter 21
Cam

Look who's back. *– caption from Cam's social media post - a video compilation of Sadie at the track before today's race, May 19th*

This race is mine. I can taste it.

Twelve laps left, and I've already passed Ludlow. Chad Green is next. I haven't raced with him as much, *but he hasn't raced with me either.*

My favorite set of turns on this track is coming up. I'll find my line and—heat nips at my heels, and not the usual heat of racing in Texas in the summer. I chance a quick look behind me.

Fire.

My bike is on fire.

Sadie must be terrified.

The heat intensifies on my heels and calves, moving up my legs.

Shit.

I've got to get this bike off the track.

My leathers are almost unbearably hot as I pull to a rushed stop on the concrete shoulder. The second I'm off the track, I set the bike down, *but the heat doesn't stop.*

My suit is on fire.

I have to get to her.

Flames lick further up my legs, intensifying the heat. Instinct kicks in, and it's a good thing because *she's* all I can think about. Dropping to the ground, I roll and pat the fire with my leather-gloved hands, but my attempts are barely enough to keep the fire from spreading. *It's not going out.* A rare twist of fear tightens my throat.

I have to get to her.

I have to put out this damn fire so I can get to her.

The corner marshals reach me, spraying foam from fire extinguishers all over my bike and suit. It's less than a minute before they have the fire out, but knowing she's watching—*and she's scared*—it feels like an eternity. If they hadn't been here, I might not have made it. *But they were here.*

I'm okay, but is she?

I have to get to her.

The overwhelming heat slowly ebbs as the guys help me to my feet, but the temperature inside my suit is the furthest thing from my mind.

She has to see that I'm okay.

I have to see if she is.

Medics rush toward me, but the second I'm up, I'm running toward *her.*

They threw a red flag to halt the race—*most likely because I leaked oil on the track*—but it clears my way as I cut across it—covering grass, concrete, asphalt, and jumping over barriers. Even cutting across it sideways, the track feels a hell of a lot bigger when I'm running than it does at two hundred miles per hour.

She's here, and I have to get to her.

My heart hammers as my pit finally comes into view.

I don't see her.

Pulling off my helmet as I step over the low wall that separates the track from the pit, I call out, "Where is she?" My voice betrays my panic.

My team is simultaneously asking if I'm alright while prepping my second bike so I can finish the race. *No one answers my question.*

"Where is she?" I repeat, breathless from the race, adrenaline, and the run.

"Over here," my best friend Luke's voice calls from the other side of the pit—by the screens—where he's sitting on the ground with his arms wrapped around Sadie's quaking figure.

She's here.

Her shoulders shake as she burrows her face in Luke's chest.

And she's not okay.

Luke is my lead mechanic, but he's not prepping my bike. He's taking care of what matters most—*her.*

The charred and warped leather of my suit protests as I fall to my knees in front of them, reaching for my girl.

"You good?" Luke asks, carefully shifting her out of his arms and into mine.

"I'm good," I assure him, pulling her to my chest and

kissing the top of her head over and over.

He nods solemnly before walking away.

"You hear that, sunshine?" I squeeze her shaking body close, stroking my hand up and down her back, but she doesn't respond. "I'm good." I kiss the top of her head again. "I'm okay."

"No, you are *not*," she says, her voice weak and impassioned at the same time.

"Look at me. I'm here. I'm alright," I urge, but she keeps her face buried in my chest, refusing to look up.

Tearing off my gloves, I shift us both so I can draw her into my lap. She leans into me but still won't meet my eyes.

"I'm not hurt." My fingers twine into her hand, which she has clutched at her chest. "Touch me. *Feel me.* You can tell for yourself that I'm alright."

She doesn't budge, but that same pained voice says, "You are *not*."

Trailing my fingers through her hair, I joke, "At least I didn't crash."

It has the desired effect—pissing her off enough that she looks up at me and glares. Her eyes are glassy, but her flushed cheeks are dry—like she's too angry to let a tear fall.

"Are you *fucking* kidding me?" Her voice cracks on the question. "You were on *fire*, Cam."

"The suit did its job. It got really hot, but I'm not burnt."

Her glare shifts from angry to skeptical. "*Really?*"

Of course, she doesn't believe me. I was on fire. She saw me on fire.

"Here," I say, carefully lifting her from my lap and into a nearby folding chair.

Her brows furrow as she watches me stand and reach for

the zipper at the neck of my leather suit, pulling it all the way down.

"*Cam*," she whispers my name in a confused scold—too overwhelmed to manage feeling only one thing at a time.

"I'm showing you," I say, peeling one arm out of the suit.

Racing leathers feel somewhere between armor and a second skin. Under normal circumstances, she'd probably laugh her ass off watching me work my body out of them. Today, it isn't until I get my second arm free and I'm shirtless, with the leather suit folded at my hips, that she cracks the slightest hint of a smile.

"*Cameron.*"

"It wasn't my upper half that was on fire," I say, unzipping each of my boots and throwing them aside.

"People can see you," she hisses, pointing behind me when I begin to push the suit past my hips.

Not caring, I push it further down.

"*Cameron Hacker, there are cameras!*"

Looking over my shoulder, I see we've drawn a crowd. My team is continuing to prep my second bike, Luke is keeping medics and Ian from *Incite Energy* away from us, and there are staff, interviewers, and cameras from the track gathered at the edge of the pit.

Looking back into Sadie's caramel-brown eyes, I push the suit all the way down my legs, so I'm standing in front of her, covered in nothing but sweat and black boxer-briefs.

"Clearly, I've built my reputation on modesty," I smirk.

Her hand flies up to cover her mouth as she giggles. *Good.* That's what she needed.

"Look at me, Sadie. I am okay." I spin in a one-eighty for

her, catching sight of the even larger crowd behind us as I do. "Not hurt. No burns."

"You're not supposed to make me laugh," she pouts.

"Since when?" I ask. "I love the way you laugh."

"Stop it," she sighs, then her jaw sets and her voice grows serious again. "This still isn't okay."

Surrounding her soft hands with mine, I draw her out of her chair and into my arms.

"Tell me what's not okay. Tell me so I can make it better," I whisper into her hair. "Please?"

"It's not that easy. *This* isn't okay," her voice cracks, and she reaches a fist up to wipe away a tear.

"I am *not* crying," she insists.

"Of course not, love," I reassure her, but my heart cracks. *I made her cry.*

For a little while, she stays silent in my arms while I trace soothing patterns on her back. Her breaths come and go in a deliberate pattern that I'm able to match with my own, so our chests rise and fall in tandem.

Luke catches my eye and nods toward my second bike with a questioning look. Behind him, Ian delivers a look that implies I'd better get my ass back on the track. I shake my head to both of them and look back to the scared woman in my arms.

"I hate this," she says, her head tilting so her eyes meet mine. "It's not okay. It's—it's—this is not okay." Her words grow more determined. "You can't keep doing this. It's not safe. It's *never* going to be safe."

My gut wrenches. *"You can't keep doing this."*

"Is going fast really *that* important?" Her voice rises, drawing attention from our audience at the edge of the pit.

"Can't you just take up running or something?"

I get the sense that her questions are rhetorical, so I stay quiet, letting her get everything out.

"Go karts," she continues. "Go karts are safe. That was fun. Is there a professional go-kart racing league you can join?" She sighs, and I hear a low chuckle from my crew. "But that's not what you want. It won't make you happy, and you deserve to be happy." A weak fist falls against my chest. "Why can't you be happy doing something safe?"

Even though *that* was rhetorical, too, I answer. "I don't think of it as dangerous." I step back just enough to make sure I can see every ounce of reaction on her beautiful face. "I know that's what's on your mind, but it's not on mine. I wasn't afraid when I realized my bike was on fire. I was prepared. I know how to handle anything that happens on that track."

She narrows her eyes. "You weren't scared at all?"

"I was scared for you."

She digs her teeth into her bottom lip, eyes narrowing even further. "Why would you be scared for me? I wasn't on *fire*."

"Because of this," I say, rubbing the back of my hand along her soft cheek—cold and wet from the tears I caused. "I knew you would hate it. I don't know how to make it better for you. I wish I did. *Fuck*, I wish so much I could take all your anxiety away."

She watches me for a long time, taking those deliberate, counted breaths. When I match them this time, her lips pull into a weak smile.

"I like it when you do that. If we're breathing together, I can feel that you're alive."

"Of course, I'm alive," I say with a low chuckle.

Her usually soft face hardens into severe lines as her voice rises loud enough I'm sure we're not the only ones who hear her next words.

"It's not an *of course*, though, Cam. It's not a given. *That* is the risk. That's it. You could *die*."

She's been careful not to say crash around me since the first time we talked about it—always whispering if she ever had to say the word. But now all bets are off, and it's a punch to the gut that I deserve.

"I could." It's the first time I've allowed myself to voice anything like that to her, and her mouth drops open in shock.

"And you'd just be okay with that?" she asks.

It *does* happen. I've known of a couple of guys who haven't survived crashes. It's a heartbreaking tragedy—an extremely rare, but possible outcome for any racer. It's a possibility I came to terms with a long time ago—long before I knew Sadie.

"No, I wouldn't be *okay* with it. I don't want to die this way. I have no intention of dying this way. That is how I *live*." I say, pointing at the track where the racers are gridding up again.

"Shouldn't you be out there?" she asks, caught between confusion, concern, and anxiety.

If I'm not out there, I won't get any points for this race. Ludlow will likely win, which means I'll be down fifteen points for the season. With only two races left, I'll have to win both, and he'll have to place lower than second on one if I want the championship. Ian is pacing where Luke has him blocked away from us. Even if I finish second for the season—when they said I only had to make top three—I'm showing everyone, including *Incite Energy*, that racing *isn't* always my top priority by staying in my pit and not finishing this race.

I may lose my spot on their team.

"No," I say, resting my forehead against hers before pressing a kiss to the tip of her nose. "I should be right here."

She huffs a frustrated sigh. "You make it so damn hard not to fall in love with you."

Fall in love with me?

"I keep telling myself I cannot fall for you. I can't let myself love you because it would hurt too much. If I love you, then this," she gestures frantically at her heart, "is how I always have to feel. But I already feel like that all the time, so…" she lets her words trail off.

"That's not what I want it to feel like for you," I say, running my thumb along the pink edge of her hair. "You deserve so much more than that."

The engines on the grid start up—my friends, colleagues, and competition ready to launch and finish this race. It's been a long time since I was sitting in the pits for a green flag, and my soul longs to be out there. But more than being on the track, my soul longs to be right here with her.

"Do you want me to stop racing?" I ask, my heart thudding as the bikes on the track take off without me.

"What the fuck?" she asks, a bewildered whisper.

"I'll do it. That can be my last race if you want." My heart breaks at the suggestion, but I mean every word.

Her head tilts with skepticism. "You don't mean that."

"I do," I say, the words landing solemnly between us. I know we're still being watched, but this part of the conversation is only for her and me. "You are the only thing that matters more than racing. So yes, if that's what you want, I'll quit." I swallow thickly. "Is that what you want?"

"Yes," her response is immediate, but her lips curl in distaste as she says the word. "No—I don't know." She sighs, resting her head heavily on my shoulder. "I want you to race, and also never be in danger. Is that so much to ask?"

A low chuckle fills my chest. "Unfortunately, yes."

"You could die out there," she repeats.

"I could die in here," I say, pressing a flat hand over my heart.

Her teeth dig into her lip, and she blows a heavy breath out through her nose. "That's why I can't ask you to quit."

"I meant what I said." I rub my hand up and down her arm. "I will quit, and I will work through whatever the hell that looks like in my life if it means I get to keep you. I'm choosing you. I want you. I love you."

She blinks, rapidly shifting from shock and confusion to a joyful blush, then back to her concerned frown. "I don't want you to have to give it up for me. If being with me would make you unhappy, it wouldn't be worth it."

Placing this decision on her shoulders is not fair, but it's the only way I know to show her my reality. "I don't think it's what you want, either," I say. "I won't be the same man you know— the same man you've been trying *not* to love." My fingers lift her chin, bringing her bright caramel eyes into focus.

"You could die out there," she says for a third time, "But I think you're right. You'd sacrifice something in here if you stopped." She rests her hand over my heart. "I don't want that. I can't allow that. I'm supposed to protect your heart." *Sadie Winslow wants to protect my heart? How did I get so lucky?* "If you'll keep doing this with me," she says, waving her rose-nailed hand in the narrow space between our bodies, "I think I can keep working out how to be okay with it."

Weaving my hand through the hair at the base of her head, I pull her body flush with mine and drop my lips to hers. Cheers sound from the audience at the edge of the pit, but when she kisses me back, all the sounds of the track and the worries that come with it fade away. I nip her ear, then whisper, "So does that mean you're not pretending?"

"I haven't been for a while," she giggles.

"Good," I say, kissing her again. "Because I never was."

Chapter 22
Sadie

Have a good boyfriend - *from Sadie's list of things she's never done*

Cam: Rubber side down, baby. Did you remember your sunscreen?
Me: Of course.
Cam: That's my girl.

He's been calling me *his girl* for months, but it feels different now that I know he truly means it. *He always meant it.*

"I am so proud of you," Devon says, jogging in place to keep her legs warm before the start of our half marathon.

"I haven't even run the race yet," I say.

"Yeah, but you trained for it. That's the hard part." She points toward the starting line. "This is the payoff."

"I don't know, Dev. I think this part is going to be pretty hard, too," I laugh, and Bea joins in from my other side.

"You didn't enjoy the training," Devon says, "But you did it anyway. You set your mind to it, and now you're here."

"What makes you think I didn't enjoy the training?" I ask.

"The look on your face every time you run," she says, dryly.

"I'm—" I start to apologize but stop myself. I don't need to be sorry. *I'm following through on my commitment. Just because I haven't connected with running the way she has doesn't mean I owe an apology.* "I'm probably never running again after this," I say.

"Good for you, angel," Bea says, pulling her headphones over her head. She and I did most of our training together, but we decided for the actual race it would be nicer to zone out to music and move at our own pace.

When the race starts, I'm reminded of the way Cam's races begin. Everyone is crowded together for about the first quarter mile, but then people find their rhythm, and everyone settles in. I'm grateful we picked a race in San Diego—the cool ocean breeze blows in from the water.

My goals today are to finish and to run the whole race without walking. If someone had told me that after my first run with Devon and Bea, I would have fallen over laughing. But we've trained hard, and I think I can do it.

Cam: You're a really sexy runner. Do you know that?

I do not know that. In fact, I'm highly aware of what I look like after every run—red-faced with blonde-pink hair plastered to my neck. *Not exactly cute.*

Cam drove down with us, and he'll be waiting at the finish line with Rhett, Allie, and Luke. He even joined me on my last eight-mile training run. It was no problem for him. A three- or four-mile run is his usual warm-up. *"What's twice that?"* he'd asked as we laced up our shoes. I had to remind myself multiple times during our run that he's a professional athlete, and I don't need to compare myself to him.

Allie: You're doing it! Go, runner girl, go!

My location is shared with her, so they can see where I am on the map.

Cam: Two miles down, sunshine!

His text comes in right as my app tells me I've hit the two-mile mark. *He knows my pace and times his encouragement perfectly.* As the race continues, a few pictures come through, including a selfie of my friends at the beach waiting for me. He sends me silly gifs and jokes as distractions, and I start saving them for when I need the boost.

My legs are tired. I'm sweaty. And I'm nowhere near the finish. *But I am doing a really hard thing,* and I'm proud of myself for it.

Checking my texts for more encouragement, the latest isn't from Cam or Allie.

Hanna: Can you send me recs for the weekend I'm there? Where are the places I have to try in Palm Springs? I need all your insider info! Can't wait to see you!

Ugh. At some point, you'd think she'd learn to take a hint. I've barely responded to her texts. Fortunately, she got moved off my team a few weeks ago, so I don't have to interact with her at work anymore. Ignoring her, I text Cam instead.

> *Me: My legs hurt.*
> *Cam: I'll give you the leg massage of your dreams tonight.*

I've never dreamt about a leg massage before, *but I am now.*
Devon was right—this is the payoff. The energy is palpable. Thousands of racers are on the course, and people line the sides with signs, cheering us on. The water stations are a godsend, too. *I love not having to carry a water bottle.*

> *Cam: Where did you land on the whole ghost thing?*
> *Me: What? What does that have to do with running?*
> *Cam: Nothing. Just wondering if you still want to see one.*
> *Me: It's still on the list.*
> *Cam: Amazing.*

It gives me something to focus on as I continue through the run. *Is there a ghost running this race somewhere? What the hell?*
Next time my phone buzzes, it's not Cam.

> *Mom: So proud of you, Sadie!*
> *Sadie: Thank you, Mom! Call you soon!*

We've talked a few times since that first night I reached out to her, and it's been amazing having her back in my life. We still need to have a heart-to-heart about everything that happened between us, but I'm okay letting that wait.

Allie: You are running a half marathon right now. You're doing it!

The final mile hits, and a burst of adrenaline floods my system. I pick up my pace. It's so close, I can feel it. And then, I can see it.

Cam: You'll see us soon. On your rose side, by the cluster of big orange flags.

On my rose side. He hasn't forgotten, and he's never once made me feel bad when I struggle with directions. I lift my hands, knowing exactly where to look.

As expected, Devon and Bea finish ahead of me, and they're waiting and cheering me on with the rest of my friends. I tear up when they all jump and cheer as I run past. *I'm doing it*, but that's not all. *They're here for me.*

After crossing the finish line, we all find each other, and despite being sweaty and gross, we hug it out.

"I cannot wait to never do that again," I laugh as Devon, Bea, and I pose for pictures with our finisher medals.

"You never have to," Devon laughs. "Don't worry."

As soon as the idea of never running again—after putting all this effort into training—settles in, I start to think I'll actually miss it. "Maybe not another half, but I'd be down for some casual after-work runs every now and then."

Bea smiles. "Thought you might."

We all head out for a celebratory late lunch, and maybe it's just the endorphins talking, but I have the most outrageously delicious burger I've ever eaten.

Allie leans across the table toward Cam. "Did you tell her

yet?"

I swallow down a mouthful. "Tell me what?"

"Whoops, guess that's my answer," she giggles. "Sorry to spoil it."

"You're not sorry," Cam laughs, narrowing his eyes at her. "But that's okay. It's time she found out." He looks at me, and I sneak a fry from his plate. "I found another way for us to check something off your list today."

"Is *that* why you were texting me about ghosts?" I ask, eating his fry.

He nods. "Found a haunted bed-and-breakfast between here and home. You and I are staying there tonight."

I do my best to stay present for the rest of lunch, but it's a struggle. *How haunted is this place? How often do ghost sightings happen? Are they nice ghosts? Did we get the most haunted room?* I get my answers when we check in via plaques and sepia-toned photos near the check-in desk. *It's super haunted.*

Our room is on the third floor, with a four-poster bed, a writing desk in the corner, and a turret window overlooking rolling hills and oak trees.

"*It doesn't feel haunted,*" I whisper.

"Don't most hauntings happen at night?" Cam asks, putting the bag of clean clothes I packed to change into after the race on the luggage stand.

"Maybe, but if there are ghosts, they'd already be here. Right?" I ask, standing closer to him than necessary.

"Right." He grabs my hand. "We'd better check."

We move around the small room, looking behind curtains and under furniture. No ghosts, but when we push open the bathroom door I gasp.

"What do you see?" he asks, concern furrowing his brow.

"That tub," I point at the claw-footed beauty beneath the window.

He chuckles. "Oh yeah, that's the other reason we picked this place."

"We?" I ask.

He explains that Allie, Rhett, and Luke helped him find it while they were waiting at the beach, keeping me company while I take a quick rinse before sinking into a glorious, steaming bath.

"You need anything?" he asks.

"What could I possibly need?" I wave my fingers through the top of the water. "I've never been happier."

"A drink maybe?" he asks. "There's a store down the street. I was gonna get toothbrushes and stuff too."

I sit up, sloshing water over the edge of the tub. "Are you trying to *leave me* while I'm naked and vulnerable in a haunted house?"

His eyes drop to my chest where my breasts have risen above the water level. "What was the question?"

"Cameron, what if a ghost tries to *get me* while you're out buying toothbrushes and rum?"

"So, you want rum?" he asks, backing out of the bathroom. "Got it."

"Don't you dare leave me," I warn, bracing my hands on the edge of the tub as I prepare to chase him.

He points out the window. "The sun hasn't set yet. Why don't you enjoy the soak, and I promise I'll be back before dark?"

I roll my lips together. "Rum does sound good."

"And pineapple juice?" he suggests.

"Fine, but hurry. If something paranormal happens when you're gone, I will never forgive you."

"Not sure if you heard, but I'm really fast," he laughs. "Promise it'll be less than fifteen minutes." He shuts the bathroom door behind him, and I'm left soaking in the tub alone. *In a haunted house. Which is fine. Why would you haunt a bed-and-breakfast if you didn't want visitors? Plus, the sun is still up. Nothing is going to happen.*

The hot water feels magnificent on my sore muscles, and before long, I'm not even thinking about ghosts. *Not much, anyway.*

Pulling out my phone, I look through all of today's pictures. There are some unflattering ones from the race, but also a few where I look strong and happy. I save those.

I should be used to being on Cam's social media by now, but it still surprises me when he tags me in something. I thought, since we agreed we're not pretending anymore, he might scale it back. But I guess he actually enjoys sharing about me because he keeps posting. Today, it was a picture of me standing between Devon and Bea after the finish, all three of us wearing our medals. His caption reads: *Could not be prouder.*

He told me he loved me during my meltdown after he *lit on fire.* I dismissed it at the time, thinking he'd say anything to calm me down—even offering to quit racing. *But the more I think about it, the more I believe he really would quit if I asked him to.* He hasn't said it again, but I think he's waiting for me to say it back—not because he didn't mean it.

He went out of his way today to make me feel special, supporting me all the way. I'm not passionate about running—

not the way Cam is about racing. But I'm passionate about *my friends. And him.*

When my phone buzzes, it startles me enough that I almost drop it in the steamy water. *Okay, maybe I'm still a little concerned about ghosts.* I look around the bathroom. The orange and pink colors of the sunset shine through the window, but I don't see any ghosts.

The notification is from Cam—a picture of rum and pineapple juice seat-belted into the passenger seat of my car.

Cam: Secured.
Me: Hurry back.

It only takes a few minutes before I hear him at the door to our room. "It's me—not a ghost!" he calls out.

"*Cameron*, what if they hear you?" I giggle.

A moment later, he comes into the bathroom with two glasses full of yellow drinks. He passes one to me and holds his up for a toast. "To crossing things off your list."

"Do you really think we could see one?" I ask, sipping my drink. "A *ghost?*"

He eyes my body through the water. "If *they're* lucky."

"You're terrible." I shake my head, loving his attention.

"I'll wait for you out there," he says, pointing to the bedroom. "You deserve to rest."

When he leaves, I sink under the water again. It feels too good for words, but I'm in a spooky bed-and-breakfast with my *not*-fake boyfriend, and the sun has just set. Taking a bath by myself seems like a wasted opportunity.

As I resurface, the lights in the bathroom flicker.

"Cam!" I call out to him.

"I'm here," he says from the next room. "You're okay."

It could be faulty wiring. It's an old house. Or, it could be ghosts—which is why we're here. My eyes search the bathroom again. I'm not sure what I'm looking for, but all I find are vintage tiles and white towels. The lights flicker again. *Yeah, bathtime is over.*

"Is that you doing that?" I ask him, stepping out of the tub and pulling the drain.

"Not me," he says.

After rushing to wrap myself in one of the white towels, I walk into the bedroom. I don't see Cam.

"Cameron. If you're hiding to scare me, it's not funny."

"Wouldn't it be a little bit funny?" His voice comes from around the corner in the turret window.

I prop my hands on my hips. "Nope."

My eyes catch the bed. It was pristinely made when I got into the bath, and now it's a tangled mess. *What is he up to?*

"Ooo—ooo—ooh," Cam's voice echoes, drawing out the words in the style of a spooky old-timey movie.

When I look over, a six-and-a-half-foot tall *ghost*—Cam, wearing a white sheet—moves toward me.

I snort a laugh.

"Sadie," he says in the same *spooky* voice, holding his arms out in a *T*-shape and waving the sheet around. "Are you *loo—ooo—ooking* for me?"

"Cam." I sit back on the bench at the end of the bed, barely able to control my laughter.

"I don't know any *Cam*." He continues to wave his arms, moving closer to me. "I am a gh—ooo—ost, and I'm here for you—ou—ou."

I stand up, backing away from him as he continues making *spooky* noises. *Can he see through that sheet?* He's got me cornered, so I jump up and run across the bed to the other side, almost losing my towel in the process.

But when I land on the ground, he's there. So I jump back onto the bed and run off the end, completely losing my towel. He chases me again, catching me when I reach the turret and wrapping his sheeted-ghost arms around my waist.

He lifts me off the ground, bringing his face to my ear.

"Cam," I squeal, kicking my legs.

His voice rumbles, "You ever made love with a ghost before?"

Made love? That shouldn't be the part I'm focused on, but it is.

"I have a boyfriend," I breathe. "I can't *make love* with a ghost."

"I don't think he'll mind," he says, kissing my neck through the sheet.

He opens his mouth, massaging my skin with his tongue through the fabric. It would be hot—*and it almost is*—but the sheet makes it tickle more than anything.

I squeal, kicking my legs again. "That tickles!"

"I wonder where else it might tickle?" he says, using his new, sexy ghost voice. He carries me over and drops me onto the bed, using sheet-covered hands to spread my legs. He buries his face between them and kisses and licks through the—now soaked—sheet.

"Can you breathe?" I ask, gasping and giggling. The wetter the sheet gets, the less it tickles, and the more... it—

"Oh my *word*," I gasp. "Get up here."

He sits up, still covered by the sheet, but his gigantic smile is visible through the fabric near his mouth. And lower, the shape of his hard cock is outlined by the sheet too.

I snort. "You look ridiculous."

He looks down at his lap, though I know he can't see anything, and uses the silly ghost voice again. "I'm here to haunt you with my—"

"Stop," I laugh, grabbing the front of the sheet and pulling it up until I can see his face. I lean in for a hungry kiss, then drop the sheet behind my head, so we're both underneath it.

"Why are you naked under here?" I ask, looking down at his cock.

He shrugs. "Because I wanted to seduce you."

"By dressing up as a ghost?" My chest bounces with silent laughter.

His brow lifts. "Worked. Didn't it?"

"Weirdly yes," I say, smirking at him in the dim light under the sheet, then drop my mouth to his length. I swirl my tongue around the head once, then spread my lips to cover him completely.

He groans my name, rocking into my mouth and hitting the back of my throat. I bring my hands to his base, moving them up and down as I suck and lick.

Suddenly, the sheet is ripped back. I look up, my mouth still full of him, to see it gathered in his hand. "I wanted to watch you," he says.

I gather more moisture in my mouth, pushing down in one slow, deep motion.

"You're incredible at that," he breathes.

I pull my mouth away long enough to say *thank you* before

diving back down to take him in again.

"You can cross that off," he moans, "taking a compliment."

I giggle around him.

"You want to race?" he asks.

The memory of the first time he brought that up rushes back. He'd been surprised I'd never done sixty-nine with anyone. *Is he offering to*—? I pull away. "I'll win," I say, returning to my task with renewed determination.

I'm going to beat Cam Hacker at this race.

He grabs my hips, pulling me toward him, and I almost lose my grip on him as he drags me back to his mouth. His lips, fingers, and tongue work in unison, skipping the usual gradual buildup.

I gasp, drawing him deeper into my mouth, pressing my chest against his lower abdomen. My body rocks in sync with his mouth. Waves of sensation wash over me, and I'm tempted to stop what I'm doing and lose myself in the pleasure he's giving me. *But then he'll win.* Pre-cum salts my tongue, making me want to taste *all of him.*

Keeping my rhythm, I slide my mouth lower over him, feeling his tip against my throat as I swallow him down. His hips jerk, and my thoughts blur, lost in what he's doing to me. My legs start to shake. I'm close, but so is he.

My mind splits between the frenzy of wanting to give him pleasure—taste him, feel him, make him crazy—and wanting to come, but fighting to hold it back.

His hips jerk again, and the instant I taste his release on my tongue, I feel myself tumbling over the edge. We reach completion together, and I roll off of him, gasping for breath as I crawl up to lay my head on the pillow beside his.

"That's *run a marathon, take a compliment, try sixty-nine,* and *win a race*," I say. "I don't think I've ever crossed so many things off in one day." I'm not ready to admit it to him, but I'm about to cross off *fall in love again* and *have a good boyfriend* too.

"Not *see a ghost?*" he chuckles. "And didn't you cross off *'win a race'* after go-karts? And *wait*—you did *not* win this race."

"I won," I breathe.

"You did not," he protests, tucking his arm under my shoulders and pulling me close. "You were already clenching around—"

His words are cut off as the lights flicker again.

"How do you keep doing that?" I ask.

"I'm not," he says, his face the picture of innocence.

The bathroom door slams shut, as if pushed by a gust of wind, but all the windows are closed.

"Okay," I nuzzle closer to Cam, raising my voice loud enough to be heard through the closed bathroom door. "I'll cross off *'see a ghost,'* too."

Chapter 23
Cam

Hell of a season racing with these two
- Cam's social media post - a picture of him,
Ludlow, and Hart on the podium after yesterday's
race, June 8ᵗʰ

"Bet you two are all kinds of nervous," Hart says, sitting on a bench next to Ludlow and me.

Today's the last race of the season. I won yesterday's, Ludlow placed second, and Hart placed third. Her results in the second half of the season have been more impressive than the first, so she's looking at finishing between fifth and sixth overall.

The championship is between Ludlow and me. After yesterday, I'm down by five points. So, in order to win the championship, I need to win today's race, and Ludlow can't finish second. If he does, we'll be tied for points, and the championship goes to the racer with the most wins for the season—Ludlow.

"At least the weather won't be an issue," Ludlow jokes, lifting a hand to the sky, which is currently dumping rain.

"Good thing we got that one practice day in a couple months ago," I laugh. "I'm sure it's all we needed to prepare for this." Being from southern California, we're not nearly as experienced with this weather as most of our competitors.

"Oh, yeah. We'll crush it out there," Hart laughs, standing up again. "See you kids on the track."

Ludlow and I sit in silence, watching the rain. It's an interesting thing, being up against a friend. I'll be thrilled for him if he takes it, and I know he'd feel the same for me. But more than that, we're both obsessed with speed and winning—for ourselves.

He stands up from the bench and extends a hand to me. "Kick some ass today, dickhead."

"Give 'em hell, asshole," I say, shaking his hand.

After I decided not to finish the race in Austin, where I was on fire, *Incite Energy* rescinded their offer. I knew it was a possible outcome, and I don't regret my choice for a second. I'll choose Sadie over anything, anytime.

I funded this season myself, so they didn't have a leg to stand on anyway. It was a tough way to learn about them, but I wouldn't want to be on a team that doesn't trust their racers to make decisions about their own safety.

"There you are," Sadie says, walking down the concrete corridor where I'm sitting. She's wearing black shorts and one of my yellow *207* t-shirts. I'll never get tired of seeing her in my race gear.

She was here for yesterday's race too—evidently without any issue.

"Here I am," I say, standing up to greet her.

"I've been thinking," she says, grabbing my hands.

"Oh yeah?" I ask.

She nods. "About race advice. I know the ones you've told me—*rubber side down, stay on the bike, head down, butt up.* But I don't like any of that for today."

"What are you thinking, love?" I ask, surprised by her words.

"I just want you to win today. So, no advice." She shakes her head. "I just want you to go out there and take what's yours. What do you think? Will that work?"

"Take what's mine?" I curve a hand around her back and pull her to me. "I like it."

She lifts onto her toes, and her mouth meets mine in a powerful kiss.

Holding her hand, I lead her toward my pit. "You know I'm yours, right?" I ask.

"I do know that," she says, leaning into my shoulder. "And you know I'm yours?"

"I do," I say, kissing the top of her head as we round the corner toward the pits.

Along with my usual crew—Luke, Allie, and Bea—are all here for today's race. Although, I suspect Bea is here more to support Sadie than me. When we get back to the pit, Allie rushes us with big hugs.

"You ready to win this race, Hacker?" she asks.

"You know it," I say, pulling my shoulders back and letting my mind shift into racing mode. *I am one lucky motherfucker. I get to do this today. This race is mine. This season is mine, and my girl just told me to go out and take it.*

The pre-race prep and interviews feel like they take forever, but before I know it, I'm sitting on the bike—tire warmers on—and Sadie comes out to meet me holding a yellow *Race Naked* umbrella.

"I know you were on this whole rebrand thing," she says, kissing my cheek. "But I like *Race Naked*. It's how I found you. I think if you can, you should keep it. I like you wild."

It feels incredible to hear her talk about next season without fear. I told her about *Incite Energy* rescinding their offer, so she knows I'll need to fund next season myself again. *Race Naked* worked for me for years, and the last viral video I was a part of—*Naked Guy Quits USMoto Race to Make Out With His Girlfriend*—makes me feel like I can keep it while also being a good man for her.

"If you like it, I'll keep it."

"Oh, good!" She braces her hand on my thigh, this time kissing my other cheek.

The clock ticks down, showing we have about twenty seconds before Sadie has to go back to the pits.

"So, I've wanted to tell you something, and I wasn't sure when the right time would be," she says.

Fifteen seconds before they take off my tire warmers probably isn't it.

"But I like now." She takes a deep breath. "I love you."

"You love me?" I ask, bewildered. *She's told me she was trying not to love me, but I didn't realize—*

Her lips turn up into a bright, dimpled smile. "I love you." She lifts onto her toes, kissing my helmet, just like she did at the first race. "Now go take what's yours."

The second the clock ticks to zero, she turns, running through the hot summer rain back toward the pits.

She loves me.

They release us for the practice lap, and the water on the track is even deeper than I expected. But I don't care, because *she loves me.*

I'm not the only one struggling in the rain, so Ludlow didn't start with pole position. He's in third, and I'm in fifth. It'll be an uphill, soaking wet battle today, but when the green flag waves, and we're finally off, *I am thrilled.*

Halfway through the first lap, the racer in second low-sides off the track. I'm not looking behind me, but I'd be shocked if there weren't a couple more like him further back in the pack. *The track is a sloshy mess.*

Finding my groove takes a little longer than usual with the wet conditions, but *I have this.*

Slow is smooth. Smooth is fast.

Sadie's non-advice advice comes back to me. *Take what's yours.*

When I finish the first lap and pass the pits, she's standing at the edge by the pit board—jumping, waving, and screaming. *She loves me.*

On the second lap, I pass the racer in front of me, bringing me into familiar territory—behind Ludlow, but he's not focused on me. He has someone to pass too.

My edge is different in the rain, and I know I have to ride it to pass him. By lap three of twelve, I still haven't found it. I've gotten close, but the perfect moment hasn't been there. *Which means, I have to look for an imperfect one.*

Coming out of the corner, I trail him, drafting so he pushes the wind and water out of the way for both of us, but when I move to launch past him, the momentum isn't enough, and I slide back behind. I try it over and over, but I'm not able to get past.

It'll have to be on the *S* turns, which isn't ideal for passing—especially in the rain. It's such a quick move to go from leaning one way, then leaning all the way to the other, then leaning back. It's easy to lose grip when you're not in the race line—exactly where I'd be if I need to pass. *Sadie will hate it.*

She's there again when I pass the pits—jumping and cheering for me. She gave up on holding an umbrella, and Allie and Bea are standing with her—all soaking wet and smiling.

Coming into the first turn of my next lap, I'm lining up to draft Ludlow again, so I can—

Hart passes me.

Shit.

Now we're halfway through the race, and I'm in fourth.

Ahead of me, Ludlow finally made his pass, so now he's in first. Hart makes it around the same racer, and after a few turns, so do I.

Now there are five laps left, and I have to find a way to pass my two best friends on the track as safely as possible in the rain.

The *S* turns are my best option to properly make the passes, but not the safest. *Sadie won't like it.* So, I wait, not taking the opportunity and trying again to draft on the straightaways. It works with Hart, and I'm able to shoot past her, bringing me into second place and closer to Ludlow, but not close enough to pass.

We're finishing the ninth lap—meaning we only have three laps left—when I'm coming up to pass the pits. But my board isn't there.

What the hell?

At the last second, it pops out, lower than usual because Sadie's the one holding it. All the numbers I usually see—distance to the racer in front of me, the racer behind me, lap number—are covered. Instead, thick letters written in marker on a piece of paper that's rapidly deteriorating in the rain read:

Like You Stole It!

My whole body shakes with a laugh. *She knew—even if it wasn't my intention—I was holding back for her. And now she's told me to knock that shit off.*

Take what's yours.

Ride it like you stole it.

I give drafting on the straightaways behind Ludlow one more chance, but it's still not enough. So, on the *S* turns, I go wide into the first curve, then dive underneath in the middle. My back tire hydroplanes slightly on my way out of the *S*, but I'm able to use it to my advantage and end up inside of Ludlow as we're exiting the turn.

Now I'm in first. I did it. I passed Ludlow for hopefully the last time this season. I have two and a half laps to go, and I have to hold on to it and hope someone back there, likely Hart, can get in front of him too so I can take the championship.

The rest of the race is like a meditative dance, leaning my bike in and out of each turn with equal parts care and aggression. When I pass the pits, Sadie is cheering for me each time, and I check Ludlow's board too. He's still behind me going into the last lap, but I don't let disappointment settle in.

It's out of my hands, so I keep racing like I stole it—just like my girl said to.

The checkered flag waves, and as I slow, I look over my shoulder.

It's Hart. She must have passed Ludlow on the last lap. Hart took second.

I won.

I took the Superbike USMoto *championship.*

I won!

Slowing my bike significantly for the cool-down lap, I lift my helmet's visor and hop up on my gas tank, swinging my legs front and back.

Hart reaches me first, yelling, "You fucking did it!" as she reaches her fist out and taps my knuckles with hers.

"*You* did it!" I call back.

Ludlow's next, riding up on my other side. "Hell, yeah, dickhead!" he yells. "You earned that shit!"

Racers congratulate me for the rest of the lap, giving me hugs, knucks, and shouts.

When I make it back around to my pit, Sadie's the first face I see. I stop my bike and run to her, picking her up and swinging her around before scooping my hands under her ass and wrapping her legs around my waist.

Her hands grip either side of my head, and she pulls me down for a rain-soaked, smiling kiss.

"Like you stole it, huh?" I ask.

"You were hesitating," she pushes on my shoulder with a playful scolding. "*Don't do that.*"

The rest of the day is a blur with podiums, interviews, champagne bottles, racers, and friends. It's a high I don't want to come down from.

Hours later, Hart approaches me with a woman I've never seen before and introduces us.

"I'm here representing *Checkers Media*," she says, shaking my hand. "We want to talk to you both about the new team we're starting next year."

Chapter 24
Sadie

Get kicked out of a bar - *from Sadie's list of things she's never done*

"Hey!" Allie stands on a stool behind the bar, addressing the entire Friday night crowd at *Voyeur Café*. "We're looking for a *USMoto* Superbike champion. Does anyone here happen to be one?"

"Ooh! Right here!" I yell, grabbing Cam by the elbow and lifting his arm high into the air. It's been almost a month, and Allie's done this every single time we've come here. Cam doesn't even pretend it bothers him. He eats it up.

He jokes and laughs with Allie as he makes his way across the bar to get us drinks, and I head to find us a table. It's more crowded than usual, but I spot one in the corner by the front window. I'm squeezing through what looks like a bachelorette party when I realize the people look familiar.

"Oh my god! I was hoping I'd see you!" Hanna yells,

wrapping her arms around me in a hug I do not want and breathing tequila breath all over my face.

"Hanna," I say, shaking her off.

"This is so perfect. You'll get to see everyone. The wedding is tomorrow, and we're all here!" she yells, though she's only a few inches from my ear.

Not a bachelorette, then. A rehearsal after-party. Great.

"Do you think I *want* to see everyone?" I ask, not bothering to mask my irritation.

"Oh, no. Maybe not," she gasps, lifting the hand that's holding her drink, narrowly avoiding spilling it all over me as she disappears into the crowd.

When I look back at the table I meant to claim, Jared's sitting there.

Ew.

"It's good to see you," he says, making his voice gravelly in a way I *think* I once found sexy. *How? Ew.*

"It's good for you to see me," I agree, turning to walk away.

When he grabs my arm to stop me, I glare at his hand, then into his eyes until he lets go. "What?" I sigh.

"Don't be like that." He steps closer, but I don't back up. I hold my ground. "Why don't we sneak out of here and have some fun?"

"Ew," I answer. People always say *"If he cheats with you, he'll cheat on you."* This creep is proof. "Aren't you married now?" I ask.

"Not till tomorrow morning," he says, making a face I imagine he thinks is sexy. *It's not, and I know I never thought it was.* "Still have one more night of freedom. How about one more good time together?"

"You and I are operating with vastly different definitions of '*good time*,'" I say, an involuntary shiver running down my spine.

"I think you and *I* have the same definition, though," Cam's taunting voice says in my ear as he drapes an arm around my waist from behind, pulling me into his chest. With his other hand, he offers me a yellow tiki drink. "You good?" he asks.

"Just want to do one more thing, then we can be done with this," I say.

Jared reaches out his hand to introduce himself to Cam. Cam—*who could also win a championship for nicest guy on the planet*—does the meanest thing I've ever seen him do. He keeps his arms tightly around me and says, "I'll pass."

My ex scoffs. "You think you're better than me? You've got *my* sloppy seconds."

"Doesn't count as seconds if you never ate in the first place," Cam says, and we both have a good laugh at Jared's expense.

It's possible I'm being petty, but it's also possible that I don't care.

Finding the person I was scanning the crowd for, I yell, "Kelee! Over here!" waving my hand high in the air to get my ex's fiancée's attention. Cam lifts his hand and waves too. Luke gives me a *hey-quit-yelling-in-my-bar* look, and I give him a big smile in return.

Kelee looks a little wary but joins our group, snuggling into a fuming Jared. "Hey, so, no hard feelings, right? 'Cause now you two are so happy," she smiles hopefully.

I could let her off the hook. She's getting married tomorrow. Hell, she's signing up for a lifetime of never getting her pussy licked. She doesn't need anything else *bad to happen. But I'm not feeling that nice.*

"Actually, *yes*, hard feelings. What you two did to me

was so shitty—like *unbelievably* shitty." I laugh, a realization dawning. "I think you might be really bad people. I'm grateful now that I'm not stuck with this asshole anymore." I point at Jared, who starts to protest. For once, *I* talk over *him*. "But neither of you gets any credit for the life I've built since then. And you *definitely* aren't part of the love I have with Cam."

Her mouth drops open.

"That was fucking rude. You're such a bitch," Jared says.

"Watch your mouth," Cam says, still holding onto me. "You will not speak about her ever—"

Jared cuts him off, "I'll say whatever the fuck I want about that—"

Cam steps out, putting himself between my smarmy ex and me, towering over him almost comically.

Is he going to hit him? Would he do that?

"No fighting!" Luke yells from behind the bar.

"Come on!" Cam yells back. "This guy sucks!"

"And quit fucking yelling," Luke responds.

After Luke's warning, Cam takes one step back, and I move in close to him again, waving Kelee to step in closer too. "Anyway, I wanted you to know Jared just tried to get me to hook up with him. If I were you, I'd want to know. I couldn't live with myself if I didn't say anything."

"Are you fucking kidding me?" she yells at Jared, slapping him hard in the face.

It's awesome.

"I said no fighting," Luke's stern voice calls from behind the bar. "You two. *Out*."

"You still good?" Cam asks me as we weave through the crowd to get away from the chaos we may or may not have just started.

"Oh yeah. I feel *amazing*."

"That was really hot," he says, a little growl in his throat before he kisses me, and not in a subtle, appropriate-for-public way. One of his broad hands grabs my ass and pulls me against him as he dips my head back, searching my mouth with his tongue. I meet him with the same fervor. When he finally releases me, I'm panting for breath.

"*That* was really hot," I say.

Still holding my body against his, he rocks his hips, rubbing his hard cock against me. "Want to do something about it?" he asks, lips tipping up in a smirk that guarantees trouble.

Rolling my body against his in every place we're already connected, I answer, "Hell yes."

Cam's hand wraps around mine, and he pulls me through the crowd toward the back door. We're only five minutes from home, but it feels like an eternity. *Maybe we can get started in the car.*

But when we reach the end of the hall, Cam doesn't open the back door to the parking lot. Instead, he shoves open the door across from it.

Allie's office.

I should protest. I should feel bad. I should not fuck my boyfriend in my friend's office. And yet, I've never done it before. So...

Cam closes us into the small room, cradling a hand behind my head as he rocks me into the hard door. Hands squeeze my thighs and roam higher with urgency that matches the press of his lips against mine. His fingertips explore my hips, and up to my waist, looking for panties I never bothered to put on today.

He groans my name, throwing his head back and digging his fingers into the soft flesh of my ass.

Bringing my lips down on his neck, first over the rose at the center, then kissing across the roaring cheetah face on one side, I suck, kiss, and nibble, devouring the tart taste of his skin.

"No panties? You've been walking around like this all night, and I didn't know?" He grips me by the waist, spinning me around and pushing me forward onto the desk.

The dress rolls up my back as I land with my chest pressed against the wooden surface, ass propped in the air. I'm wildly exposed, and not a bit of the nerves or shyness I once felt remains. Lifting onto my toes, I arch my back, giving him the best view possible. When I look over my shoulder, I see he's stepped back, staring at me slack-jawed.

"You're so wet for me already," he says, running his finger through the slickness between my legs. "Another minute and this would have been dripping down your legs."

"I want *you* dripping down my legs," I say.

He steps back again, licking the taste of me from his finger. "I like the sound of that," he says, eyes focused on my sex.

"Are you going to stand there and stare all night, or are you going to fuck me?" I ask.

His hands immediately drop, unfastening his pants and releasing his straining cock. I only get a second to enjoy the sight of it before he steps forward, gripping my hips and slamming into me.

I cry out at the sharp sensation, but it quickly fades into hot, intense pleasure. His fingertips dig into my soft skin as he thrusts into me again and again. He picks up a punishing pace, drawing whimpers from my mouth each time he drives forward. The desk crashes against the wall with every thrust, and before long, he's rocked me so far forward that my toes no longer touch the ground.

One of his hands digs in even harder, almost to the point of pain, but when he taps the front of my hip, encouraging me to lift, I understand. His fingers slide underneath, reaching my clit, starting with slow strokes that only heighten my pleasure. It doesn't take long before he builds to a pace that has me on the edge of losing control.

I whimper his name.

"You want to come for me, baby?" he asks.

And it's that—the slight difference between being *told* it's time for me to come and being *asked* if it's what I want—that sends me over the edge. I scream, and it's not until I come down that I remember we're in public—at a bar our friends own, fucking on Allie's desk. When I look over my shoulder at him again, the fire in his eyes has me not caring anymore. He's not done, and I'll stay here as long as it takes for him to experience pleasure the same way I just—

There's a loud bang on the door that sends my heart racing. *Shit. We're caught.* My eyes shoot to Cam's, but he doesn't look the slightest bit concerned.

He smirks as he pulls out of me and covers me with my dress. He has just enough time to help me flip over to a seated position before the door bangs open, and Luke walks in, immediately covering his eyes with one hand.

"Are you fucking kidding me?" our bar-owner-friend asks.

My boyfriend stands in front of me, though I'm *technically* decent now, and his pants are still down around his ass. He covers his cock with one hand, and props the other protectively on my knee.

I grab onto the sides of his shirt and hide my face in his

back.

"On Allie's desk?" Luke asks, sighing with exasperation. "Why do I keep having to kick people out of my bar tonight? *Get out.*"

Cam and I both stifle laughter as Luke shuts the door behind him.

"Oh, my word," I mutter, "I cannot belie—"

Luke opens the door again. "Get out *now*. But you're coming back tomorrow morning to sanitize that desk."

When the door shuts again, Cam and I burst into a full laughing fit, doubled over and wiping tears from our eyes. Once he regains his composure, he pulls up his pants, covering his still-hard cock, slick from the hard fucking he just gave me.

"You can check getting *kicked out of a bar* off your list now," he says, grabbing my hand.

"Does it really count if your friends own the bar?" I ask.

He scoffs. "It counts twice as much."

Glancing at the length of him straining through his pants, I say, "I feel bad you didn't get to come."

"I don't have to come every time," he replies, helping me down off the desk. He keeps hold of my hand as he leads me out of the office. When we reach the parking lot, he kisses me again, squeezing my bare ass under my skirt. "And I'm *definitely* not done with you tonight."

"We got kicked out of the bar, right?" I ask, licking my lips and eyeing his hard cock.

"But not the parking lot," he grins. "Exactly."

Chapter 25
Cam

Family dinner - *caption on Cam's social media post - a video of Sadie, Allie, Luke, Bea, Rhett, Devon, Betty, Spaghetti, Dandy, and Boo around the dining table in Sadie and Cam's backyard, July 9th*

Sadie scoops Boo up off the ground, cradling him in her arms as we stand in the front doorway, waving goodbye to our friends. I installed a cat door for him a couple of days ago, and he's been in and out ever since. He's still skittish, but he likes Sadie. *I get it.*

"Do you think we should tell them?" she asks, after I shut the front door and we move back inside.

"Tell them what?" I ask.

She sets the cat down, and he darts down the hallway. "That when we first got together, we were only pretending?"

"Maybe *you* were only pretending," I say, sinking onto the

couch. "I always wanted it to be real."

Sadie opens the little wooden box on the table by the television where she keeps her weed. She pulls out the cutest damn pipe I've ever seen—a yellow and pink, hard-candy-shaped glass piece the size of her palm—and packs us a bowl.

"Did you really?" she asks.

"I did. I would've asked you to date me for real on that first night if I'd thought you'd go for it," I say, leaning back on the couch.

"No, you wouldn't have." She waves me off.

"I would've," I insist. "I always wanted you, from the first moment I saw you—and even more once I knew you."

"You have no idea how true that is," she says, passing me the hard-candy pipe.

"What do you mean by that?" I ask, taking a hit.

She smiles at me, looking wistful, then devious, then delighted. "Hold on," she says, running down the hall toward her room.

It turns out I was right when I made up the story about us fighting over whose bed to sleep in. Mine's bigger, but her bedding's nicer. We switch back and forth almost every night, and we still haven't moved all of our things into one room together.

My phone buzzes with a text.

> *Shane: I still can't believe we get to be on a team together next year.*
> *Me: Me neither. It's going to be amazing.*

The woman from *Checkers Media* turned out to be legit. The company wants to fund a superbike team, and they liked the way Shane and I work together. I get to scale way back on my social presence, and I'll be paid to mentor Shane. It's worked out perfectly—

Sadie walks down the hall, and my thoughts melt away. She's wearing tiny cut-off denim shorts, rolled over at the waist, and a pink shirt cut to show the underside of her boobs that says *Show Me Your Willie*. She even twisted her hair into space buns.

Leaning on the doorframe between the living room and hallway, she asks, "Seem familiar?"

"You're dressed up like my tattoo," I answer, probably drooling.

"Not quite," she laughs, picking up the *hard-candy* pipe from the table and taking a hit. "In the original costume, my shorts weren't folded over, and my shirt wasn't cut off. But this *is* the original shirt."

"What do you mean, the original?" I ask.

"It was ten years ago, so I can't totally hold it against you. But I have to say, I'm a little offended you haven't put it together yet." She sits on the couch next to me, her eyes sparkling with mischief.

The original costume. Is she saying—Could she be?

She passes me her phone, and on it is a picture of her with blonde space buns. She's wearing—I look up and down from her shirt to the photo and back. *It's the same shirt.* This is *the* picture.

"*You're* the girl I used for reference for my tattoo?" I chuckle, pulling her in for a kiss.

She giggles against my lips. "Yeah, I'm pretty sure I am."

"Fuck me. That's incredible." I lean back, unbuttoning my

pants. "You're going to love this."

"*Damn*, I knew you'd like the outfit," she laughs. "But I didn't think it would be this effective."

"It *is* that effective," I say. "But that's not why I'm taking my pants off." I pull down my boxer briefs too, showing her the pinup girl who now has pink space buns.

"Cam," she gasps, trailing her fingertips along the tattoo. "When did you—why did you?"

"I had her do it while you were on the phone with your mom. I've been waiting for you to notice. I'm surprised you never did, but I guess I do a good job of keeping you distracted by other things when I have my pants off."

"But why?" she asks, looking back up.

I pull my underwear and pants back up. "I wanted her to be you."

Her lips turn into a touched pout. "But I won't always have pink hair."

"But you had pink hair when I fell in love with you, and that's what I wanted to remember."

She swings her leg around, so she's straddling me. "Did you know one of the things on my list is keep a secret?"

"I don't think so," I say, running the backs of my fingers under her partially exposed breasts.

"It is, and I wanted it to be that. I thought it was funny that I knew, and you didn't. But I'm glad I told you. I like it better this way." She leans forward, kissing the back of my ear.

Why did I bother putting my pants back on?

"What if the fact that we were pretending to date in the beginning is your secret?" I ask.

"Ooh, I like that," she says, popping back off my lap.

"Hey, wait! I wasn't done with you," I call as she runs back down the hall.

When she returns with her *Try It* notebook in hand, she tucks herself under my arm. "I've got to cross that off."

I watch as she flips the pages, looking for the correct entry, and when she lands on *have a secret*, I see lower down on the same page, she's crossed off *have a good boyfriend*.

Leaning down, I hook my finger under her chin and pull her lips toward mine. What I intended to be a soft, sweet kiss turns into something loaded and passionate. She turns toward me, grasping my shoulders, and my fingers dig into the soft flesh of her ass as I pull her across to straddle me.

"You have *ride it like you stole it* on that list, baby?" I ask, rocking my hips into her.

"Not yet, but I think I better hurry up and add it," she giggles.

Epilogue

Sadie

> One month later, two miles down a dirt
> road - *Mojave Desert, California*

"You gonna tell me why we drove out to the middle of nowhere this late at night?" I ask, accepting Cam's hand as he helps me hop down from his truck.

"We're crossing something off your list," he says, dropping a kiss on top of my head before stepping back and pulling his shirt off.

Is have sex in the desert *on my list? I don't think so.*

"You gonna start taking your clothes off, or do you want my help?" he asks with a *please-say-yes* smirk and a raised brow.

When I continue to stare at him, confused, he chuckles and unbuttons his pants.

What am I missing?

Tossing his jeans onto the seat of his truck, he points up at the sky. My eyes follow his finger straight to the bright, shining moon, and then it clicks. *Dance naked under the full moon.*

"You're going to dance with me?" I ask, finally catching on, and lifting my sundress over my head.

He leans against the truck, and a moment later, *Dreams* by Fleetwood Mac starts playing through the speakers. When he turns back to face me, I toss the dress at him.

His eyes widen as he takes me in—standing in the desert in only my bra and panties. "Unless you'd rather I sit back and watch," he says, setting my dress down and then reaching for his underwear.

"No, I think it's more fun this way," I say, rushing to get the rest of my clothes off and kicking off my sandals. The sand—still toasty from the day's 112-degree heat—is soothing under my feet, and the still desert air is warm enough to keep me comfortable as I spin in a flowing circle, lifting my hands to the sky.

A moment later, one of Cam's warm hands grasps mine, and he spins me around and around. I sway my hips as he moves me loosely in and out of his hold, matching the easy, sultry beat. Before long, my cheeks ache from smiling, and he pulls me in for a giggling kiss.

Lifting onto my toes, I whisper into his ear, "Even though we're crossing this one off, I think we should do it again next month."

Cam

> Five months later, Sadie and Cam's garage
> - *Palm Springs, California*

"Isn't she gorgeous?" I ask, stepping back to admire my

new royal blue race bike, wrapped in its custom *Checkers Media* branding, sitting on stands in our garage.

"I'm unsure what qualifies a motorcycle as attractive, but sure." Sadie smiles sleepily, tucking a wild strand of hair behind her ear. The call about the bike being delivered woke us up earlier than usual. She insisted on coming outside to see it, though the news didn't give her the same adrenaline rush it gave me. She lifts her chin toward the bike. "Let me see how you look on it."

Swinging my leg over the back of the bike, I settle onto the seat. *I'm going to win championships on this machine.* I lean forward, feeling the handlebars in my grip for the first time, then run my hands over the gas tank and look back at my girl.

Her eyes sparkle, and her lips curl into a sexy smirk.

"See something you like?" I ask.

"No matter how hard I tried, I never could bring myself to hate the way you look on a motorcycle," she giggles, stepping closer to me.

I shift back, making more room on the seat in front of me. "Want to help me break it in?"

"I'm not riding on the back of that thing," she scoffs, as though I've lost it.

I spread my legs wider to make space for her and pat the seat in front of me. "That's not what I was inviting you to ride."

The look on her face shifts with each thought that crosses her mind. I wish I could hear them, but I think I'm getting better at guessing. Based on the way she tugs her lip between her teeth and narrows her eyes, I bet she's caught between *I've never had sex on a motorcycle before* and *what if it falls over?*

"It's steady. Promise I won't let us fall," I say, shifting my weight side to side to show how the stands hold the bike.

She takes another step closer, her sleepy expression gone—replaced with flushed cheeks and a sexy smirk. "Okay," she says, patting her hands on the gas tank and seat before looking up at me. "How do I get up there?"

I guide her to brace herself with a hand on my thigh and a foot on the peg, helping her lift herself onto the bike, facing me, with her ass resting on the gas tank and her legs draped over my thighs—on either side of my hips.

She slides down, aligning herself over my thickening cock and rocks against me. "I've never had sex on a motorcycle," she breathes out, teasing me.

"Neither have I," I groan, using my hands on her waist to press her down, increasing the pressure between our bodies.

"Really?" Sadie lifts her face, pressing her lips against mine in a hot kiss.

I've had opportunities to fuck on a motorcycle before, but it never felt worth it until now. "Was saving it for you," I say. It takes some effort, but between kisses, I manage to pull off her shorts and panties while keeping her balanced on the bike.

Her fingertips push at the waistband of my pajama pants until the *Ride it Like You Stole It* lettering is visible. She traces an agonizingly slow, teasing line across the words. "I think I'd like to," she whispers.

When my fingers dip between her legs to get her ready for me, I find her already soaked.

She pushes my hand away, instead reaching to free me from my pants. "I want your cock *now*," she says, pressing a hand to my chest as she lines herself up and slowly lowers down, surrounding me with her tight heat until she's filled herself completely.

Propping her hands on the gas tank behind her, she lifts and lowers herself—giving me an obscenely perfect view of her sex as it's filled by my hard length.

The strap of her tank top falls off her shoulder as she picks up speed, riding me for her pleasure and mine. Somehow, the fact that she's still wearing that tiny shirt makes this even hotter.

With my feet planted firmly on the ground, I keep the bike steady as she finds a more fervent rhythm—rocking my cock into her g-spot, sending us both into wild, panting climaxes.

She collapses against my chest, breathing heavily.

"If that's not riding it like you stole it, I don't know what is," I chuckle, amazed by her. "If I say something about you stealing my heart, would it be too cheesy and ruin the moment?"

"Oh, my word, Cameron," she laughs, tilting her head back to meet my gaze. "No, that would be adorable."

"Well, then," I say, running my fingers through her hair before cupping her soft cheek in my hand. "Of course, you ride me like you stole me. You have stolen my heart, Sadie Winslow. I am yours."

Sadie

Six months later, Sadie and Cam's kitchen
- *Palm Springs, California*

"Hey, gorgeous," Cam greets me as he walks into the kitchen.

"Hey, *you*, gorgeous," I reply, licking frosting off my fingertip as my eyes trail over all six and a half feet of his bare skin.

When we first moved in together, I thought Cam just loved walking around shirtless. Turns out I was wrong. *The man loves to be naked.* Shirtless, with sweatpants on, was a courtesy for me when I was his roommate and fake girlfriend. Now that I'm his *real* girlfriend, he rarely bothers with pants—usually just boxer briefs, and sometimes—like right now—not even those.

I admire the muscular cut of his ass as he walks past me. *Wait. Is that...?* There's black ink on it that I've never seen before.

"Did you get a new ass tattoo?" I ask, stepping closer for a better look.

"What do you mean?" he asks, spinning around like a dog chasing its tail.

"Stop being ridiculous," I laugh, pressing a hand to his hip to still him. "You totally did. Right here," I tap his ass cheek where there's definitely a new tattoo—high up, just a few inches away from his pinup tattoo.

"Oh, that?" he says, his blue-green eyes lighting up, and a grin spreading wide across his face as he looks over his shoulder at me. "I'd almost forgotten. What do you think of it?"

The tattoo is still fresh, the black lettering large and swooping in script. *It looks like it says—but that can't be—would he? Does he? What else could it say, though? He's really—he wants to—oh my word, I'm tearing up over a damn ass tattoo.* After a few stunned moments, I finally admit it to myself. It really says what I'd hoped it would.

Marry me, sunshine?

My voice barely escapes, a stunned giggle accompanying my question. "Are you proposing to me with an ass tattoo?"

He turns around and drops to one knee. "I am. Didn't want anyone else to see it and think it was for them." His smile turns shy as he says, "Marry me, sunshine?"

I nod, tears welling up as I repeatedly nod, and finally, I find my voice. "Yes." I fall into his arms, and we tumble to the kitchen floor, laughing and kissing. He's stark naked, and I'm wearing an apron splattered with frosting. *It's perfect.*

"There's a ring, too," he says, squeezing my hand and pulling it to his chest. "But I don't have it on me."

"I'd hope not," I laugh.

Cam

> Ten years later, a bowling alley - *Palm Springs, California*

The *"Things I've Never Done"* lists have become a family tradition. Sadie has one. I have one. We have a shared one, one for the whole family, and the kids even have their own. There are only two holdouts left from Sadie's original list, and she's *so damn close* to crossing one of them off.

She's one of the best bowlers in our league—a hell of a lot better than I am. Six months ago, she even bowled a 298.

We've been here a few times before in the last couple of years—only one strike to go—and every time, the pressure has been immense. I've tried offering encouraging words, standing by her side, even trying to quiet the alley, but nothing has helped.

Everyone knows what's happening, and she's gathered a crowd. The thing is—part of succeeding at this *is* pulling it off under pressure.

My heart races as she lines it up, swings the ball, and sends it down the lane. The two seconds it takes to reach the pins feel like an eternity, but it looks *good. It looks like she's got it.*

The ball hits, and all ten pins go flying.

My girl spins around, throwing her hands triumphantly in the air and screaming, "I did it!"

I rush to her and lift her up in a tight hug. "So fucking proud of you," I whisper before setting her down so she can soak up the congratulations flooding in from everyone around us.

Hours later, when the celebrating has settled and we're walking to our car, I squeeze her hand and say, "Now, if you'll just let me cross '*bake a perfect cookie*' off, your original list will be finished."

"Maybe someday," she giggles.

What's Next?

You've just finished *Revved Up & Ready*, book three in *Heartbeats in the Heat*, a series of interconnected standalone spicy romantic comedies. Allie and Luke's story is in book one, *Voyeur Café*. Devon and Rhett's story is book two, *How Dare You*.

The fourth and final book of the series will be Bea and Teddy's love story, releasing 2025.

The best way to make sure you have all the details for Jasmine Grace's new releases is to sign up for her newsletter at www.JasmineGraceAuthor.com.

Acknowledgments

Thank *you* for reading Sadie & Cam's story. There are always more books we want to read than we actually have time for, so it's huge to me that you made Revved a priority. It feels incredible that I get to share these characters with you.

Gary, it's hard not to dedicate every book I write to you. You love me exactly how I need and how I want to be loved. Because of you, I get to draw from real life when I'm writing beautiful love stories. Thank you for designing the cover, floor plan, formatting everything, listening to every idea I bounce off of you, and helping me think up ways to get out of the corners I write myself into. I never feel alone in this process because you won't allow it. Thank you for getting up early and staying up late to sit with me while I write when I need it. I think part of the reason Cam is so special to me is because he's special to you. I loved all the ideas and passion you had for his story as I was working through it. I hope I did your favorite character justice. We made it through our third rodeo, and I couldn't have done it without you.

Ari, I look forward to your comments while I'm writing! Your feedback, thoughts, and excitement for my characters give me so much joy and encouragement. Thank you for being a safe person to share my stories with early, always promoting my books, and helping me in every way imaginable.

Ashli, I love how every time I meet a new friend of yours, they've already read my books. I lean on your belief in me whenever my own belief isn't enough—so, every day. Thank you for listening to me read through the raw version of chapter one that one night with Lauren. It helped me finish this story.

Caitlin, you are an absolute dream come true of a friend. Thank you for always supporting me and my stories, and sharing your thoughts and comments. You help me improve as a writer and a person all the time.

Emily, your advice is always so helpful. I look forward to your thoughts every time I get to see you. Thank you for your support on this book and for being such a good friend.

Jamie, thank you for being so supportive of my stories. I love working beside you.

Jenica, it's been so special to share these stories with you. Your support and feedback for this story and my writing career in general mean the world to me.

Lauren H, you are a fervent supporter of me creatively and otherwise. You always make me feel cherished and never judged. Thank you for listening to me read through the raw version of chapter one that one night with Ashli. It helped me finish this story.

Lauren S, you're always on my side, and knowing you're proud of me helps me keep going.

Pip, you are a bright spot in my life. I always appreciate

your excitement, feedback, and support as I'm working. Thank you for helping with Sadie and Cam's story!

Steph, I love hearing your thoughts on story and characters. You're always so insightful! Thank you for supporting me, listening to me, and sharing my books.

Sophia, most importantly, thank you for turning me into a cat person. Without you, Sadie and Cam wouldn't have gotten the pet the deserve. And, thank you for drawing that beautiful kitty for the back cover! Thank you for helping me think things through and giving me real, objective feedback on my stories.

Banjo, Shadow, and Matcha. Y'all don't read, since you're animals. But I couldn't do this without you, so I wanted to say thank you.

About the Author

Jasmine Grace

Jasmine writes feel-good romance filled with swoony moments and good communicators. Her characters get together and stay together. (No third act breakups!) Romance has always been her favorite escape, and she is thrilled that life has led her to a place where she gets to share her stories.

She lives in Denver, Colorado with her husband Gary, stepdaughter Sophia, dogs Banjo and Shadow, and cat Matcha.

I'd love to hear from you!
TikTok - @JasmineGraceAuthor
Instagram - @JasmineGraceAuthor
Email – Jasmine@JasmineGraceAuthor.com
Website – www.JasmineGraceAuthor.com